The MIDNIGHTERS

The MIDNIGHTERS

Hana Tooke

VIKING

VIKING

An imprint of Penguin Random House LLC, New York

First published in the United States of America by Viking,
an imprint of Penguin Random House LLC, 2022
Published simultaneously in the UK by Puffin Books, Ltd.

Text copyright © 2022 by Hana Tooke
Illustrations copyright © 2022 by Ayesha L. Rubio

Viking & colophon are registered trademarks
of Penguin Random House LLC.

Visit us online at penguinrandomhouse.com.

Library of Congress Cataloging-in-Publication Data is available.

Book manufactured in Canada

ISBN 9780593116968

1 3 5 7 9 10 8 6 4 2

FRI

Design by Opal Roengchai
Text set in Monticello LT Pro

For Dylan and Felix,
the centers of my universe

PRAGUE, KINGDOM OF BOHEMIA, DECEMBER 12, 1877

I t was a night so dusky the streetlamps looked like fallen stars. A night seized by a fierce frost, which crept up the spires of Prague until they glimmered like diamond stalagmites, then inched across the Vltava River until its entire surface was as smooth as marble.

It was a night that would bear a new small life.

And, alas, a *smidge* of death.

The Vaškov residence stood—tall, wide, and regal—on the southwestern corner of Big Old Town Square, looming smugly over the ancient, brightly painted zodiacs of the Astronomical Clock just across the street. Despite the late hour, all twelve of its ornate windows were aglow, revealing a well-to-do household abuzz with nervous activity.

On the ground floor, maids raced between rooms with buckets of water and fresh linen.

On the first floor, Karel Vaškov sat in his leather armchair, puffing profusely on a Toscano cigar while the three eldest Vaškov children played cards by his feet.

On the second floor, six younger children were eating a box of Swiss chocolates they'd pilfered.

On the third floor, a tired-looking nursemaid was slumped in the rocking chair, having given up on trying to get the two smallest, crib-scaling children to sleep.

And on the fourth floor, Milena Vašková lay in bed, surrounded by midwives, wondering what was taking this baby so much longer to appear than all her others had.

The already large Vaškov family was about to grow by one.

Across the frozen river, another residence stood—narrow, crooked, and forlorn—at the bottom of a dark street below the lamplit castle. All its weather-beaten windows were dark, except for the round one just below the gabled roof. It glowed like a single golden eye, staring ominously out into the gloomy night.

Beneath the creaking rafters of the attic room, the soon-to-be-born child's grandmother, Liliana, lay in her bed. Yellow candlelight trembled across her age-weathered face, revealing the feverish sweat that glistened on her forehead. A man wearing oil-spattered overalls sat on the edge of the bed, frowning down at Liliana in concern.

"Milena's new child is on the way," Josef said, dabbing his mother's brow with the cleanest corner of his handkerchief. "Isn't that wonderful, Maminka?"

"It's terrible," Liliana muttered. "Worse than terrible, in fact. Nothing short of *hellish*."

"That's no way to speak of a new grandchild. The other eleven children all seem perfectly tolerable. I'm sure this one will be too."

Liliana seemed not to hear him. "It's bad enough that it's the twelfth child. But born on the *twelfth* day of the *twelfth* month too."

"A mere coincidence—"

"I caught you eating twelve fruit dumplings this morning."

"You can hardly blame me. Those things were divine."

"There were *twelve* crows circling the Týn spires."

"You're giving me twelve different headaches right now."

Liliana's eyelids fluttered weakly; her voice dropped to a raspy whisper. "This new child . . . I sense—"

"Maminka, let's not get into prophecies again; it wears you out—"

"I sense dark shadows. And I see"—she squeezed her eyes closed, then immediately snapped them open again— "an eyeball."

Josef let out a long sigh. "Just the one?"

Liliana's bleary gaze sharpened as she turned it to where many ink-smeared words had been scrawled on the wall. "This new child is the one I've been dreaming about."

Josef pinched the bridge of his nose. "You should sleep. The doctor said you'd feel better in the morning."

"The doctor was wrong," Liliana whispered, summoning a weak smile. "My time is nigh, and I am more than ready."

"Don't say that."

"One day you'll believe me again," Liliana rasped. "One day, you'll see I'm not the foolish old woman your sister thinks of me as."

"I don't think you're foolish, but you are rather pale."

Across the river, the clunking gears of the Astronomical Clock echoed through Big Old Town Square. Despite being too far away to hear it, Liliana turned her gaze in its direction.

On the top floor of the Vaškov residence, the scream of a newborn baby filled the air, and at the very same moment, in the candlelit attic room, Liliana sagged into her pillow.

The baby's first breath had coincided — *precisely* — with Liliana's last.

The Astronomical Clock began to chime the hour.

Twelve strikes.

Midnight.

The twelfth child born into the Vaškov family was a girl with hair the color of spider silk and candle-smoke eyes, flecked with the palest blue. As those eyes fluttered open for the first time, her family peered down into her crib, as if studying a rare and mystifying scientific phenomenon.

"She has Máma's small, twitchy nose," said a younger girl.

"And Táta's perfectly symmetrical dimples," said an older boy.

The baby hiccupped, her gaze drifting toward a shadow on the wall.

"Her eyes, though," said another child. "Where did *those* come from?"

They all looked to their mother, waiting for her to offer a hypothesis. Instead, they were greeted by a frown.

"We've examined this little specimen enough for now,"

their father said quickly. "I'm sure we can all agree she's splendid, and that it's time for breakfast."

All eleven children nodded in agreement — some with their father's first statement, some with his second. A few hours and pastry-fueled negotiations later, the children had settled on a name for the newest sister.

Ema.

No one was more taken with the littlest child than the eldest child, Františka. Before Ema's first morning was over, Františka had fashioned a sling out of a scarf and tucked Ema inside it. "I will take her everywhere I go," she declared. "And I will show her all there is to see."

When Milena opened her mouth to protest, Františka silenced her with a shake of her head.

"You feed her milk; I'll feed her wisdom," said Františka decisively. "Besides, every child in this family has a twin, except for me and little Ema here. I see no reason why we cannot form our own, unconventional twinship."

And so it was that Ema found herself nestled in the arms of a ten-year-old philosopher each day, listening to her soothing commentary as they roamed the house.

"A *normal* drawing room would be full of elegant chairs, a beautifully woven carpet, and gossiping ladies in frilly dresses. But Máma is a meteorologist and prefers entertaining ideas, rather than people. You'll notice *these* chairs all have chemical burns that no amount of patching up will cover, and Máma has painted the periodic table on the floorboards, to save her having to squint at the one on the wall."

"Are you criticizing my decorating skills?" Milena said, peering up from her clutter-strewn desk.

"Not at all," Františka said. "I'm merely giving Ema her first lesson in the unlikely beauty of chaos."

Milena chuckled softly, and Ema was carried up the marble stairs, where Františka informed her that *normal* bedrooms *weren't* full of equipment, excited mutterings, and the occasional loud bang.

"Each one doubles as a laboratory," Františka explained. "I don't need a laboratory. The only tool a philosopher needs is her mind, and maybe some kolache. Speaking of which, there's a bakery by Charles Bridge that I must show you. On the way I'll introduce you to trees and towers and ducks."

Outside, Ema's candle-smoke eyes blinked furiously, taking in the color and scale of the city.

"It's a big old universe, isn't it?" Františka said. "Don't worry, though—we'll find your place in it."

As far as Ema was concerned, Františka was the center of the universe. For the next three years, she never left her sister's orbit.

Ema's first word was "Tiška," her second word was "biscuit," and with a lot of encouragement, her third and fourth words were *almost* recognizable as "Aristotle" and "Socrates."

As soon as Ema got the hang of joining words into complete sentences, she discovered the magic of asking questions.

"Where do bubbles go when they pop?"

"Why can't ducks talk?"

"Who invented horses? Was it Táta?"

Whatever the question, Františka answered it with a radiant smile that made Ema giddy with delight. Until one day, when Ema asked a question that left her insides itching unpleasantly.

"Tiška, where are you going?"

Her sister stopped packing her green portmanteau and lifted Ema onto her lap. "I'm going to school in Vienna," Františka answered, with a smile that looked as if it were *not* for Ema. "I'll get to study philosophy every single day and maybe even win trophies and go to university."

For the first time in her life, Ema wished she'd never asked.

"I'll be back for the holidays," Františka continued. "But I'm thirteen now. It is time I find my place in this big world. I wish we'd been actual twins, Ema, so that we could start this journey together. Your time will come, though — I promise. And in the meantime, Marek and Magdalena have agreed to continue your education."

Františka carried her into the next bedroom, where the eldest set of twins was hunched over a table covered with broken pots. Ema eyed them warily.

"Máma and Táta will take her each evening as they always do," Františka said, setting Ema in Marek's arms. "But she needs someone to give her lots of attention during the day. We can't let her curiosity go to waste."

Ema scratched at her stomach, wondering why she couldn't reach the unbearable itchiness inside. It was still bothering her the next day, as the family gathered on the station platform to see Františka off.

The steam train hissed, its wheels screeching as it and Františka disappeared, and then the itching finally stopped. In its place, however, was the painful realization that Ema's entire world had tilted on its axis.

For the next year, Ema followed her new custodians as if she were their much smaller, much too talkative shadow.

"We can't teach you about anthropology if you keep asking random questions," Marek said one day, in one of Prague's many museums.

"Why don't we *tell* you all about the ancient Egyptians?" Magdalena said, patting her lap. "You can just sit and listen."

Ema sat, as instructed. The listening part proved harder.

"*. . . in the early dynastic period . . .*"

Her mind was still preoccupied with her unanswered questions.

"*. . . Ema, why aren't you blinking . . . ?*"

They buzzed around her brain like trapped wasps.

"*. . . let's take her home; she's drawing looks . . .*"

Marek and Magdalena left for school the following autumn, eagerly passing Ema over to the next set of twins. Ema felt an itchy sense of unease as Kryštof and Kateřina explained that they would *tell* her all there was to know about zoology.

"No questions," Kryštof whispered, as the three of them crawled through the undergrowth of the local woodlands. "You'll scare every creature off."

"Yes," agreed Kateřina. "Stealth is key."

Ema was, it turned out, exceptionally good at stealth. Kryštof and Kateřina seemed not to notice when Ema stopped following them to the woods, choosing instead to study the creatures she found the most mysterious, curious, and fascinating of all . . .

Her parents.

For an entire week, she got up early to hide beneath a cabinet in the library, so she could study her father working. Karel was, she quickly decided, the human form of a well-wound clock. He arrived at the strike of nine each morning to sit at his clutter-free desk. He would work silently for precisely two hours, smoke precisely four cigars in that time, and then get up at the strike of eleven to neaten his already neat bookshelves, before returning to his desk for another hour of work and a further two cigars. And then at precisely midday, his neatly groomed face would appear beneath the cabinet to smile at Ema and tell her it was time for lunch.

Observing her mother's routine, on the other hand, was like trying to chase a storm. The only time her mother's energy stilled was when she noticed someone about to leave the house. She'd hurry to the hallway and declare things like "You'll not need that thick coat—the wind is about to die down, but you will need an umbrella as it'll have started raining before you even leave the square" or "Be back by six p.m., as that is when both the incoming snowstorm and your supper will arrive."

Her mother was *always* precise about the weather.

And she was *always* too distracted to notice Ema lurking beneath the cabinets of her drawing-room laboratory— which was precisely where Ema was when one of Milena's chemistry experiments went awry. As her mother pulled the curtains from their rods and flapped them over the smoldering remnants of her paperwork, an old box was sent tumbling off the top of a shelf.

The fire was quickly extinguished, but the contents of the box exploded—photographs, drawings, and several lace handkerchiefs scattered across the floor. Ema watched in astonishment as her mother started to weep, then dropped to her knees to gather it all up again.

One photograph had landed right by Ema's nose.

A moment later it was in her hand, and her eyes were

gazing down at the age-faded image of a man and a woman — the latter of whom had the same pale gray eyes that Ema had.

Ema's gasp of surprise was followed swiftly by Milena's shriek of shock.

She was watching Ema with a look of panicked horror on her face. "Beruška, what are you doing?"

"Who are these two?" Ema asked. "One looks like me, but more old, and the other one looks like you, but more mustachey."

"That's your grandmother, Liliana, who is dead now," Milena said, pushing her lips into a tight smile. "And your uncle, my twin brother, Josef, who is traveling the world on a bicycle, I believe."

"Why are you smiling if you're so sad?"

Milena took the photograph from Ema's fingers and put it back in the box. Ema looked down at the dark shadow pooled beneath her mother's feet, feeling as if it were seeping into her own shadow. Tears prickled in the corners of her eyes.

"I'm not sad, beruška."

"Yes, you are. In fact, you're getting sadder and sadder. I can feel it."

"Nobody can *feel* other people's emotions, Ema."

Later that night, Ema lay in bed feeling more confused than she'd ever felt before. Why had her mother lied about feeling sad? And what did her shadow seemingly have to do with it?

Ema was handed over to the next set of twins — Hedvika and Jana, who were studying archeology — the following year. Their thrill at having a tiny acolyte to share their passion for digging up old things with lasted almost an entire month, until one day they came home with Ema slung over Jana's shoulder, crying her eyes out.

"We took her to the Bone Church in Kutná Hora," Hedvika explained, as Milena and Karel looked at their weeping daughter.

"She insisted on it," Jana quickly added. "She said she had a hypothesis she wanted to test, and that her insides were itching to go there. We just thought she had an unusual way of expressing her excitement, but she keeps scratching at her stomach — look."

Ema was, indeed, still scratching her stomach and feeling an inexplicable sense of dread spreading through every inch of her skeleton.

"Anyway, it wasn't the *bones* that upset her," Hedvika said. "It was the people in the graveyard *outside* the church, gathered for a funeral, that upset her. She started whispering about dark shadows. Then bawling her eyes out."

They all turned to Ema and waited for her to explain herself.

Ema shuddered. "I felt their sadness . . . and my shadow . . . it's still dark. Just like yours was, Máma, when you were looking at that photograph of Liliana and Josef."

Her mother's face darkened like a storm cloud, and the itching inside Ema turned into an uncomfortable thrum that vibrated through her. It was the same feeling she'd had just before Františka had left—as if something bad was about to happen.

"Was this your hypothesis, Ema?" Milena asked quietly.

Ema reached into her satchel, pulled out a bundle of papers, and handed them to her mother.

"Shadowology?" Without looking at any of Ema's carefully collected notes and observations, Milena handed the papers back. "You will stop this . . . *research* . . . right now."

Ema realized then that the itching inside her had stopped and that the most calamitous thing since watching Františka's train chug away from her had just occurred.

She'd upset her mother.

Hedvika and Jana left a few months later, and Ema was sent to study physics in her father's library with her brothers Benedikt and Lubos.

By now, all Ema wanted was a subject of her own to study. But the memory of her mother's disapproval still felt like a fresh wound. It took Ema several more months before she felt another spark of curiosity that would not cease tugging at her.

"Ema, why are you shining that light through your arm?" her father asked.

He, Benedikt, and Lubos were peering over their wire-rim spectacles at her.

"I was trying to see my bones," Ema explained.

"Have you decided to take up anatomy?" Benedikt asked.

"No," Ema said. "I call it intuitive osteology. I learned that word from Hedvika. It means the study of bones, but I added the 'intuitive' bit because I'm convinced there's a sixth sense hiding in my bone marrow that warns me of impending doom."

Her father and brothers blinked.

"Yesterday, I couldn't stop scratching my left humerus bone," Ema continued. "I *knew* something bad was going to happen. And then something bad *did* happen." She lifted her sleeve to show the nasty scab on her elbow. "I tripped over a cat. I'm still collecting data to prove my hypothesis, but I'll soon be able to show Máma how she does what she does."

Her father and brothers frowned.

"What has any of that got to do with Máma?" Lubos asked.

"She *predicts* the weather," Ema said, confused that they hadn't worked out the obvious. "Just like I predict bad things."

The library fell uncomfortably quiet.

"Beruška," Karel said finally, "your mother uses barometers and other such equipment to predict the weather. Her skill comes from observations, not hunches. Promise me you won't let your mother hear this new hypothesis of yours. I suspect it will upset her."

Ema felt a tickle of despair in her chest. "I promise."

That night, Ema found herself confused once again. If she couldn't observe her bones to prove her hypothesis, then what *could* she observe?

Soon, the only twins left were Jasmína and Nina—whose offer to teach her astronomy Ema politely turned down. She was too busy trying to find an answer to what was responsible for her intuition.

Though the quantity of siblings in the house had steadily diminished, the quantity of trophies they sent home was increasing—almost entirely filling the hallway. Ema wondered what kind of trophies—if any—she would one day receive . . . and if there'd even be enough space left in the hallway for her parents to display them.

Ema began to feel as if she were haunting her family's

home, instead of living in it. She wanted nothing more than for her scientific calling to fall into her lap.

Instead, Ema fell into bed with a vicious fever. "Something awful is going to happen," she rasped as her mother mopped her brow. "I can feel it."

"Fevers can cause delirium," Milena said. "Everything will be fine, I promise."

For the next week, Ema slept fitfully—her dreams were dark and scary; her bones felt electrically charged.

The fever broke on her eleventh birthday.

The dread that had been coursing through her stilled too but left Ema feeling weak and wobbly. She stumbled downstairs in her sweat-drenched nightgown. Her mother and sisters were gathered around the table, chatting happily.

Nothing *looked* wrong.

Ema's confused staring was interrupted by a scream as one of the maids entered. Everyone followed the maid's gaze to Ema.

"She just appeared in the doorway like a ghost!" the maid said, clutching her chest. "What are you doing, sneaking around like that!"

"I didn't sneak," Ema said.

"Oh, beruška," Milena said. "Come and have a seat; you look awful."

Ema stood there, shaking her head. "Has something awful happened?"

"Everything is fine. Just like I promised."

Just then her father came into the room, holding a telegram in his shaking hands.

"What is it?" Milena asked.

"It's Františka," Karel said, his face pale. "She's had an accident."

Ema heard a faraway shriek that sounded an awful lot like her own voice. Dizziness finally overwhelmed her, and everything turned dark.

When Ema came around the following morning, Františka's face was staring at her in concern from the next pillow.

"You're alive!" Ema said, reaching out to wrap her arms around her.

"Don't!" Františka said, wincing as she held up a hand. "I have a broken arm and three fractured ribs, so I'm afraid I am ill-equipped to give you the hug I so desperately wish to."

"You look awful," Ema said, staring at her sister's pale face and bandaged body.

"You look awfuller," Františka said, giggling.

"What happened?"

"I tried to climb a tree in roller skates," Františka said. "In my defense, it was the first time I'd tried this bizarre new invention. I'd just got the hang of not falling over every three seconds when the biggest dog I've ever seen came charging toward me. There was an oak tree nearby. I forgot I had wheels on my feet. It did not go well. The silver lining is that now I get to see you in person! What's wrong? Why are you trembling?"

Ema *had* been right about disaster looming. She opened her mouth, ready to share her ponderings with her sister, but stopped herself. What if Františka responded the same way as her parents? Ema didn't think she could bear to see disappointment on her sister's face. And so, Ema swallowed her questions down again.

"Nothing is wrong," Ema said. "I was just worried about you."

"Ema," Františka said, suddenly much more serious. "Máma and Táta are worried about *you*. They've told me about your . . . studies. You know how I feel about being curious, but . . . please, don't ask questions about Liliana. Some things are better buried in the past."

Ema swallowed down a hard lump and nodded.

"Now! How about we gorge ourselves on kolache?" Františka said, grinning again. "That'll cheer us both up, I'm sure."

Ema forced a smile, feeling it settle over her face like a mask.

She wore that very same mask the day that Františka left, taking the last of Ema's siblings with her. In the thunderous quiet that followed their departure, Ema felt hollow.

The great enigma of her life had presented itself: How was she ever supposed to understand a world that didn't understand her?

The Ema
Enigma

2

Ema had been dreading her twelfth birthday. When the day arrived, despair hummed through her, vibrating every atom of her being.

She spent the morning on her bedroom windowsill with a monocular spyglass pressed to her left eye, scanning Big Old Town Square for a person she'd never seen before, but whom she knew she would recognize as soon as she saw them.

One by one, each grinning market vendor and rosy-nosed customer appeared in the brass circle of Ema's spyglass. She could almost taste the toasted walnuts that were lifted toward cold lips and feel the warmth of steaming honey wine as it was ladled into cups. But it was a blurry figure entering the square from the side of the Church of Our Lady before Týn that finally caught her attention.

Ema tweaked the spyglass's focus until the figure sharpened. Nothing about this person appeared extraordinary except for one clue: the way they walked — commanding the crowds to part with nothing more than a determined lope.

"That's her!"

As the woman strode past the towering Christmas tree in the center of the square, the grinding of large gears shattered through the quiet.

Clunk-clunk-clunk.

Ema turned her spyglass toward the Astronomical Clock across the street. Beside the bright zodiac dial, the skeletal figure of Death began to ring its bell. But Ema already knew — in her very bones — exactly what time it was.

Twelve o'clock.

"Oh no."

The twin doors above the zodiac creaked open, and the mechanical figures of the twelve apostles began rotating into view. As the first chime rang out, there was a *knock-knock-knock* on the front door.

Ema snapped her spyglass closed as she tumbled off the windowsill. She staggered on numb legs across the room, pausing only to check herself in the mirror. She judged herself perfectly presentable, except for the bright red circle around her left eye, courtesy of the spyglass.

Knock-knock-knock-knock.

Grabbing her leather satchel, she ran from her room.

The house was eerily quiet. The clocks had been stilled and the maids furloughed until spring. The only noise that followed Ema as she hurried past her siblings' empty bedrooms was the jinglejangle of the new bell around her neck.

At the top of the final stairs, Ema came to a breathless halt. Her parents emerged from opposite doorways: Karel from the library, a cigar clamped between his teeth as he neatened his already neat necktie, and Milena from the drawing room, hastily arranging her hair with a pencil.

Knock-knock-knock—

Ema made it to the foot of the stairs just as the eleventh *knock* struck. She sucked in a hopeful breath, then blew it out in a defeated sigh at the final—twelfth—*knock*.

Her father threw the door open.

The twelfth chime echoed into their hallway.

Ema stared wide-eyed at the woman on their doorstep.

Dagmara Bartoňová was exactly how she had imagined the headmistress of an exclusive academy for young female scholars would look: nothing short of a marvel.

Her blue travel cloak was unremarkable, her brown hair was plain as could be, but her eyes gleamed like cut glass. She had the look of someone who could stare deep into the cosmos and uncover its deepest mysteries in just a few blinks.

"Dobrý den," Dagmara Bartoňová said. "What a joy it is to see you both again."

"We appreciate you visiting on such short notice," Karel said. "You have no idea just how grateful we are."

"Oh, I have some idea," Dagmara said with a wry smile. "But I was in the city anyway."

She stepped forward, and Ema's parents sprang apart to let her through. Ema's mouth twitched, ready to offer the headmistress a smile, but those cut-glass eyes glided right over her.

"I don't have much time. I want to be back at school before dark."

"Of course," Milena said. "Follow me."

The three of them swept into the drawing room, leaving Ema blinking in bemusement.

The jinglejangling of her bell collar was the only noise she made as she followed meekly after them.

Dust sheets covered the furniture. There was no sign whatsoever that this was a room in which science was celebrated. The only thing that remained uncovered was the periodic table painted on the floor, and the four chairs set out around it. Ema sat herself in the chair nearest the headmistress and cradled her satchel to her chest.

"Yes," her father was saying to Dagmara Bartoňová, cutting the tip off a fresh cigar. "We learned that the curatorship Vendula promised us has gone to some astronomer nobody has heard of. So, we've decided to join our eldest daughter on her expedition to the Alps. You remember Františka, don't you? After finishing her degree in philosophy, she started another one in glaciology."

Those sharp eyes twinkled, and the headmistress smiled softly. "A teacher never forgets a student as brilliant as Františka. You must be so proud."

Milena and Karel beamed, and Ema felt a familiar knot tighten in the pit of her stomach.

"We couldn't be prouder," her mother said. "Františka's research is helping our own immensely. This trip might just provide us with the data we need to silence our critics."

Dagmara nodded knowingly, but then her smile dropped. "But while you're gone, you need a babysitter for your youngest child. Don't you have maids for that?"

And just like that, the gleam of pride in her parents' eyes dulled, and their smiles became fractionally more strained.

"We need her in school," her father said. "Nearly five months without instruction would be such a waste."

"She wasn't due to be interviewed until June," Dagmara said. "You know my rules. I will not take a student on until she is ready."

"She's *definitely* ready now," Karel insisted, in a voice that oozed sincerity.

"Just like her sisters were," Milena added, with a smile that radiated integrity. "We're certain of it."

Dagmara Bartoňová's steely gaze bored through Ema's parents.

Ema leaned forward in her seat, wondering if the headmistress could also see the tiny twitch under her father's left eye, or the slight pinch at the corner of her mother's mouth. Their true feelings were as clear to Ema as a cloudless sky—they weren't certain about Ema's preparedness in the slightest.

Surely, those cut-glass eyes would see what Ema could see?

Finally, however, Dagmara gave them a single nod.

Ema wasn't sure if she was disappointed or relieved.

"All right," Dagmara said. "Please send for her."

"I'm right here!" Ema said, with more bite than she'd intended.

"Sweet saints!" The headmistress clutched at her chest as she finally turned her gaze to Ema, staring at her as if she were looking at an apparition. She blinked, then turned back to Ema's parents. "Does she always sneak up like that?"

Her parents' apologetic smiles said it all; yes, their daughter did have an uncanny tendency to move about unnoticed, and no, they weren't sure how she managed it.

"If I may, Professor Bartoňová," Ema said, as contritely as she could, "I didn't sneak up. I was there in the hallway when you arrived. Surely you heard my bell necklace?"

Dagmara blinked down at the necklace in question. "I thought I heard a cat."

"That often happens," Ema replied glumly. "I clearly need to come up with a different method of amplifying my movements. Tap shoes, perhaps?"

Dagmara frowned, then turned to Ema's parents. "You may wait elsewhere while I interview her."

Karel's and Milena's hopeful smiles twitched almost imperceptibly. They looked to Ema with matching expressions of near-invisible panic. Near invisible to everyone but Ema, it seemed.

"It's all right," Ema said, patting her satchel before offering up the biggest lie she'd ever told: "I'm ready."

With synchronized nods, her parents left the room, leaving Ema wilting under the scrutiny of the most intimidating eyes she had ever seen.

"So," Dagmara said. Her gaze flicked, dagger quick, to the satchel cradled in Ema's lap. "Is that your research proposal for admittance to my school?"

Ema nodded, withdrew a neat bundle of papers, and passed them over — curling her hands in her lap as Dagmara began to read.

"Ah," the headmistress said. "A geological study into the rock formations of the Bohemian Forest."

"Yes. We spent last summer there."

Dagmara skimmed through two more pages. "And rock formations are your great scientific passion, are they?"

Ema kept her smile fixed expertly in place. "My father says that geology provides a very grounded career."

"Aren't fathers amusing," Dagmara said, without any twitch of amusement that Ema could detect.

"And my mother says my drawing is acceptable enough to capture the details with ninety-four percent accuracy. I'm sure I could improve that with practice."

"I have no doubt you could."

Ema watched every inch of the headmistress's face: the small crease between her brows, the way her right eye was slightly more narrowed than her left, and the barely perceptible tilt of her chin. Ema could see that the headmistress was anything but impressed. This fear was confirmed when, on reaching the twelfth page, Dagmara dropped the papers on the floor beside her.

Ema flinched as they hit the floorboards with a slap. "There's another thirty-three pages of—"

"Rocks, Ema. Which, in the hands of an ardent geologist, can be a highly invigorating subject. But all I see here is lots of rocks, and some impassionate observations about their properties. Tell me what, exactly, is it about rocks that has you filling out forty-five pages on them?"

With great effort, Ema sat a little straighter. "My parents—"

"Yes, I thought so."

"But—"

Dagmara Bartoňová held up a hand, and it was as if she'd sucked all the air out of Ema's lungs. All Ema could do was try to hold on to her carefully curated composure as she felt herself being studied with intense scrutiny. She couldn't help but feel in awe of this woman, as well as utterly terrified of her.

"The difference between you and your parents, Ema, is that they spend their days speculating at great and passionate length about carbonic gases, and how our Earth will soon become dangerously warm. A subject considered utterly ridiculous by many of their peers. Personally, I never dismiss a hypothesis just because it seems implausible. But I need to see one key thing in my pupils."

Ema's mind flicked automatically to the wall of photographs and trophies in the hallway.

"Exceptionalism?" Ema asked quietly.

"We all have the ability to be exceptional . . . but to get there, we need passion. I interviewed all your sisters, and none of them were exceptional at that point. But they were, each one of them, full of passion and potential."

Ema swallowed a hard lump as Dagmara leaned forward.

"Just one question, Ema. Answer it with full conviction and you may yet fulfill your parents' dreams of attending my school."

Ema nodded.

"What is it in this world, or beyond, that mystifies you to such an extent that it makes your very soul burn with determination to solve it?"

"I—"

"Think carefully before you answer."

Ema had rehearsed what she was meant to say for nearly a week; she knew she should talk about tectonic plates and Earth's lithosphere. Instinctively, however, she returned her gaze to her leather satchel. There was another bundle of papers in that bag. Another, secret, body of research. But not one she could ever present to such a woman and expect to be taken seriously.

Ema licked her dry lips. "Rocks—"

The headmistress's chair scraped loudly as she stood, sending the pulse in Ema's ears into a clamorous crescendo.

"Wait!"

Those crystalline eyes glinted down at her once more. Ema stared up into them and could almost see what would happen next play out like a series of moving, flickering pictures. Dagmara would throw open the doors, her parents would stand there with twin expressions of disappointment, and Ema would drop to her knees in despair.

She couldn't let that happen. "I have something else . . . a quandary I cannot solve no matter how hard I try, but that will not cease tugging at me, demanding I find answers."

The headmistress blinked, once, like a camera shutter. She sat down again. "And what is this mystifying quandary of yours?"

Ema's heart continued its chaotic jitter.

She took a breath.

"The mystery . . . is *me*."

"Pardon?"

Ema reached for her satchel, pulled out a thicker bundle of papers, and dropped them in Dagmara's lap. The headmistress stared down at the title page in bewilderment.

"'The Ema Enigma'?"

"Yes. I am an enigma. Not the good, interesting kind of enigma—like the birth of the universe. But the bad, frustrating kind of enigma—like how one sock always vanishes in the laundry."

Dagmara opened her mouth as if to respond, but her jaw hung loose instead and stayed there.

Ema pressed on. "It has been clear to me all my life that I'm not like everyone else, so I decided to start developing new scientific fields of study to try to explain the phenomena I experience."

Ema flipped to the first page.

Dagmara settled her skeptical gaze on its contents. "'The Happy Birthday Paradox'?"

"As of today, I've only had twelve birthdays, so the data is limited in scope, but there's a clear pattern emerging. I haven't had a single birthday that hasn't ended in catastrophe."

"It's your birthday today? Happ—"

"Don't! You mustn't say it. Whenever people say that, things tend to go momentously badly . . . Here, look." Ema leaned forward and flicked a few pages. "It's my *twelfth* birthday, on the *twelfth* day, of the *twelfth* month—"

Dagmara read the next title. "'Dodecaphobia'?"

"There is something very troubling about the number twelve," Ema said gravely. "My observations today provide further evidence. There were twelve hairs on my pillow this morning, I hiccupped twelve times during breakfast, twelve bicycles cycled through the square this morning, you arrived at the very stroke of twelve, and then you knocked twelve times."

"Are you calling me a bad omen?"

"I would never. Please, read on."

The headmistress sighed, then flicked the page again. "'Intuitive Osteology'?"

"Yes. I can *feel* disaster looming. Whenever I get that feeling, something bad usually follows. Like Františka's accident last year."

"Accidents happen all the time, Ema."

"That wasn't an isolated incident, though." She nodded at the paper. "It's all recorded there, every instance where I've felt disaster before it's struck."

Dagmara's right eye narrowed even more. She flicked another page and blinked down at it. "'Twitchology'?" Flick. "'Unseenology'?"

"Those are my newest fields of study. The former is a study of whether I might be a human lie detector; the latter you witnessed yourself when you failed to notice me . . . When I'm out in the city, I'm constantly being bumped into and trodden on. When I'm home, it seems I'm always startling someone with my presence. That's why I got this bell collar . . . but I've come to realize that no matter what I try, no one notices me. There must be a scientific reason."

Dagmara clucked her tongue again.

Flick. Pause. Frown.

"What on earth is shadowology? No, let me guess. You're afraid of your own shadow?"

Ema held the woman's gaze.

Just.

"For good reason."

Dagmara looked down to the shadow pooled beneath her, but Ema couldn't bring herself to do the same.

"I know this all sounds wildly ridiculous," Ema said, with a wildly ridiculous squeak to her voice, "but there is something to be uncovered in all these phenomena I experience. I can tell you that for certain."

Dagmara sighed. "Well, I can tell *you* for certain that these provide more than twelve reasons why I cannot enroll you in my school."

Ema felt the room sway around her. "But you said you don't dismiss hypotheses—"

"This. Is. Not. Science," Dagmara said, tapping the papers for emphasis, then setting them down carefully on the floor. "It is a list of things you are afraid of, Ema."

"But—"

"I'm not saying you're a lost cause. You are bright, articulate, thorough. I see plenty of potential for potential in you, but you're not ready to join my school. Perhaps your parents were right about the rocks—maybe they would be . . . grounding."

Ema squeezed her eyes tightly shut as Dagmara left the room. She heard the door swing open, she heard her parents groan with disappointment, and then she heard the front door shut with a decisive thunk.

After that, all she could hear was the rushing in her ears.

She waited for the unbearable thrum of dread to finally break like a fever now that the catastrophe she'd been expecting had finally come to fruition. Instead, however, the feeling intensified—until every bone in her body itched with unease.

A cold certainty swelled inside her. Dagmara Bartoňová's rejection wasn't the only thing her birthday had to offer.

Something bigger was on its way.

T he silence that descended after Dagmara Bartoňová's departure was deafening. Ema's parents greeted her with forced smiles and soft mutterings of comfort, and she did her best to appear unperturbed. Then she went up to her room, where she spent the rest of the day observing the thunderous quiet with ringing ears.

As dusk oozed into night, that looming sense of dread persisted. What could be worse than ruining both her interview and her parents' plans? Dagmara had arrived at twelve o'clock, and that had gone disastrously wrong. Surely, then, whatever else was on its way, it would arrive at midnight?

The moon was reaching its peak when Ema heard footsteps. Giddy with fear, she forced herself to investigate. She peered out of her room to find her parents clambering down the stairs. Two pairs of skis were slung over her father's left shoulder and two fur-lined sleeping bags over his right. Her mother was cradling her camera equipment with both arms and clenching a pair of gloves between her teeth. Both wore their woolen breeches, canvas jackets, reindeer-skin boots, and ushanka hats with smoked-glass snow goggles perched on top.

They were dressed for adventure, not bed.

Ema followed them down to the hallway.

"We have no time for more inventory checking, miláčku," Karel said. "The carriage will be here any moment."

"You're leaving *tonight*?" Ema asked, startling them both. She reached up to her bare neck. "Sorry, I took the bell off."

"Ah, you're awake." Milena balanced her camera atop a case labeled METEOROLOGICAL INSTRUMENTATION. "It's taken us hours to pack, but I think we're ready."

"But it's . . ." Ema swallowed. "It's nearly *midnight*."

"We're already two days behind Františka," Karel said. "If we don't leave now, we'll never catch up."

Ema looked to the large stack of luggage by the front door and noticed they'd packed her red portmanteau.

Hope ignited in her chest. "Am I going with you?"

"No, beruška," Milena said, pulling Ema into a hug. "Much as we'd love to take you, a glacier is no place for a child."

Ema's insides began to itch. "Where will I go, then?"

They looked at her the same way Ema looked at every algebra problem: with unwavering devotion, but also as if viewing an unsolvable dilemma.

"We're certain we'll find you a tutor to stay with tonight," said Karel. "We've already sent inquiries across the city. Don't you worry; everything will be just fine."

"No, it won't," Ema said ominously, but her words were drowned out by the clip-clopping of horses and the squeak-rattle of carriage wheels on the street outside.

At half past eleven, after the luggage had been secured onto the carriage roof, a letter arrived. Her father slipped some coins to the messenger as her mother took the letter from his fingers.

"Just one reply?" Milena asked. "No others?"

The boy shook his head.

Ema watched her parents carefully as they read the letter. She saw the small crease between her father's brows, the tight line of her mother's mouth, and the split-second pause they each took before plastering on entirely false smiles.

"She'll be perfectly fine there," Karel said. "It's only a few months."

Milena's smile twitched. "Very well."

Ema peered up at the Astronomical Clock. In twenty-five minutes, her midnight birthday catastrophe would finally catch up with her.

Where were they sending her?

Ema opened her mouth to ask her question, but her voice was stuck. Instead, she settled into the farthest corner of the carriage and wrapped her arms around herself. Her parents scrambled in with her, and the carriage lurched forward, carrying them out of Old Town, toward the Vltava River. Ema sat in anxious silence, watching the city pass in the eerie glow of the streetlamps.

During the day, Prague was a phantasmagoria of color. The spires gleamed, the red-tiled rooftops battled the turquoise church domes for attention, stone gargoyles grinned downward, and saintly statues gazed upward. At night, the lamplit city looked like it had been dipped in liquid gold. It was no less magical to behold, but tonight Ema felt the edges of the darkness closing in on her.

Time ticked loudly in her eardrums.

Twenty minutes until midnight.

The carriage rattled over Charles Bridge, flanked by looming statues of saints, and into the Little Quarter. Ema caught a glimpse of the castle halfway up on the hill before the carriage lurched left, then right, then left again, slowing as it turned into a cobbled street so narrow Ema could see the detail in each brick they passed.

"I never thought I'd see this street again," Milena whispered as they came to a halt, and Ema pressed her face against the glass. She gazed up at an empty-looking house with several boarded-up windows and shuddered.

On the other side of the carriage, her mother's window squeaked open.

"Brother," Milena said in a somber voice. "You look well."

"Sister," said a quiet voice from beyond. "You look like you have a dead badger on your head. Those goggles are rather fetching, though."

The panic in Ema's chest gave way to confusion, then straight back to panic again.

They must be truly desperate to be free of her if they were sending her *here*, to the uncle she'd never met before, to the house where Ema's *unmentionable* grandmother had lived.

A thousand questions threatened to burst from her lips, but Ema bit each one of them down again.

Don't ask questions about Liliana.

Ema looked from her mother to her father. Karel was watching Ema with a concerned frown.

"Your uncle has agreed to take you in until we return," he said quietly. "He'll take good care of you until spring."

There was a small twitch of uncertainty under her father's left eye that set Ema's heart thundering with worry. Why were they leaving her here when they were both so clearly uneasy about the idea?

Ema checked her pocket watch. Quarter to midnight.

"We love you and we'll miss you, beruška," her mother said.

Ema studied their shadowed faces, feeling the tiniest bubble of relief at the sincerity that gleamed in their eyes. They weren't lying about that, at least.

Her mother pulled her into a tight hug. "Just remember everything we've taught you, Ema. You are a brilliant scientist in the making, and just because today didn't go as planned does not mean that you won't ever realize that dream."

"We'll be back before you know it," Karel said, tucking a strand of spider-silk hair behind Ema's ear. "We will bring you souvenirs and stories of our adventure. Who knows, you might find adventure here too."

"All right," Ema said, her voice little more than a croak.

She hugged them both fiercely before climbing out of the carriage and hauling her things with her. As she turned, there was a sharp rap on the carriage roof, followed by a tongue cluck from the driver as he urged the horses on. The carriage rattled away, haloed by street-lamps and chased by its own shadow, revealing what would be Ema's home until spring.

Right across from the abandoned house, her uncle's house looked barely more inviting—narrow, crooked, and hopelessly forlorn. Even the moonlight, which kissed the top of every other building in the city, seemed to shy away from it. Ema wanted nothing more than to get as far away from it as she could too, but she didn't have a choice.

Like the house, her uncle was shrouded in darkness. As he stepped forward into the lamplight, Ema recognized him from that photograph she'd seen all those years ago. He looked pretty much exactly like her mother would, if Milena were able to grow an impressive mustache, and if she had a fondness for oil-stained overalls. Despite this familiarity, however, he felt so very alien to her.

He stared after the carriage, looking completely bemused at the seemingly empty street it had left behind.

"Hello, Uncle."

With a small start, he turned. It took a moment for his confused gaze to settle on her. "Oh, there you are."

He smiled strangely, his lips jerking as if they were uncertain how to perform the act. Despite the awkwardness of him, Ema could see the same soft kindness in his eyes that she saw in her mother's.

She racked her brain for something polite to say. Instead, what slipped somberly out of her mouth was "It's my birthday."

"Ah, yes. Happy birthday."

Ema blew out a shaky breath and reached for her portmanteau.

"Oh, um, wait," Josef said, nearly tripping over his own feet as he rushed over. "Let me carry that for you."

He heaved her portmanteau up and nudged the door open with his foot. The bell above the door jinglejangled. Ema's legs felt heavy as she followed him inside. Warmth greeted her skin, and the smell of oil and wood tickled her nostrils—she shuddered and sneezed.

Her uncle led her down a hallway lit not by a chandelier but by a single oil lamp. The floor was wood, not marble. The hallway was narrow enough that Ema could reach each wall by extending her elbows.

"Did we come through the main entrance?" Ema asked.

"Only the one entrance. I suppose that makes it the main one."

"Oh."

He nodded to a dark green door as they passed it. "I'll show you the workshop tomorrow. It's late; let's get you settled for the night, shall we?"

Ema wondered what sort of workshop lay beyond that door but found she was both too tired and too worried to ask. They walked on, past a short, angular doorway built into the wall beneath a staircase. Ema had never seen anything like it.

"Does that lead to the maids' quarters?"

She heard a soft chuckle ahead of her. "That, beruška, is a broom closet."

"Oh."

Another trembling oil lamp lit the stairwell. Each step groaned beneath Josef but didn't elicit so much as a squeak beneath Ema. They emerged in another narrow hallway, and Josef nodded to an open door as they passed.

"The grand kitchens."

Ema could just make out the dark shapes of a small cooker, a table with a crooked leg, and four mismatched chairs. She hurried to catch up with Josef, who was already halfway up to the third floor.

"This is where the lord of the manor resides," Josef said with a wink. "M'lady's quarters are on the next floor."

Ema caught a glimpse of a neatly kept bedroom through the first doorway and a clutter-strewn study next door. Then she followed Josef as he squeaked and creaked his way up an even more rickety staircase.

"You really have *no* hired help?"

"Maid, cook, *and* uncle," he said, grinning as he set the portmanteau down at her feet. "Three for the price of one."

Ema realized they'd climbed as many stairs as the house had to offer and were now under the arched eaves of the roof. A single door loomed before them.

"An attic room?"

"The biggest room in the house. Your grandmother loved it. I hope you will too."

"This was *Liliana's* room?"

"Indeed."

Ema offered him another weak smile. He offered her another awkward one.

"Well. Goodnight then, Ema."

"Goodnight, Uncle."

She waited until he was down the stairs and out of

sight before turning — very slowly — to the door to her grandmother's room. Her *dead* grandmother's room.

It all made sense now. Whatever doom awaited her, she'd find it beyond that door.

Ema looked again at her pocket watch. Five to midnight.

Reluctantly, she nudged the door open. The room was long and narrow but drenched in lamplight. Most of the furniture was draped in dust sheets, but Ema could see evidence that her uncle had made a hurried effort to make it somewhat cozy for her unexpected arrival.

The bed had nicely plumped pillows, a thick blue quilt, and a round fur cushion at the foot, like the one her father used to warm his feet on particularly cold nights. There was even a fresh, if somewhat messily arranged, bouquet of flowers shoved in a mug and placed on the bedside table.

Realizing she had no other option, Ema half carried, half dragged her portmanteau to the bed. She dropped it with a solid thunk on the floor. A cloud of dust shot out from underneath it. Coughing, she checked her watch again.

Four minutes.

Wafting the air, Ema began to pull at the dust sheets, revealing a green velvet armchair, then an ornate dresser.

Three minutes.

Ema continued to yank each sheet away. There was a bookcase filled with novels, another filled with trinkets, and one filled with shelf upon shelf of identical red leather journals. A final sheet tug revealed a mirror standing up on silver duck's feet.

Ema made a slow circle, expecting some sort of monster to jump out at her at any moment, or for a bookcase to come tumbling down upon her, but apart from a gentle draft blowing around her, the room was eerily still. After a few turns, she realized the ticking sound in her ears was not a product of her imagination but emanating from an ancient mantel clock.

It told her she now had two minutes left.

Ema's bones itched unbearably as she counted down in her head.

One minute.

The draft picked up slightly, swirling the dust around the room and into Ema's face. She staggered to a round window and opened it and had just blinked the last of the dust from her eyes when she heard clockwork gears stirring from the mantelpiece.

A surge of terror coursed through her.

Midnight had arrived.

The abandoned house stood opposite, but the window across from her was not boarded up like the others. It was an attic room, much like her own, but emptier.

But not *entirely* empty.

The clock gears clunked one final time. Ema stared wide-eyed and frozen-limbed at the sight before her. Deep in the gloom, the outline of a girl dangled upside down from the rafters like a giant bat. And as the first chime rang out, a pair of dark, hollow eyes snapped open and looked directly into hers.

Ema blinked, but the shadowy figure was still there when she reopened her eyes, and still staring straight at her. The girl—if it was a girl—appeared to be around her age, with dark auburn hair that cascaded down in long waves, and thin arms crossed over her chest.

One ridiculous word pushed itself into Ema's mind.

Ghost.

It was, Ema knew, the most illogical explanation for what she was seeing, but she was too gripped by horror to grasp on to a better one. As the chimes rang on, Ema wondered if the figure would ever move, even though she herself had forgotten how to. Then the shadowy specter reached one arm slowly up to the rafter and performed a quick flip to land on the floor as the last chime heralded midnight.

She drifted slowly toward the window, moonlight catching her features—flushed cheeks, twitching nose, and that unblinking stare. It was the rise and fall of the girl's shoulders, however, that tugged sharply on the reins of Ema's galloping heart.

She was *alive*.

Ema sucked in a breath of relief, but some lingering dust swirled up her nose.

She sneezed.

The girl shrieked. As Ema pressed the tip of her nose to stop another sneeze, the girl shook her head, snorted, then doubled over with laughter.

And with that, the spell was broken.

The buildings were close enough that Ema could hear the small wheeze between each fresh bout of laughter and see each wrinkle between the girl's eyebrows as she tried and failed, several times, to pull herself together.

Ema felt her cheeks warm. "What's so funny?"

"I thought you were—" The girl goose-honk laughed.

"You thought I was what?"

"I thought—" She blew out a breath, then another few, until finally she seemed able to breathe properly again. "Oh saints, I thought you were a *ghost*."

"Oh. I thought *you* were a ghost."

"No." The girl shook her head and leaned out the window. "You're much more ghostly than me. Your hair is so pale. And your eyes are like smoke. I nearly wet myself when you appeared. Which would have had unfortunate consequences considering I was upside down."

Ema noticed the girl's clothes, and embarrassment gave way to curiosity. Layers of tulle skirts, a black shirt with a ruffled collar that reached right up to her ears, a midnight-blue waistcoat, and silver ribbons woven through the length of her dark hair. She looked extraordinary.

Ema became slowly aware that the girl was studying her just as carefully.

"You snuck up on me," the girl said, her smile gone.

Ema felt a familiar knot tighten in the pit of her stomach. "Sorry. I—"

"No one has ever snuck up on me before." She grinned again. "That's astonishing." Still clutching her left hand to her chest, the girl climbed onto the windowsill, seemingly unconcerned about the long drop down. "I'm Silvie."

Ema leaned carefully out of her own window, feeling her vision swirl as she noticed how far up they were. "I'm . . . I'm Ema Vašková."

"Are you scared of heights, Ema Vašková?"

"It would seem so. Aren't you?"

"It would seem not." Silvie moved farther forward and cocked her head. "What are you doing up in a dark, dusty attic if you're not a ghost?"

"I'm staying here. Why is your house all boarded up? And why were you upside down?"

"It's not my house. I was—oh, I suppose there's no

way of explaining myself without sounding ridiculous. I was hoping to befriend a colony of bats."

Ema's eyebrows climbed up her forehead.

"This seemed like the perfect place to find them," Silvie continued hastily. "I thought hanging upside down might make me more agreeable to them, but I've been waiting hours with no luck. Told you it was silly."

"It's not silly."

"Really?" The girl beamed.

"It's almost entirely brilliant."

"What do you mean *almost*?"

"Well, those rafters look like a bat-roosting paradise, and the upside-down bit . . . well, when dealing with any shy creatures, it's wise to try to camouflage with them. My siblings Kryštof and Kateřina once covered themselves in dung and grass to get close to a herd of bison in the Carpathian Mountains. So, really, there's just one problem with your plan."

Silvie leaned eagerly forward. "Which is?"

"Bats hibernate in winter," Ema said, feeling an unfamiliar tingle of pride at the gleam of awe in the girl's eyes as she spoke. "They'll have moved underground or into a cave, and they're almost impossible to find at this time of year. I'm afraid you'll have to wait until spring."

The girl's face fell.

Ema's newfound confidence evaporated.

"I can't wait that long," Silvie whispered.

"Why not?"

Silvie gently lifted her hair away from where her hand was still clutched against her chest. Her fingers uncurled, and a tiny, almost skeletal hand emerged. The squashed face of a bat appeared a moment later.

"I found him last night, shivering in a puddle. I put him in my pocket to warm him up, but he doesn't seem to want to leave. I named him Béla. I was hoping I could find his family."

Now it was Ema's turn to watch in awe as Silvie gently stroked the soft fur on the bat's head.

"I imagine that pocket of yours is comfortingly dark for him, which is why he doesn't want to leave it. Perhaps you could find him a cool, dark place where he can sleep for the next few months. Somewhere hidden and safe, where no one can find him."

Silvie's smile wavered, though only for a moment. "I know just the place."

Ema squealed as Béla suddenly flapped one leathery wing at the night air. Silvie cooed to the bat until he stilled, then smiled up at Ema. "Scared of bats too?"

"There isn't much I'm not scared of."

Ema regretted the words as soon as they'd left her mouth. She waited for Silvie to roll her eyes or mock her. Instead, Ema was rewarded with another grin.

"Well, it just so happens that I am an expert in conquering fear." Silvie beamed, twirling her feet in the air. "Perhaps it is destiny that we met."

"There's no such thing as destiny."

Silvie shrugged. "If you say so."

Ema reached for her pocket watch. Twelve minutes had elapsed since midnight, and yet here she was in one piece. No catastrophe in sight, just a dazzling girl and a tiny bat.

It made no sense.

And yet, the relentless thrum of dread was . . . gone.

Ema scrambled to change the subject. "Do your parents know you're here?"

Silvie's grin vanished, and the night felt darker in its absence. She tucked Béla carefully into her breast pocket. "I should go."

"No, wait!" Ema cried, horrified with herself for somehow ruining the moment. Despite her fear, she leaned farther out of the window. "I . . . oh saints, this is terrifyingly high."

"And yet you're grinning."

"Am I?"

"Indeed."

Ema pushed herself back again. There was another thrum coursing through her veins now, but as she lifted her hands to her cheeks, she realized Silvie was right about the grin. It left Ema so confused all she could do was stand there holding her cheeks, wondering what had come over her.

"There's a very fine line between fear and excitement, Ema Vašková," Silvie said, her expression thoughtful. "I think perhaps you need some nudging over that line. Let's meet at this time again tomorrow, but not here."

Ema dropped her hands from her cheeks and shook her head. "At *midnight*?"

"Adventures are best served with a drizzle of moonlight and a sprinkling of stars, Ema Vašková. Midnight is the perfect time for our fear-conquering quest to begin."

"Are you sure we can't meet earlier? How about at midday?"

"No."

"But—"

"Do you have trouble staying up that late?"

"Actually, I can never sleep before midnight—"

"Aha! See, destiny at play again."

"No, it's called insomnia. Look, I'm sorry, but I can't meet you in the middle of the night."

"Never believe you can't do something, Ema Vašková. Nothing is impossible, with a little imagination."

Silvie leaned farther forward, then farther still, until Ema was certain that the girl would tumble off the windowsill, down onto the cobbles far below. She seemed not to notice the peril, however, and merely studied Ema intently.

"I see I have my work cut out with you," she said finally. "But it just so happens I love an entirely impossible challenge. I'll send you an invitation with instructions on where to find me. It'll be *splendiferous*."

"But I haven't agreed—"

"Lesson one, Ema Vašková," Silvie said, standing on the ledge, grinning like a cat. "Less worrying, more daring. I will see you tomorrow."

With a rustle of skirts and a shimmer of silver and gold, Silvie somersaulted backward off the window ledge into the empty attic. As Ema watched Silvie merge into the abandoned house's deep shadows and disappear, her heart started hammering again, at Silvie's reckless daredevilry, at the absurdity of her proposition, and at the even more absurd bubble of excitement Ema felt at the thought of taking her up on that proposition.

It was a cold gust of air that finally brought her back out of her thoughts. Shivering, she closed the window, kicked off her shoes, and clambered into bed—too cold and overwhelmed to change into her nightclothes. She pulled her blankets up to her chin and wriggled her feet beneath the large fur cushion, and her shivering soon stopped.

But as she stared up at the unfamiliar shadows

creeping across the unfamiliar ceiling, her mind continued to whir. Midnight had come and gone, and Ema was overcome by the profound sense that something had indeed changed considerably in her life. What she couldn't work out was what exactly that something was, and how exactly it would, inevitably, lead her to disaster.

Was it the unbearably long stay with her bumbling uncle, who was so like her mother, and yet somehow so *not* like her?

Was it the lingering legacy of her mysterious grandmother, and whatever had caused the rift that still haunted the family to this day?

Or was it the girl with the star-speckled eyes, the mere thought of whom filled Ema with a confusing mix of worry and wonder?

5

Ema woke the next morning to an eyelash-ruffling breeze, and a feeling that she was being watched. It took a few moments to remember where she was: in a large bed, in her uncle's attic — and unable to feel her legs. She sat up and realized that somehow the large fur cushion from the end of the bed had moved across her knees while she'd slept. In the middle of the cushion was a single yellow button.

The button blinked.

A strangled noise clawed its way out of Ema's throat. As she pulled her numb legs free, the cushion extended a huge paw and sank long claws into the quilt. A feline head appeared from under what Ema now realized was a furry leg. An unbelievably giant cat uncurled itself, sporting an impressive amount of ear fluff, a generous under-chin mane, and a decidedly furious expression.

Astonishingly, the beast had not eaten Ema while she'd slept.

The creature bared its long fangs in a yawn. Ema hastily staggered out of bed toward the door, fumbled with the handle, and darted through, pulling it tightly shut. Then she stumbled down all the rickety stairs until she reached the ground-floor hallway, just as Josef was coming out of his workshop.

"Ah!" Josef exclaimed, jumping when he noticed her. "Morning, Ema."

Ema steadied herself on the wall as she caught her breath. "There's a wild cat in my room! I think it might be a lynx or a bobcat, though lord knows why it's in Prague. Perhaps it escaped from a circus!"

Josef raised his eyebrows. "A wild cat?"

"Indeed. It's huge. We should call the policie—"

"Ema. That isn't a wild cat," Josef said, fighting to contain a smile. "It's Ferkel."

"Ferkel?" Ema recognized the German word but struggled to comprehend what her uncle was saying. "It's definitely not a piglet!"

"No, but I named her that for good reason." Josef nodded to the stairwell. "I don't suppose you opened the kitchen door on your way down, did you? I'm sure I had that steak safely stowed away."

Ema turned to find the cat-beast sauntering down

the steps, her jaws wrapped around a slab of meat.

"But I locked her in my room!"

"It seems she's getting better at operating door handles," mused Josef. "She's a Maine coon. As far as I'm aware, she has no appetite for human flesh, so please don't look so horrified. I have baked us some breakfast. If we're quick, we can eat it before she does." He held up a plate with two wheel-shaped pastries on it.

"You bake?" Ema asked.

"Apricot kolache." He beamed proudly, handing her one before nudging open the workshop door. "Now, come and peruse the magical mayhem of the workshop."

Ema pressed herself against the wall as Ferkel ambled smugly after him. Eyeing the workshop door, Ema began to fret about what *magical mayhem* might be lurking beyond it. Was he some sort of strange alchemist who still believed it was possible to turn iron into gold? Or worse — was he going to have her making useless potions and hexes to sell to gullible clients?

Josef appeared in the doorway again, looking concerned. "Is everything all right?"

Ema nodded, then forced her legs to move and tried her hardest not to wince as she finally stepped through the door. As she saw the room beyond, however, there was no stopping the gasp of surprise that burst out of her.

"You're a . . . *bicycle maker*?"

Josef frowned. "You sound horrified at the prospect."

"Not at all," Ema said. "I'm . . . relieved." Then, as his frown deepened, she added, "I've always wanted to learn how to ride one but never found the time. Though I see you weren't lying about the mayhem."

The workroom smelled of varnish and oil. Wheels in various stages of construction were strewn all over the room, some as tall as Ema, others reaching only halfway up her shin. Tools hung from nails on the walls, as did bicycle saddles. There was a penny-farthing in the center of the room, its frame painted yellow and its spokes alternating between black and gold. Beside it was a child-sized replica.

"Yes, well, tidiness isn't my strong suit. Neither, it seems, is making bicycles that people are a hundred percent happy with. There's always something amiss — not fast enough, not smooth enough, not enough wheels . . . We could tackle the untidiness together, but I'd appreciate your mathematical skills for my design concepts, if you think that would be an interesting way to spend your time here?"

Ema summoned a smile. "It wouldn't be the worst way to spend my time here," she said truthfully.

Then, nibbling the puffed edge of her kolache, Ema crept around worktops, piles of bicycle parts, and Ferkel, who had finished her stolen steak breakfast and was weaving through Josef's legs, yowling.

Ema balanced her breakfast on a saddle and squeezed past a teetering pile of paint cans. Half-buried behind a stack of spokes was an entirely wooden bicycle. Its wheels were not quite equal in size and were almost touching, with pedals protruding from the middle of the front wheel. It looked so unremarkable compared to its flamboyant cousins, and yet—for that very reason—all the more beguiling.

"Ah, the boneshaker," Josef said, pulling the bicycle out and swatting away some cobwebs. "The wooden frame and wheels make riding it a rather rattling experience." He beamed down at it. "First bicycle I ever made. I'd forgotten it was there, to be honest."

"I think it's magnificent, even though the mathematical dimensions are a little strange."

"Then let's call it a slightly belated birthday gift."

Ema's stomach gave a little, unexpected flutter of delight. "Really?"

"Yes, really. We'll take it out later, so you can ride it. But first, eat up."

Ema smiled again, then reached for her kolache—only to find it had disappeared.

As had the cat-beast.

Any relief Ema had felt earlier that day that her uncle might not be as ominously peculiar as she'd feared was quickly doused the moment they stepped out of the house.

"You do realize that it's customary to walk *dogs* on

leashes, not cats," Ema said, eyeing Ferkel warily as the cat-beast dragged her uncle down the road, and she pushed the boneshaker along after them.

"I'm not sure Ferkel has realized that she's a cat yet," Josef said, by way of explanation. "And—although they haven't told me this themselves, of course—the local squirrel population seems to be greatly appreciative of this leash. Now, how about we take that new bicycle of yours up to the park on Petrin Hill? Ferkel loves it up there. Don't you, Ferkel?"

As they were climbing the seemingly endless steps up past the castle, Ema had—out of the corner of her eye—made some worrying observations about her uncle.

Josef tapped every chimney sweep they passed on the shoulder. Every time they happened upon a black cat, a white horse, or a single magpie, Josef would stop, take three small steps backward, and spit three times. And as her uncle stopped to give some coins to a beggar, she noticed a small fish scale tucked inside his wallet.

It took all her willpower not to ask about any of these things as they carried on up the hill, having realized that there really was a reason her mother had been so uncomfortable leaving her with him.

Josef was incredibly superstitious. As Ema knew all too well, superstition was the one thing Milena did not tolerate.

Finally, they arrived at a parkland that overlooked the city, and Ema found herself worrying about something new entirely. She'd never ridden a bicycle before, and now that she was faced with the prospect, all she could think about were the many ways in which she could fall off it.

It was Ferkel who saved her from her predicament.

No sooner had Ema positioned herself on the bone-shaker's wooden saddle, given Josef a shaky smile, and found herself frozen with terror as she willed herself to begin, than the cat-beast yowled.

Only, the yowl had come from far in the distance.

Josef was staring down at the empty leash in his hand with a confused frown. "How did she—"

A scream sounded from behind a row of rhododendrons, and her uncle pinched the bridge of his nose. "You go home when you're finished here," he told Ema. "I'll meet you there. It might take me a while to find Ferkel."

As soon as he disappeared in pursuit of the yowls and screams, Ema climbed off the boneshaker, shaking with relief.

By the time dusk arrived, Ema was sweeping up the last of the workshop's debris, and Josef staggered in, dragged by the furious momentum that was Ferkel on a leash.

"She caused some minor mayhem, but at least I eventually found her," he said, releasing the leash and rubbing his wrist. "Oh, I think this might be for you."

He passed Ema a tiny scroll, about the length and width of her little finger, sealed with what looked and smelled suspiciously like half-chewed toffee. Scrawled next to the seal was her name. A confusing combination of intrigue and unease swept through her.

"What mysterious friends you have. I noticed a small hand tuck this into Ferkel's harness, then disappear."

"Thank you," Ema said, holding the scroll to her chest. "I think I might go to bed early tonight, if that's all right?"

"Don't you want dinner?"

"I'm too tired after all that cycling."

"Oh."

Their awkward silence was interrupted by a massive belch. Ferkel vomited a paintbrush head, then looked up at them accusingly.

Ema hurried up the stairs to the attic room, carefully peeling away the half-chewed-toffee seal. The handwriting was beautifully neat, but the ink was so faint she had to squint to read it.

> *Dearest Ghost Girl,*
> *I hereby invite you to seize the night with me.*
> *Charles Bridge at precisely midnight.*
> *Dress sensibly.*
> *Yours splendiferously,*
> *Silvie*
> *P.S. Don't be late.*

P.P.S. Don't be early.
P.P.P.S. I like your giant cat.

As Ema began to crumple the absurd invite in her fist, a breeze whistled around her, and the first few pages of the Ema Enigma documents blew off the bedside table. The memory of Dagmara Bartoňová's rejection slammed into her, pushing hot tears out the corners of her eyes.

This is not science. It is a list of things you are afraid of, Ema.

She looked up at the duck-foot mirror, seeing her pale reflection blinking back at her. As the breeze ruffled the wispy ends of her hair, a shiver ran through her, and a new sense of purpose bloomed in its wake. Slowly, she uncrumpled Silvie's invite.

6

The house was eerily quiet by eleven thirty as Ema emerged from under her blankets already dressed. Per Silvie's instructions, she had chosen her most sensible outfit: a puffed-sleeve woolen dress, her favorite hooded cloak, and a pair of suede boots with green silk laces.

Glancing at herself in the mirror, Ema noticed a tiny, hopeful smile tugging at the corners of her mouth.

She crept downstairs, pausing briefly outside her uncle's bedroom door to make sure he was asleep. To her relief, there were two distinct sets of snoring coming from his room — a nose-whistling one just like her mother's, and a softer, purring one.

The floorboards were perfectly silent as Ema made her way to the front door and pulled it open. The cold darkness of the night wrapped around her, and she stood on the threshold, unsure whether to step forward and close the door behind her, or step back and close it in front of her.

A city at night was no place for a child. What would be lurking out there in the darkness? Ema could think of at least a hundred terrible things.

She stepped backward, ready to shut the door on the cold night and pretend she'd never even contemplated going out into it, but the memory of Dagmara Bartoňová's cutting gaze stopped her. It was Ema's fear that had cost her a place at Dagmara Bartoňová's school.

Silvie was offering to help get rid of that fear.

"Less worrying, more daring," Ema whispered, taking a night-seizing step out of her uncle's house.

An icy wind wrapped itself around her, sending a loose strand of shimmery hair flying and her heart fluttering.

She took another step.

Then another.

And another.

Her feet passed silently over the mosaic sidewalks as she hurried toward the river, under arched walkways and down winding streets. There were more people than she had expected, wandering alone or in small groups, chattering loudly or singing drunkenly. Ema was glad no one paid her any attention. The wind pushed her onward until she arrived—cold nosed but warm limbed—at the crenelated bridge gate.

Charles Bridge was deserted, except for saintly statues silhouetted against the moody purple sky. Halfway across, Ema stopped, uncertainty crawling over her skin as distant church bells tolled the twelfth hour. It was midnight, but she and the ancient saints were the only figures on the bridge.

Where was Silvie?

Ema made a slow circle. A brief flicker of movement drew her attention to a nearby statue, which was oddly out of proportion to the others. It was shorter, for one thing. And although its palms were pressed together in prayer, there was no golden ring above its head. It also seemed to be wearing a tricorn hat.

As Ema took a tentative step forward, the statue leaped from the wall and dropped into a crouch on the cobblestones in front of her. Ema swallowed a yelp of surprise.

"Hello, ghost girl," said a familiar voice. "I knew I'd be able to sneak up on you this time. Although I'll admit, I didn't notice *you* until you were right in front of me. It was like you materialized out of thin air."

They both stepped forward into a ring of lamplight, then raised their eyebrows.

"What are you wearing?"

"What are *you* wearing?"

Both girls spoke with identical tones of astonishment.

Silvie wore an oilskin jacket that reached her shins, boiled-wool trousers tucked into boots, and the tricorn hat, which kept slipping down toward her nose.

"You look like a fisherman who has lofty dreams of becoming a pirate," Ema said, unable to stop herself giggling.

"*Indeed*," Silvie said with a grin, pushing the hat from her eyes. "Which means I'm perfectly waterproof. You, on the other hand, look about as waterproof as a sponge."

"Why do I need to be waterproof?"

"I told you we were meeting on the bridge. Surely that's suggestive of a watery adventure?"

Ema peered down at the dark river. "Watery?!"

"Don't look so horrified." Silvie linked her arm in Ema's. "The plan is to avoid falling in, but you can never be too careful. I'll explain it all properly once we get there."

Ema tried to look less horrified. "Get where?"

"You'll see."

Silvie led her back toward the Little Quarter, where the lamplit castle rose up from the hill behind the gate tower Ema had just come through. Before they reached the gate, Silvie tugged her down some steps onto Kampa Island—the biggest of the narrow islands nestled in the Vltava. They followed the riverbank for a few minutes until Silvie finally came to a halt.

"Ta-da!" she said, waving her arm at a plank of wood that jutted out from the riverbank wall.

It stretched across a small river lock, its other end

resting on the wall of the narrow slip of island just opposite. Ema looked at it skeptically.

"Can't we use the bridge farther down?" she asked. "It's a much more reassuring feat of engineering—"

"Tonight we are *pirates*." Silvie sprang up onto the wall with the ease of an acrobat. "We can't have a pirate adventure without walking a plank."

She walked halfway along the plank, turned, grabbed her hat with one hand, and then winked at Ema before performing a series of one-handed cartwheels until she reached the other side.

Ema's mouth opened and closed a few times.

Silvie giggled. "Now I've proved that the plank is sturdy, get up here before your brain convinces you otherwise."

"It's too late for that."

"Can you swim?"

"Yes, but—"

"Excellent! There's no current on this side of the island. The worst that can happen is that you fall in, and I fish you out again."

"That's not comforting in the slightest."

"Aren't you even a little bit curious to find out what it's like? Aren't scientists like yourself supposed to be curious about things?"

Ema leveled her with a glare, but this only made Silvie's grin widen. She walked slowly back toward Ema.

"If I squint, it's like I'm walking across water." Silvie beamed, then held her hand out. "Now, I refuse to believe I haven't tickled your curiosity, so up you get. Curiosity is the best antidote to fear."

"I can't —"

"Don't!" Silvie said sternly. "That word is not allowed."

With a groan of resignation, Ema let Silvie pull her up onto the wall. One pointed boot was hovering over the plank when a wave of ice-cold dread shuddered through her again.

"Be curious," Silvie whispered, then let go of Ema's hand and ran across the plank to stand on the opposite side of it. "All you have to do is walk to me."

Silvie's smile of encouragement seemed to light a fuse in Ema's stomach. Adrenaline coursed through her as she put her boot down on the wood.

"That's it. Now another step."

The plank groaned and bent. Ema noticed the bounce in her legs and the air wrap around her. For a glorious moment, she felt exhilarated. She took another step, then another. And then she looked down at the cold, dark water beneath her and wanted nothing more than to be on firm ground.

Ema jolted forward. The plank ends rattled, but her focus was on Silvie's startled expression as she crashed into her. They tumbled backward in a tangled mess of skirts, hats, oilskin, and hair.

Silvie wheeze-laughed, untangling herself and getting to her feet. Ema lay on her back, her heart humming like an electric charge. Her ragged breath caught in her throat when she looked up. She'd been so focused on crossing the plank she hadn't noticed the many tiny lights strung up in the trees.

"What is all this?" she asked, sitting up and gazing around her in wonder.

"Fluvius Incanto."

Ema blinked. "The enchanted river?"

"Oh good, you speak Latin." Silvie's dark eyes danced with delight, then her expression turned serious. She leaned forward until they were almost nose to nose and whispered, "Have you heard of Vodník?"

"The water goblin?"

"Indeed," Silvie said, leading Ema through the trees and toward the wall on the other side of the narrow island where the Vltava rushed past in all its might. "It is said Vodník lurks in the depths of the river here."

Ema scoffed. "Vodník is nothing more than an old fairy tale."

"Perhaps. Or maybe he really is deep down in that murky brown void, lying in wait."

"In wait for what?"

"Someone to fall in, of course. It is said that he traps the souls of the drowned in upturned teacups."

Ema narrowed her eyes.

"What?" Silvie asked indignantly.

"You just . . . you look so serious. Like you actually believe a goblin traps souls in teacups. There's no truth in fairy tales."

"Oh, how wrong you are, Ema Vašková." Silvie stepped away from the water's edge. "Fairy tales breathe truth into the world. They are more real than even you and me." She nodded toward the river wall. "Go on, look for yourself."

Ema looked down at the water. The reflection of tiny lantern lights danced merrily on its surface, as did the wobbly reflection of her own skeptical face.

"All I see is murky river water, no gobli—"

Her words were cut short as something began to rise from the depths of the riverbed. A long-limbed figure with thick strands of weed-like hair. Its long twiggy legs kicked behind, and Ema heard a tiny cackle.

The figure broke the surface and lurched up at her. A scream leaped from Ema's throat. But just as its twig-like arm reached toward her, the figure collapsed and began flailing about on the surface of the river.

Behind her, Silvie let out a small curse.

Ema turned to see her holding a broken piece of rope in her hand. Its severed half was snaking steadily toward the river and the goblin effigy it was attached to. Ema's terror trickled away as she watched the goblin's head get swept in one direction by the river's current, its limbs in another. The cackling returned, and Ema crossed her arms as she met Silvie's glinting eyes.

"Did you honestly think you could trick me into thinking that bundle of twigs and rags was a real goblin?"

"I believe I *did* trick you. And I also believe you found it amusing too, as you're grinning again."

"It was a fine spectacle," Ema conceded. "If the rope hadn't broken when it did, I might have believed it for a full ten seconds longer. Bravo."

"Thank you." Silvie gave a little curtsy.

"What's next? I hope you're not planning on dangling me in the water to lure real goblins?"

"I think we've done enough fear-conquering for now," Silvie mused. "And I promised you a pirate's adventure. How about we find some treasure instead?"

Ema followed Silvie to a large bundle of fishing nets on the other side of the island. With a practiced fling, Silvie cast a net over the side of the wall, tying the ends of it to a small sapling.

"Now we sit and wait," she said, settling herself on the wall and patting the space beside her. "And you can tell me how a girl who lives in a dusty attic room above a bicycle shop came to speak Latin."

"Only if you tell me how a girl who befriends bats

and hunts water goblins in the middle of the night happens to not only speak Latin but also turns cartwheels like a trained acrobat."

"I asked first."

"Fine. I usually live in Old Town," Ema said. "In a house filled with science and learning. Until my parents sent me to stay with my uncle while they're off on a research expedition. So now I'm helping my uncle make bicycles."

Silvie's eyes narrowed. Ema felt like she was being studied.

"Have you always wanted to be a bicycle maker?"

"No."

"What do you want to be?"

"A scientist," Ema said with such conviction it startled her.

Silvie smiled. "What kind of scientist?"

"I—I don't know yet."

"Hmm, an I-don't-know-yet-ist," said Silvie thoughtfully. "Well, this certainly is the perfect city for you to find out in. Prague is home to some of the greatest minds in all of Europe."

"And what do you want to be?" Ema asked. "Other than a goblin-hunting pirate, of course."

Only a hint of moonlight touched Silvie's face, and Ema could just about make out a small crease between the girl's brows. Silvie reached up to her neck, and Ema saw the silvery glint of a thin chain underneath the collar of her oilskin jacket as she held her hand over the hidden necklace.

"I've had the most brilliant tutors anyone could hope to have. They've taught me so much, but . . . I'm just like you. I haven't yet found my true calling."

Silvie's grip on her hidden necklace tightened. Ema realized she was staring hard at Silvie, trying to work out how this endlessly confident girl could suddenly sound so . . . lost.

Ema averted her gaze. "Let's hope the water goblins deliver us the answers we need, then."

Silvie smiled, but it seemed strained. They sat there for several minutes, with no sound except the gurgling river. Then Ema had an idea. She reached into her pocket and took out her monocular spyglass.

"Perhaps we can spot Vodník with this?"

Instead of bringing Silvie's dazzling smile back, as she had hoped, it caused the girl's eyes to widen. She took the spyglass from Ema, turning it over in her hands. "Where did you get this?"

Silvie asked the question calmly, with an air of polite curiosity, but there was a subtle bite to it that caught Ema off guard.

"My . . . my parents gave it to me a few months ago."

As Silvie handed the spyglass back, Ema looked down to where their shadows pooled beneath their knees.

Silvie's was suddenly dark and heavy. It filled Ema with such skin-crawling dread that she tore her gaze away again, to find Silvie smiling beatifically once more.

Ema blinked, trying to work out what had just happened, then Silvie shot to her feet.

"Oh, I think we've caught something. Help me, would you?"

Together they tugged at the net, heaving it over the side of the wall and letting it drop in a sloshing pile on the ground. Icy water splashed all over Ema's feet, up over the edges of her boots to soak her socks, but she barely noticed. Silvie moved lightning quick, pulling things out from the net and setting them down on the ground.

"Wow," said Ema. "That's some treasure."

They delved through the assortment before them: a bull's-eye lantern, its glass intact but encrusted in brown river slime; several boots in various stages of decay; enough twigs and rags to make many more goblin effigies; and a disgruntled fish.

"Let's put you back where you came from, shall we?" Silvie said, scooping the fish up with both hands and lowering it back into the water.

"Um, Silvie?" Ema giggled as she began to untangle the last bit of netting. "You missed this."

For the second time that night, Ema delighted in the look of wide-eyed surprise on Silvie's face. In the bottom of the net was a small upturned teacup.

"Looks like we caught ourselves a trapped soul!"

Silvie dropped to her knees beside her and gently turned the cup the right way around. "There," she said. "It's free now." She sighed deeply, and then looked up at Ema. "You've walked the plank, escaped the clutches of a water goblin, and freed a soul. How do you feel?"

"Worried," Ema said, looking out across the darkened city. She gazed up at the light-scattered spectacle around her. "Exhilarated." And then she looked back down to the mysterious, improbable, and entirely bewildering girl grinning up at her. "And endlessly curious."

"That is the *perfect* alchemic combination for adventuring. Make sure you bring those feelings with you next time."

"Next time? There's more?"

Silvie's grinning face was lit up by the drizzle of moonlight and the sprinkling of stars above them.

"This, dear Ema, is only the beginning."

Every morning in the weeks that followed, Ema woke to the smell of spiced milk being placed on her bedside table by Josef. Then she would wake more fully to the sound of the same milk being slurped by Ferkel. After rescuing her drink, Ema would sip at it while the cat-beast stared unblinkingly at the wallpapered wall behind the bed, and the attic room breeze whistled around them.

Following breakfast, she and Josef would work all day in the workshop, painting frames, attaching wheels, and discouraging Ferkel from disemboweling saddles. They took turns scouring the neighborhood each time the cat-beast stampeded her way through a customer's legs and out the door.

After dinner, they would bake.

Ema learned that Josef's baking was born from necessity, rather than enjoyment.

"Do you think this babovká will do?" he asked one evening, holding up a large donut-shaped cake. "It's for the postman."

"Yes," said Ema. "A cake that big will certainly make him forget all about those packages Ferkel destroyed."

"Excellent. I'll deliver it now, then. You should probably have a bath. I say this with utmost respect, but you look like something a wild cat dragged in."

Ema's hair smelled faintly of varnish no matter how much she washed it, her forehead was usually paint smeared, and her elbows attracted a daily buildup of oil, sawdust, and cat fluff. She felt a universe away from her life in Big Old Town Square—but every now and then, her new world would collide uncomfortably with her old one.

"There's no need to dress for an Arctic expedition," Josef told her one day before their afternoon walk. "You'll boil alive in that outfit."

She looked down at her fur-lined snowsuit, then at his more modest coat, and shook her head. "It's blizzarding out there!"

"Not for long. Here, watch." He steered her toward the workshop window, beyond which snow swirled and roared furiously. "It's about to clear—you'll see."

Ema peered through the furry edges of her hood at him. He had no barometer—she'd searched for one. But he did have the same look of satisfaction that Milena would have as the snow suddenly stopped and blue sky appeared once more.

Ema swallowed down the urge to ask how he'd known, certain she would not like his answer, and quietly went to change her outfit.

Swallowing questions became a daily practice. Each one sat heavily in her stomach like an undigested lump. These were mostly questions about her grandmother — especially about the bookcase full of journals in the attic room, which Ema had taken to covering with a dustcloth so she wouldn't have to think about them. Františka's words were ever present in her mind: *Don't ask questions about Liliana.*

For all her uncle's bumbling awkwardness, he was clearly trying hard to make her feel welcome. Ema felt it was the least she could do to not let him see just how desperate she was for her stay in this house to come to an end.

Each day, she plastered on a smile.

Sometimes, it worked. Often, it didn't.

"Ema? Hello? Are you all right? I think you've mopped that patch of floor enough now. Why aren't you blinking? Is there something stuck in your eyes?"

Ema jolted out of her reverie to find her uncle staring at her in concern. She'd been thinking about Silvie and the Midnight Manifesto they'd scribbled on the back of an empty soap packet that night by the river.

They would meet under the full-ish moon, each month, at midnight, on Charles Bridge.

Silvie would provide three nights of fear-conquering adventures.

Ema would provide three nights of snacks.

As keen as she was for her parents' return, she was just as desperate to see her new friend again. The weeks had seemed like an eternity.

"I wasn't in a trance," Ema said. "I was just admiring the moon."

Josef stared at her a moment longer. "Yes, it's a beautiful full-ish moon tonight, isn't it?"

Ema nodded, her heart giving a little flutter of anticipation, then ducked with a shriek as a small projectile soared through the window and over her head. Peering out, Ema caught a brief glimpse of dark curls and heard a distant giggle as a small figure darted off.

Josef picked the small toffee-sealed scroll up from the floor. "Your friend needs to be introduced to the concept of letter boxes."

He chuckled as he handed it over. Ema settled her features into their usual mask of composure, hoping he couldn't see the heart-thrumming excitement coursing through her, nor the guilt she felt about sneaking out.

"Silvie doesn't like putting things in boxes. She says the world would be a better place if we weren't so limited by such mundane predictability."

"She sounds wise beyond her years." Josef yawned. "And I am tired beyond belief. Goodnight, Ema."

"Goodnight, Uncle."

The moment he was gone, Ema unrolled the soap-packet invitation and held it up to the moonlight to read. A small hiccup of joy burst from her.

Ema hurried through the night, under the January full-ish moon, feeling horribly cold, chillingly terrified, and unbearably curious as to what adventures Silvie would have in store.

"I'm sure my invitation said to dress like an explorer," Silvie said, emerging from the shadow of Saint Ivo, wearing a beige jacket over puffed breeches and a wide-brimmed hat.

Just like on their first adventure, Silvie's necklace was tucked into her collar. Ema resisted the urge to ask about it.

"This was as close to an explorer as I could manage," she said instead, waving a hand at her paint-spattered overalls, velvet cloak, and woolen hat. "Is it all right?"

"It's splendiferous. And once again, I didn't notice you arrive until you were right in front of me. One day, I'll work out how you do that."

Then Silvie looked pointedly at the brown-paper parcel in Ema's hand. Ema opened it up to reveal some crescent-moon-shaped biscuits. The smell of vanilla and hazelnut wafted around them.

"Mmm, rohlíčky are my favorite!" Silvie shoved one in her mouth and smiled a biscuity smile. "Payment accepted. Now, on with our expedition."

The girls climbed slumbering trams to conquer Ema's fear of heights and raced wood lice up Ema's bare arms to beat her fear of insects. Some such fears were easy to address; others took a little more imagination.

"Being wrong can be *more* exciting than being correct," Silvie said the following night beneath the stone arches of Charles University, dressed in a woolen snowsuit and a spangled top hat. "You should be thrilled about making mistakes, not scared of them." She reached out, plucked a hairpin from Ema's head, then held up two closed fists.

Ema tapped the hand that had taken her pin.

Silvie opened it to show an empty palm.

Ema giggled. "Did your tutors teach you to do that?"

"They teach me the very greatest wonders of this universe, illusion being one of them. How boring would magic tricks be if they were predictable?"

By the third night, however, Silvie's tricks were beginning to lose their effect.

"How do you keep guessing correctly?" Silvie huffed. "Are you psychic?"

"'Definitely not. Your nose twitches a fraction of a millimeter when you're trying to divert my attention, your eyes dart to the left when you lie, and you never quite manage to conceal that smile quickly enough when you think I'm going to choose incorrectly."

Silvie blinked at her in astonishment. "That's frustratingly brilliant. How am I supposed to trick you if you can read my face like an open book?"

"You could wear a mask."

Silvie's grin returned, lighting up the dark night. "I'm still convinced there's a hint of psychic-ness you're keeping from me."

Ema put her own mask on — a smile she hoped would hide her discomfort. "I assure you, I'm perfectly normal."

"Normal is the biggest illusion of all, Ema Vašková. I don't need to be psychic to know that you are *splendiferously* peculiar." Ema struggled to keep her smile firmly in place as Silvie leaned in closer. "I'm making an amendment to our Midnight Manifesto," she said. "We will banish these fears of yours, but we will also banish the idea that normal is something worth striving for. I will make you *proudly* peculiar."

The following weeks felt like a never-ending sequence of impossibility. Ema couldn't stop the attic room breeze, no matter how many holes she plugged. Ferkel wouldn't stop trying to outdo her own mischievousness, they couldn't bake enough apology pastries, and Ema couldn't help counting the days until her parents' return. But most of all, Ema found waiting for the next full-ish moon to arrive so impossibly frustrating she thought she might burst.

"It's impossible!" Ema blurted out one frozen February afternoon.

Her voice filled the workshop and was followed by a small shriek of surprise. Standing at the workshop counter beside Josef was a woman in a green bustled dress, a woolen shawl, and a foul mood.

"I beg your pardon?" the woman said, eyeing Ema with obvious unease.

The woman had spent the last hour complaining about anything and everything she could think of—too much dust in the room, too much snoring from Ferkel, too many paint colors to choose from. Her insufferable petulance had cut through the very last of Ema's nerves.

"You want my uncle to build you a bicycle that—and I quote—glides smoothly across the city like a swan on water. That's simply . . . impossible."

"And what would you know?" the woman asked peevishly. "You're a *child.*"

"Would you like me to explain the physics of cobbled streets and metal wheels to you?"

Josef made a small noise, somewhere between a squeak and croak. "What my niece means is that we will need some time and some very complicated calculations to get the design just right, Frau Kraus."

"Very well," Frau Kraus said. "I shall return in a few weeks." After leveling Ema with a satisfied smirk, she sashayed out of the workshop like a goose.

"Is everything all right, Ema?" Josef asked, worry creasing his forehead.

"Yes," Ema lied, settling herself down on a stool. "I suppose I'd better get started on those complicated calculations?"

His eyes narrowed. "Yes, I suppose you should," he agreed reluctantly. "Do you have any questions about — "

"Was Liliana a witch?"

The question burst unexpectedly from her lips. She couldn't swallow it back down again, however, so she settled for blushing profusely.

Josef stared at her.

Ema racked her brain for something to say but ended up spitting out another question. "Those journals in the attic — are they spell books?"

Josef blinked. "How much has your mother told you about her life here?"

"Precisely nothing."

"Your babička wasn't a witch. She was just very . . . intuitive."

Ema winced. "Was she a fortune-teller?"

"More like a *mis*fortune-teller. I'm sure she'd have been a lot more popular had it been fortunes she'd read and not vague prophecies of doom. People generally like their mystics to be a bit more optimistic. Those journals aren't spell books; they are divinations."

Ema's mind swirled with *many* questions she didn't dare ask. What kind of misfortunes had Liliana given? Why had her mother stopped speaking to her? Was it *more* than just Milena's aversion to the unscientific?

"Is that expression on your face just curiosity," Josef asked, looking at her so intently she couldn't help but squirm, "or is there something you want to tell me?"

Ema kept her mouth squeezed shut and shook her head.

Josef looked at her in a way that was becoming all too regular—like he was studying a rare and mysterious creature that he was so very desperate to understand.

"I just need some fresh air," Ema said, quickly summoning a smile. "How about I take Ferkel for a walk?"

"It's going to rain," Josef said, his eyes narrowing further still. "Heavily. Any moment."

Ema looked out the window at the cloudless sky and sighed. "Very well. In that case, I shall find a quiet place to sit and work on those *impossible* calculations for Frau Kraus's *impossible* bicycle."

The quiet place Ema found was the broom closet. She wedged herself in beside a mop and several spiderwebs, and squeezed her eyes closed. It was cramped, but at least her uncle would not be able to study her.

The next day, Ema headed straight to the broom

closet again, only to find it transformed. All mops, buckets, and old shoes had disappeared—replaced by a scattering of cushions, a flickering oil lamp, and a sleeping cat-beast.

"Your own private study," Josef said when he found her staring at it in astonishment. "I couldn't bring myself to rehome those spiders, though."

"Thank you," Ema said, feeling a confusing mixture of gratitude and discomfort.

His beaming smile made Ema feel even more uncomfortable as she ducked into the closet and closed the door—sealing her uncle away. He had been so kind, but he was becoming far too observant. What if he saw through her mask? Perhaps it was for the best that she avoid him as much as possible until her time here came to an end.

When the February full-ish moon finally arrived, Ema felt giddy with relief. Even when she found herself blindfolded and guided down a slippery ladder.

"'Where are we?" she asked nervously as her feet hit the ground with a squelch. "It smells like wet cat down here."

"Did you know that Prague's ground was raised by several meters about a hundred years ago?" Silvie whispered. "You can find hidden basements, tunnels, streets . . . there's an entire city hidden beneath your feet, Ema Vašková. If you know where to look."

Silvie tugged the blindfold off. They were in a crypt, with vaulted stone ceilings that curved high above their heads. Silvie set her bull's-eye lantern on the floor, directing its light against a moss-covered wall. Two large shadowy hands crept up the wall, morphed together to form a shadow bat, then proceeded to flutter around in a frenzied dance.

Ema chuckled. "You're trying to frighten me with a shadow puppet show?"

The shadow bat halted mid-flutter and broke apart into two separate hands again, and then Silvie appeared before her, frowning in bemusement.

"I thought you were scared of shadows?"

Ema's smile wavered. "That's not on my list. What makes you think I'm scared of shadows?" She'd been careful not to mention the Ema Enigma.

"You *are* scared of shadows," Silvie said assuredly. "I've seen you staring at them several times. I've even seen you leap away from some."

Ema swallowed around a hard lump. "Let's focus on the list, shall we? What's that behind your back?"

Silvie grinned and held up a folded piece of soap-packet paper. "This should convince you that being invisible is nothing to fret about. In fact, the way you can sneak about is nothing short of magic, Ema."

Ema unfolded the soap packet, then frowned. "It's blank."

"Smell it."

Ema lifted it to her nose and breathed in.

"Lemon? Why—oh, I see."

Pressing the paper against the lantern, Ema waited as the invisible ink began to appear in familiar, elegant letters:

TA-DA . . . MAGIC!

Ema smiled. "This is science, not magic."

"Can't it be both?"

At the start of March, color burst across the city. Leaves burgeoned, flowers bloomed, and the usual scent of smoke and horse dung developed a fragrant undertone that helped take the edge off. It was with happier nostrils that Ema followed Silvie through the small patch of woodland just above the castle one midnight. She felt a niggling itch of unease, but she tried her best to ignore it.

"Did you know there are plants that eat flies and even small animals?" Silvie said, dressed like a woodland fairy in an emerald-sequined leotard, with small wings protruding from her back. "And in Sumatra they have a corpse flower that smells like rotting flesh."

"You're supposed to be giving me fewer things to worry about, not more."

"Don't worry—Bohemian botany is less macabre, mostly."

"Mostly?"

Silvie pointed her bull's-eye lantern down at a mossy spot on the ground, illuminating a large mushroom oozing what appeared to be blood. "The Devil's Fingers," Silvie said, clearly delighted by Ema's horror. "It's juice, not blood."

Ema shook her head in disbelief. "You really do have peculiar tutors. Magic tricks, fairy tales, macabre botany— you haven't escaped from a circus, have you?"

Silvie's smile dropped, and the knot in Ema's stomach hardened. She was starting to realize that she hadn't been the only one wearing a mask when they'd met. Any time she asked Silvie anything personal, it was met with the same awkward silence. But Ema also knew that if she wasn't willing to share her own secrets, she couldn't expect Silvie to share hers.

Silvie took her by the arm. "Come, I have a splendiferous spectacle for you tonight."

They climbed the hill and came to a stop at the base of the Hunger Wall—a medieval structure that wove down the hill toward the city like a giant stone snake. Ema craned her neck to take in the crenelated brickwork looming above them.

"You want me to climb that, don't you?"

Silvie scaled a nearby tree, tiptoed her way along a thick branch like a dancing sprite, then hopped onto the wall. She beamed down at Ema. "Less worrying—"

"More daring, yes, yes, all right." Ema scrambled onto a tree branch, then crawled onto the wall. "But all this daring seems to come with bruises. Why do we need to—oh!" Her breath caught at the sight before her.

The city lay like a glittering map below them, and the moon cast an orangey glow across the terra-cotta rooftops.

"I wonder if this is where Libuše stood," Silvie said. "She was the daughter of the first ruler of Bohemia and able to see the future." She shot Ema a sly look, which Ema returned with narrowed eyes. "Legends say that a thousand years ago she arrived on a rocky cliff, high up above the Vltava, long before this city was built, and the prophecy she spoke that day came true." Silvie pointed to the Church of Our Lady before Týn, whose sixteen spires stabbed the night sky, then continued in a whispery-prophetic voice: *"I see a great city whose glory will touch the stars."*

"I suppose she *was* right," Ema admitted. "I have a prophecy of my own, if you'd like to hear it?"

Silvie looked at her in astonishment. "I thought you didn't believe in prophecies?"

Ema smiled mischievously. "I believe in this one, be-cause I've already seen compelling evidence to back it up."

"Go on then, tell me."

Ema cleared her throat, then tried not to giggle as she stared deep into Silvie's star-speckled eyes: *"I see a girl whose light will cast all darkness aside, who will change the world with her endless enthusiasm, and who will make us all see what fools we are to find fear instead of delight."* Ema lowered her voice and hardened her stare. *"She will be . . . an impresario of impossibilities."*

Ema's giggle finally burst free from her lips but trailed away as Silvie blinked up at her in wide-eyed silence, her lower lip trembling.

"It's just . . . I've been thinking about your true calling," Ema said quickly, suddenly nervous. "I don't think you will ever truly know what you've done for me, Silvie. You make me see everything in a new way. I think that's what you're meant to do . . . you're a fixer. A fixer of people."

Still Silvie said nothing.

Ema began to fret. "Did I overdo the spooky voice? I was just being silly—"

"Ema Vašková. You are anything but silly."

They sat there for a few minutes, watching the city slumber. Then Ema noticed Silvie wiping away a tear.

"Silvie, what's wrong?"

"Nothing."

Ema saw the lie dance across her friend's face. Once again, Silvie's hand reached up to the hidden necklace.

Despite months of knowing each other, there was a side to Silvie that was so mysterious she felt like a stranger at times. Silvie most likely felt the same way about her. And so Ema had decided that it was time to finally let Silvie *see* her.

Ema took a large envelope out of her cloak — inside of which was her entire collection of papers on the Ema Enigma.

"What is that?" Silvie asked.

"This is the most frightening thing I've ever done," Ema said, setting the envelope down on Silvie's lap. "Don't open it until you get home later. We can talk about it next month. And maybe, afterward, you can tell me what it is that's worrying you?"

Silvie stared hard at her, then shrieked as a sudden fluttering of leathery wings beat the air above them. The girls huddled together as small dark shapes flitted frantically upward.

"Ema, look!" cried Silvie in delight. "They're out of hibernation! Perhaps Béla will be too. Oh, you've gone impossibly pale. What's wrong?"

Every atom of Ema's skeleton itched with horror as she counted. One, two, three, four, five, six, seven, eight, nine, ten, eleven . . . *twelve* bats.

This time, it was she who offered up a small smile and a big lie.

"Nothing."

After that night on the Hunger Wall, Ema woke each morning from the same nightmare: stumbling through darkness, ducking away from bats, and endlessly trying to find Silvie, who always seemed to be dancing away from her, one step ahead. Ema became keenly aware that the small knot of worry that had started that night with Silvie was now becoming a churning tangle of dread.

What catastrophe was coming her way?

Would her family arrive to collect her in the next few weeks and be disappointed by her lack of accomplishment? Other than being able to ride the boneshaker, which surely would not impress them much. Would Josef see past her mask and decide that she was just like her grandmother? If so, would he tell her parents? Had she made a huge mistake in giving Silvie her Ema Enigma documents? Would Silvie—despite her assurances to the contrary—decide that Ema really was beyond hope?

Day by day, Ema cocooned herself in her makeshift study. "More calculating?" Josef would ask, jolting her out of her own thoughts. It was clear that he knew her mind had been far away from calculations, and Ema felt a conflicting mix of guilt and relief that he was trying hard to let her have the bits of privacy she so clearly needed. But as Josef's new bicycle began to take shape and the late-March sun spread warmth through the trees, towers, and winding streets of Prague, Ema could not rid herself of the incessant chill of foreboding.

She wanted nothing more than to see Silvie again, urgently.

"Just a few weeks," she would whisper to herself, watching the waning moon become steadily slimmer. Then, after the new moon was over and the waxing moon had plumpened once more: "Just a few more days."

But when Silvie's invitation turned up a day early— tied with a silver ribbon to the boneshaker's handlebar— the intense sense of dread became an icy grip of terror.

Silvie *never* asked to meet her before a full-ish moon.

Silvie *never* asked to meet her anywhere other than Charles Bridge.

Something was wrong.

The sky was a purple haze of mist-smudged star glow as Ema arrived at the graveyard gates a little before midnight to find Silvie already waiting for her. Beyond the iron bars, statues and headstones loomed like pieces on a giant macabre chessboard.

It was the sight of Silvie, however, that made Ema's teeth itch with worry. Silvie was wearing a plain black dress, with her hair plaited neatly around her head and the somber look of someone in mourning. Her flamboyant friend was barely recognizable.

"Silvie, what's going on?" Ema asked. "And why are you—"

"Quick," Silvie interrupted, grabbing Ema's arm and ushering her in through a small gap in the gates. "We don't have long."

"Don't have long for what?"

"I'll explain when we get there."

Ema shuddered with unease. "Get where?"

Silvie tugged her along the gravel path, running past row upon row of weeping angels and towering crosses, toward a long line of mausoleums in the distance. The darkness was as thick as soup, and were it not for the tight grip Silvie had on her, Ema would have thought she was in one of her dreams again, especially when a bat swooped down over them, making Ema yelp in surprise.

"That's just Béla," Silvie said. "He's been following me all week now that he's out of hibernation. Come. It's not far."

As Béla fluttered away again, Ema dug her heels in and pulled Silvie to a stop.

"Silvie, no—please! I don't think we should be in here."

Ema could barely see her friend's face, but she was suddenly overcome with a sense of sadness and despair. She looked down at her friend's heavy, darkened shadow, and every last bit of breath left her lungs.

"What you said that night," Silvie said quietly, as if she too were struggling to find the air to speak. "About facing the truth . . . and then those papers you gave me . . . You're far braver than I am, Ema Vašková. You always have been. All this time I thought I was helping you become braver, when really it was you who was helping me."

"Silvie," Ema rasped. "You're not making the slightest bit of sense right now."

"You said I could tell you anything. Did you mean that?"

"Of course I did—"

"Then come."

Silvie led her, slower this time, past a stone gargoyle, to the very edge of the cemetery. They came to a halt outside a huge mausoleum; with a mere sliver of moonlight peeking through the clouds to see by, Ema could only just make out the vague, pointed-roof shape of it. Her heart was now hammering so hard she felt dizzy. Silvie stepped toward her so that their faces were close enough that they could breathe each other's trembling breaths.

"I've spent every day reading your research," Silvie said solemnly. "I know you hoped I could find an answer in it for you, but I couldn't. Not yet, anyway."

Was this why she was so full of sadness? Was she mourning any hope either of them might have had that Ema could one day be fixed? Before Ema could find the breath to respond, Silvie leaned ever so slightly closer, her eyes shimmering with unshed tears, but also a glint of something inscrutable.

"You truly are an enigma, Ema Vašková," Silvie said gravely. "But the most *fascinating* kind, like the birth of the universe or . . . giraffes."

Finally, a word burst past the heavy lump in Ema's throat. "Giraffes?"

"Nothing about them makes sense either, but you must admit they're brilliant. *You're* brilliant, Ema, but you never finished testing your original hypotheses—"

"That's because they were absurd—"

"That's your mother speaking, not you. You've absorbed *her* fear and denial of these things. What I saw in those papers of yours was curiosity about the very real, very mysterious, but utterly remarkable way you see the world. Perhaps it's supernatural, perhaps it's not—perhaps you're an alien from the moon—"

"There are no aliens on the moon."

"That's a debate to be had another time; my point is that you *need* to finish testing those hypotheses, Ema—even if they do turn out to be wrong. You and I are living proof that fear and denial never get us anywhere."

Ema felt a sudden swell of sadness, which washed over every inch of her. Her gaze dropped to the shadow that surrounded them both and seemed to be getting darker and darker.

"You can feel it, can't you?" Silvie whispered. "Every time I tried to hide it behind smiles and cartwheels, you could *feel* that I was hiding something. You can feel my despair . . . my grief . . . right now, can't you?"

Ema nodded. "I can also feel that we shouldn't be here, Silvie. Something's going to happen tonight, and it's going to happen here, in this graveyard."

"You're right about that." Silvie looked up as the almost full-ish moon appeared from behind the clouds. "But it *needs* to happen tonight."

Ema cast a nervous glance at the shadowy mausoleum. "You want me to go in there and test my shadow hypothesis, don't you?"

"Yes, Ema. Perhaps these shadows you see *are* the dead kind."

"Silvie, what you're asking—it's too much."

"I know," Silvie said. "But it's safe to explore that possibility with me. Ghosts or no ghosts . . . and I'll accept you as you are, no matter what. Instead of running away, we could face the truth *together*."

Sincerity radiated from every inch of her friend's face, and although Silvie's words bloomed warmly through her, they did not lessen the dread that had taken root in Ema's very bones. This was not just about her own fears, she realized, but Silvie's too.

"What is this secret you want to tell me?"

Out of her sleeve, Silvie pulled a single white tulip. "Floriography," she whispered, holding the tulip up between them. "Red roses for love, heather for luck, sunflowers for loyalty, and a perfect white tulip for forgiveness. It's a way of apologizing when you can't find the words to say sorry. There is someone whose forgiveness I need more than anything else in this world."

"Who?"

Silvie's hand reached up to her necklace, then dropped again. "I'll explain inside, if you'll come with me?"

It was the silent but desperate look of hope on Silvie's face that made Ema nod her head. And it was Silvie's tiny, grateful gasp of relief that made Ema follow her friend up the mausoleum's stone steps.

Warm, gusty air wrapped around them as the door creaked open and the clouds parted, pouring moonlight into the darkness beyond. The mausoleum smelled of old stone and damp dust, and was filled with several ancient-looking tombs, as well as one very new-looking one. It was that tomb that Silvie steered Ema toward, and as her bones trembled in unease, Ema could find no strength to resist. Her gaze darted around the dark room, and she felt as if her entire skeleton might shake itself into dust.

The walls were coated in cobwebs that shivered in the breeze, and the floor was dusted with dirt — through which two sets of footprints carved a speckled path toward the middle of the room. It was the smaller set — Silvie's — that Ema's eyes followed, until her gaze finally settled on the newly carved stone effigy that Silvie was peering down at.

The stone man's face looked serene and peaceful, with marble arms crossed delicately over his chest. Ema had to squint to read the plaque on the side of his tomb:

ALOIS BLAŽEK

APRIL 3, 1866–NOVEMBER 5, 1889

Ema frowned. He'd died a few weeks before the first time she'd met Silvie — and so young.

"Silvie, who is this?"

"There is so much I haven't told you," Silvie whispered, in a voice Ema had never heard before. It sounded almost broken. "So much I've wanted to tell you —"

The door slammed shut behind them and the room plunged into near darkness, except for a thin column of moonglow that streamed in through a circular window above the door. It beamed down on Alois Blažek's stone face like a spotlight, and another shudder of dread coursed through Ema. She squeezed her eyes closed, willing her bones to be quiet. Wishing she were anywhere but here.

"Silvie, please can we just go somewhere else? You can tell me everything—"

"No, it has to be right here, and it has to be right now."

"Why?"

"Because in just a few minutes it's Alois's birthday. He always said that birthdays act as a channel for the spirit you're trying to reach. Alois was the greatest ghost whisperer there ever was, so he must be right. Here, look, he even gave me this."

Silvie reached into her collar and tugged on the chain of her necklace. Ema leaned in closer, expecting to see some sort of locket. A shriek left her lips as Silvie pulled the necklace free, and she realized that in the center of its clasp was a perfectly formed human eyeball.

"It's not real," Silvie said. "Or at least I'm pretty sure it's not. Alois told me it's made of porcelain and is at least a hundred years old." She tapped the eyeball, and her fingernail made a solid, clinking noise. "It's what Alois used when he first started ghost whispering. He wasn't sure why, but it always made him feel closer to the spirit realm when he held it."

Ema shook her head. "You want me to *hold* that thing?"

"Ema, please?"

It was the choking sob in Silvie's voice that had Ema cautiously reaching her hand out. She ran her fingertip over the eyeball's cold, solid iris. One by one, every hair on Ema's arm stood on end. She pulled her hand away, clasping it to her chest.

"Did something just happen?" Silvie asked, eagerness in every syllable. "Did you feel something? You did, didn't you! Try again. Please."

Ema stared at the eyeball.

The eyeball stared back at Ema.

Then the faintest crack of a twig had her spinning around to face the door. Every nerve in Ema's body began to scream.

"Someone's coming!"

Silvie sucked in a sharp, hopeful breath. "Is it Alois?"

"No—someone alive, I mean. I—"

In the distance, beyond the mausoleum's stone walls, a clock struck the first chime of midnight. The mausoleum door groaned open, and a gust of cold air blew around them.

In the groaning wake of the opening door, an arc of silver moonlight widened out across the mausoleum. Ema pushed Silvie backward into the shadows, away from the light, as it inched toward them. As the second chime of midnight sounded, she and Silvie squeezed into a narrow gap between the ancient tombs. Ema watched a hooded silhouette step inside, a star-shaped brooch glinting at the base of its neck.

The third chime struck loudly.

Behind Ema, Silvie trembled. The figure walked, boots scuffling loudly across the stone floor, right up to the very spot where she and Silvie had just been standing; then it came to a halt and let out a long, deep breath.

By the fourth chime, Ema was certain this was no ghost—but this did nothing to quell the terror surging through her.

Whoever it was, Ema couldn't let them find her and

Silvie. If they had been seen sneaking in here, then they'd be found after just a quick search.

Her eyes flicked to the open door.

She used the fifth chime to muffle their footsteps as she nudged Silvie along behind the tombs. Her eyes never left the figure, and the fear of being caught outweighed the horror of cobwebs clinging to her cheeks, dust falling down the back of her collar, and shadows swallowing the two of them whole.

They paused at the last tomb as the sixth chime tolled.

The figure was still staring down at Alois's tomb, and the open door was just a short stretch across the patch of moonlight. Finally, Ema turned her gaze to Silvie. Her friend looked so terrified that, for a moment, Ema barely recognized her.

Ema squeezed her hand as the next chime sounded.

Go, she mouthed, then gave Silvie a firm nudge.

Silvie staggered across the room, through the doorway, and out of sight. Confident in her own silent movements, Ema started inching her way after her before the eighth chime struck. She had one foot out the door when she spotted Silvie's white tulip lying limp in the middle of the floor. Surely this figure would notice it when they turned around. Ema, haloed in the light, snatched the flower from the floor and ran out.

The last few chimes chased the girls as they ran past statues and headstones, all the way back to the graveyard gate. They slipped through it, still shaking, and hurried over to Ema's boneshaker.

"Here," Ema said when they were on the other side. "I picked up your flo—oh."

There was already a white tulip in Silvie's hand.

Silvie stared at the second flower, her mouth moving but no sound coming out.

"I thought you'd dropped it," Ema said. "It was right there in the middle of the floor."

Silvie looked back toward the cemetery, and Ema saw a whole series of emotions parade across her friend's face: surprise, horror, confusion, sadness, uncertainty, and—as she noticed Ema watching her intently—discomfort.

"What is it?" Ema asked. "What's wrong?"

Without warning, Silvie flung herself forward and wrapped her arms around Ema.

"You're the best friend I've ever had," Silvie whispered into the tufts of her hair. "I'm sorry I dragged you here to-night, and I'm sorry I scared you. I should never have asked this of you."

Ema squeezed her back. "Let's just go somewhere else—"

"No. We should go home."

"But you wanted to tell me—"

"I should have listened when you said something was wrong. And we should listen to that intuition now. We'll revisit all this another night."

"Should we look for Béla, at least?"

"He'll find his own way home."

"But—"

"I'll go straight home too." Silvie squeezed her again, tighter this time. "I promise."

Silvie finally let go and avoided Ema's gaze as she tucked the eyeball necklace back under her collar.

A moment later, she was gone, and Ema was left standing on the dark and gusty street alone. She hurriedly climbed onto her boneshaker and pedaled hard all the way back to her uncle's house. It wasn't until she was climbing under her covers that she realized she was still clutching the second tulip tightly in her hand, and every bone in her body was still shivering with a sense of impending doom.

Something was *still* wrong. But what, Ema had no idea.

The attic room breeze whistled around her, turning her shivers into shudders. A growl of frustration climbed out of her throat.

"Stop it!"

The breeze stopped.

The following day, Ema woke to the *flap-flap-flap* of leathery wings and a near inability to breathe. Her eyes snapped open, expecting to see the dark night sky, fluttering bats, and cloaked grave robbers she'd been dreaming about. Instead, she was greeted with sunlight and fur.

Ferkel was sitting on her chest, her yellow eyes fixed on the wall above Ema's head.

Only this time, something was different.

Flap-flap-flap-flap-flap.

Heart thundering, Ema scanned the attic room for winged creatures. Then Ema finally spotted the source of the sound—above her head, directly where Ferkel was staring, was a small piece of wallpaper that had been scratched loose by very sharp, very muddy claws. The breeze was back—and moving the scrap of wallpaper in a most agitated fashion.

Ema glared at Ferkel. "You've turned to destroying my room now, have you? What is it about the wall that's offended you?"

She waved her hand in front of the cat-beast's face, but Ferkel didn't so much as blink. Ema nudged the cat-beast aside.

At the sight of the white tulip on her bedside table, memories of the previous night came flooding back to her: Silvie's unusual behavior, the mausoleum, the hooded figure. After all that awfulness, her insides were still a maelstrom of unease.

Ema shivered as she climbed out of bed, and not just thanks to the relentless breeze that had once again ripped away the dust sheet covering her grandmother's journals. The white tulip's petals were already beginning to drop, several of which were snatched up by the draft and sent fluttering around the room. Ema blew one from her mouth, swatted another one away, and then found herself watching a third one spiral gracefully onto the bookshelf, before finally settling on one of the plain red leather journals.

The breeze was gone as quickly as it had appeared, but Ema stood there, frozen to the spot, her hand reaching for the journal, then away again, then for it, and away again.

An hour later, she made her way to the workshop, the journal clutched tightly to her chest, and stood in the doorway, silently watching her uncle as he painted their bicycle design a glimmering swan white.

"Good morning, Ema," Josef said without turning. "Is something the matter?"

Ema stepped in, her feet noiseless as she walked toward the workbench and dropped her grandmother's journal down on it with a thunk. Josef turned and frowned.

"Did my parents stop talking to Liliana because of misfortune number three hundred and seventy-two?"

Her uncle's eyebrows erupted in a quick sequence of twitches — shock, confusion, disbelief — and then he gave an almost unnoticeable gulp of panic, which he tried to cover with a grin.

"I — um, I don't know what you mean."

Ema narrowed her eyes at him. Just as with her mother,

Ema could see Josef's lie twitch the corner of his mouth.

"Then let me explain further." Ema cleared her throat and read the page in front of her: "Misfortune three hundred and seventy-two, Milena, May 14, 1867, reads as follows: 'No matter how hard you work, no one will ever, in your entire lifetime, take your work seriously.'"

Josef looked unbearably uncomfortable. "Um, well—"

"Her research means *everything* to her. Why would Liliana say such a thing?"

Josef sighed. "She said it because she believed it."

"So, it *is* why they stopped talking?"

"Yes." Josef sighed again. "No one wants to believe that their entire life's work is a waste of time. When your grandmother kept on insisting Milena's fate was sealed, Milena decided she no longer wanted to listen. Their estrangement was heartbreaking . . . for all of us."

"There's only one entry for you. And it's not even a *mis*fortune."

"Oh, I'm not so sure it isn't."

"Why? Here, let me read it." Ema cleared her throat. "'You needn't go far, and you needn't feel bleak, for under your feet, you'll find all that you seek.' That sounds the very opposite of gloomy to me. It even rhymes!"

"Yes, well, I spent twelve years seeking that fortune across the world, with nothing to show for it other than very sore legs and a cat-beast who is probably, at this very moment, causing mischief. I should go and look for her, and you should stop worrying about this book."

"She's upstairs, clawing at the wallpaper above my bed—"

Ema yelped as her uncle sprang to his feet, knocking over the paint pot as he scrambled to the door.

"What's wrong?" Ema called after him as he bounded up the stairs two at a time.

"Nothing at all, beruška," he called back. "You stay down there; I'll deal with Ferkel."

Ema ignored him and hurried up the stairs in his wake. She arrived, panting, in the attic room to find her uncle holding the tattered remains of the wallpaper in his hands.

Ferkel was nowhere to be seen.

"At least you don't have to bake an apology cake for yourself," Ema said. "Why are you hugging the wall like that? Is that *writing*? What are you hiding?"

"Nothing," Josef lied. "Go back downst—"

"Show me!"

They stared at each other for a long moment, and, despite the evident despair on her uncle's face, Ema held his gaze steady, trying to ignore the thrumming dread coursing through her. Finally, her uncle sighed and stepped aside.

Ferkel had torn several more long, jagged strips right off the wall while she'd been downstairs, and Ema could now see messy scrawlings on the paint beneath. Spurred on by her churning insides, Ema tore the rest of the wall-paper away, revealing a scattered array of seemingly random words.

shadows
lost
lies
white tulip
midnight
find her
moon
murderer

Ema stared at the wall, unblinking and unmoving, trying hard to ignore the bone-deep sense of certainty creeping over her.

"That's my misfortune, isn't it?"

"Why on earth would you think that?"

"It's dated the day I was born."

"Oh."

"Indeed."

"She was very ill, Ema. It's just a bunch of nonsensical scribblings. Look, none of them even rhyme."

"Then why didn't you just paint over it?"

Josef was silent, his expression pinched.

"For the same reason you won't get rid of her journals, right?" Ema said. "You think it's bad luck?"

"We could paint over it now if you like?"

"No!"

They were silent again for a long moment, both ignoring the breeze that whipped around them. Ema stared at the words, feeling each one settle over her skin with an itchiness she couldn't scratch away.

"Your parents will be home very soon," Josef said. "Perhaps it's best we forget all about—oh sweet saints, where did *this* come from?" He held the half-wilted white tulip up, then glanced at the wall with a look of horror on his face.

Ema felt herself become steadily more light-headed.

How could her grandmother have possibly known about the tulip?

What did the tulip *mean*?

And the other words—"murderer," "lies," "lost"—were these the catastrophes headed her way?

"You're right," Ema rasped, turning away from the wall and plastering on a smile that wouldn't stop twitching. "We should forget all about this. I'll clean up the paint downstairs, and you should probably go and find Ferkel, in case she's causing more destruction to the house decor."

"But—"

Ema hurried out of the room again, chased by her own overwhelming sense of impending doom. The only thing that kept her from climbing into the broom closet to curl up into a ball of despair was the thought that *tonight* was the full-ish moon.

Silvie would know what to make of all this.

Silvie would know what to do.

They'd face it together.

As dusk began to creep in at the edges of the horizon, Ema peered out the workshop window, waiting for the full-ish moon to rise above the rooftops. Josef came through the door, looking particularly glum.

"No sign of Ferkel?" Ema asked.

Josef shook his head. "No, but this arrived in the most peculiar fashion." He held up a fancy envelope. "It came through the letter box."

Ema's heart gave a little flutter as she reached for the letter. The handwriting was definitely Silvie's, but the envelope was made of paper, with stars embossed in the corners, not the usual soap packet. And the seal was made of black wax, not chewed toffee.

Ema Vašková
c/o Josef Kozar's Velocipedes
The narrowest street near the Church of Our Lady Victorious
Fourth house on the left, with the bright green door
Unless you come from the other side of the street, in which case,
it's the twelfth house on the right, with the bright green door

"Thank you," Ema said, excusing herself.

She hurried into her broom closet study and shut the door, her insides itching as she unfolded the letter and began to read:

Dearest Ema,

I'm afraid we're going to have to put the Midnight Manifesto on hold. I'm leaving the city for a little while and I don't know when I'll be back. Everything is fine, I promise. I'll write again when I can.

Yours splendiferously,

Silvie

No P.S.

No P.P.S.

No P.P.P.S.

Ema stared at the letter, trying to make sense of it and quell her rising panic; unable to do either, she stared harder at the fancy stationery Silvie had *NEVER* used before, the shakiness of some of the words, and the ominous formality of its tone. Not an atom of this letter made sense, and Ema knew why: it was full of lies.

Silvie had *NOT* left the city.

Everything was *NOT* fine.

Something was *desperately* wrong.

≋ 10 ≋

U nder the guise of feeling unwell—which wasn't a
complete lie—Ema bid her uncle an early goodnight.
To Ema's relief, Josef seemed preoccupied with finding
the wayward cat-beast, which meant he'd be less likely to
notice the fact that she had absolutely no intention of
going to bed at all.

The moment she'd concluded that Silvie was lying
about everything being fine, she'd decided that she was
going to scour the city for her friend.

Tonight.

It was the memory of Silvie's dark sadness and her
desperation to tell Ema her secret that spurred her up
the stairs to her attic room, where she faced the wall of
misfortune with a racing heart. The dread of looming
catastrophe still hummed through her, but underneath
there was something sharper and more potent.

Determination.

"Is that *my* misfortune," Ema asked the empty room, "or is it Silvie's?"

The only answer she got was a goose-bump-inducing gust of air. Ema read the scrawled words silently, over and over, until each one was seared into her mind. It may have looked like random nonsense to Josef, but to Ema each word struck a spine-crawling chord inside her.

shadows
lost
lies
white tulip
midnight
find her
moon
murderer

She forced the final word shakily from her lips. "Murderer."

The memory of the cloaked figure in the mausoleum pushed into her mind, as did the terror on Silvie's face. And then the long hug Silvie had given her, as if saying good-bye . . . but also, perhaps, to make sure Ema didn't see the lie on her face when she'd promised to go straight home.

Had Silvie gone back into the graveyard?

Had she been caught?

Why would she go back?

Ema's legs threatened to give way, but she held herself firmly in place. Silvie had written this letter—she was sure of it—so she was still alive. But that didn't mean she wasn't in dire trouble. Ema needed to hold herself together if she was going to be any use to her friend. She needed to focus.

"The soap packets," Ema whispered, shivering as the breeze picked up around her.

Ema hurried over to her dresser and pulled open the drawer that held the Midnight Manifesto, the goblin's soul teacup, and every soap-packet invitation Silvie had ever sent her. She lifted one of those invitations up and uncurled it.

Ema's eyes settled on the tiny print in the bottom corner:

Devil's Canal Soapery,
Kampa Island, Prague

The breeze stopped, and Ema felt a tingle of hope bloom in her chest.

"I'll find her," she said, unsure if she was speaking to herself or some*thing* else.

A few minutes later, she had constructed an Ema-shaped lump under the blanket on her bed, dressed herself in dusk-colored clothing, and snuck out of the house as Josef was knocking on neighbors' doors asking after Ferkel.

The full-ish moon was beginning to climb up above the spire-strewn skyline as she pedaled down the hill, through the Little Quarter, under the bridge gate, and down onto the lamplit street that led to Kampa Island. On the edge of the Devil's Canal, next to a disused water-wheel, was the soapery. Ema parked her boneshaker on the small bridge outside and realized, to her delight, that there were still lights shining through the small steamed-up windows.

She pushed a side door open and stepped into a warm, humid room.

The overwhelming lavender scent made her dizzy.

It smelled of Silvie.

Rows upon rows of huge round tubs lined the long room, each with a man or woman stirring the steaming contents with wooden paddle-like spoons.

As Ema wove nimble footed around the steaming tubs, desperately searching for any sign of her friend, no one paid her any attention. When she found no such sign of Silvie, she settled on a lone figure sitting in a wingback chair with his feet propped up on a wooden crate and his nose in a *Czech Dreadful* magazine.

Judging by his overt idleness, Ema decided he looked like he was in charge.

If anyone here knew Silvie, it would be him. Or perhaps he knew Silvie's parents—maybe they worked here? When he didn't look up at her arrival, Ema leaned forward and tapped him gently on the shoulder. The man jumped an inch off his chair.

"Can I help you?" he asked, blinking up in surprise at Ema.

"I'm looking for Silvie."

"Who?"

"Silvie," Ema repeated. "My age-ish, my height-ish, dark hair, dark eyes, likes acrobatics and daredevilry, sometimes dresses like a pirate?" She paused to take a breath. "I believe she's in great danger. Do you know where I can find her?"

He looked at her as if she were speaking gibberish, blinked a few times, then—with his mouth full—he shook his head.

Ema looked at the empty sweet wrappers in his lap, and the way his jaw seemed glued together, and gasped.

"She eats those toffees! Well, half eats them and then uses them to seal letters. And she always smells of lavender and writes messages on the back of these very soap packets. You must know her!"

Finally, he swallowed. "Half the city buys this soap,

child. These toffees too, no doubt. I do not know all my customers individually. I'm sorry, but I can't help you as I don't know any such girl."

Ema studied every inch of his face as he spoke. She could detect no sign of him lying, but he did, however, seem to be growing increasingly disconcerted by her staring.

Ema racked her mind for what to do or say next. She could press him further — explain how the soap packets, the lavender smell, the toffees, and the proximity to Charles Bridge were, in combination, far too unlikely to be a series of mere coincidences. Silvie *was* connected to this soapery, whether this man knew it or not.

"Are you all right?" he asked, shifting uncomfortably in his seat. "You're not blinking."

Ema blinked. "Um, yes, I'm fine. Thank you for your help. I'll see myself out."

Silvie had told her to trust her intuition, so that's exactly what she intended to do. As soon as she stepped outside, Ema hurried back over the little bridge, stashed her boneshaker behind a bush, and climbed in after it.

Darkness now cloaked the city, but the full-ish moon was bright enough for Ema to see clearly as she put her monocular spyglass to her eye and hunkered down to watch the soapery's front door. One by one, workers emerged, looking tired and soggy and ready for sleep.

Ema watched each one closely, waiting for some sort of sign or feeling to appear that might tell her they were connected to Silvie somehow. But as the toffee-chewing man emerged, locking the soapery's door behind him, Ema realized no such sign or feeling was coming.

The only feeling she had left now was the bone-deep certainty that somewhere around here there would be a clue that would lead her to Silvie.

That was when she saw the bat.

"Béla?"

Ema took a few steps after him, then stopped.

It could be *any* bat.

Black wings fluttered over her, diving down toward the water, disappearing, and then reappearing from behind her.

And yet, it *could* be Béla.

Ema followed the creature as it zigzagged over the bridge and down toward the canal. The bat flew past the derelict waterwheel, along the ivy on the soapery's wall, then buried himself deep within the leaves. When the bat didn't reappear, Ema suddenly remembered the very first conversation she'd had with Silvie.

Perhaps you could find him a cool, dark place . . . Somewhere hidden and safe, where no one can find him.

I know just the place.

Ema climbed over the bridge and lowered herself

carefully down onto the waterwheel, then stretched toward the spot where the bat had disappeared and pushed the ivy aside. Hidden behind the vines was an old broken window.

It was just about large enough for a twelve-year-old girl to crawl through.

So that's exactly what Ema did, pausing only briefly to marvel at the fact she hadn't so much as hesitated before doing so.

She was met with complete darkness as she pushed her upper body through the hole. She heaved herself in and lowered herself down slowly. Her feet landed on a hard stone floor.

The darkness was disorienting. She patted her pockets for her matchbox, lit a match, and held it up, squinting as she made out vague shapes: crates, narrow walls, a lantern.

Ema lit the lantern and blinked away the sudden brightness.

She was in a tiny storeroom, blocked off from the rest of the soapery by stacked crates of soap boxes, beyond which Ema could just about make out the hissing and gurgling of a steam boiler. Two of the stone walls were draped in bedsheets, and someone had painted brightly colored trees and star-filled night skyscapes over them. In the middle of the stone floor was a large laundry tub, which, judging by the fact it was filled with blankets and a bundle of mismatched pillows, doubled as a bed.

The bat seemed to have disappeared.

"Béla?"

Ema rounded the laundry-tub bed and came to a sudden halt.

Tucked beside it was a large wooden trunk. On top of it was a familiar bundle of blue velvet. Ema lifted the cloak up and breathed in the lavender scent she had come to know so well.

Shaking, she unlatched the trunk and threw the lid open. A small yelp caught in her throat. Inside were bundles of clothing—bejeweled ruffled shirts, tulle skirts, a pirate's eye patch, reams of shiny ribbons, and hats of all shapes, colors, and designs. On the very top was the envelope containing the Ema Enigma documents.

Confusion, clarity, despair, and relief all crashed into her at once as she stared around her, making her sway on her feet.

This was, without a doubt, Silvie's room.

Her friend lived here in this cold, dark storage room. Alone.

Ema felt like she was staring at one of her mother's most challenging algebra problems, or worse, a *riddle*. Why would someone like Silvie—with her finely tailored outfits and vast array of talents and peculiar knowledge—

live in a laundry tub behind a stack of soap boxes?

Ema could see only one logical conclusion: Silvie was a runaway.

In fact, Silvie had used that very word more than once, Ema realized.

Instead of running away, we could face the truth together.

But *what* had she run away from? And did that "what" have anything to do with why she had disappeared now?

There is so much I haven't told you. So much I've wanted to tell you . . .

Ema felt a sharp sting of guilt that she hadn't pushed Silvie harder to open up about whatever it was that had been troubling her. But perhaps Silvie's things could tell her what she had wanted to say or lead Ema to wherever Silvie was now. For all her clever tricks and expert sleight of hand, Silvie always left clues that only Ema could find.

She settled herself in front of Silvie's trunk and sifted through sequins, tulle, and velvet. As she reached the bottom of the trunk, she found a small wooden trinket box. With a determined flick of her fingers, she unclasped the latch and lifted it.

Laid out neatly inside was a small assortment of items: a tiny mechanical raven, a pack of magician's cards, a pouch full of stage makeup, the Midnight Manifesto, and two neatly folded pieces of paper. Letters — both on the same star-embossed paper as Silvie's letter.

She stared at the two letters uneasily.

It wasn't right to read someone else's letters; she knew that. But she also knew that Silvie needed her help. Swallowing down her shame, she opened the first one.

Dear Silvie,

I am writing in response to your very impressive application and am pleased to hereby offer you a sponsorship to join me in Prague.

You will begin on the lowest tier, naturally, but I have every faith in your ability to progress to the status of acolyte in no time at all.

Welcome to the Midnight Guild.

Yours splendiferously,

Alois Blažek

P.S. Please pass on my regards to your parents. I'm sure they'll be so very proud of you.

P.P.S. Your train to Prague is on the next full-ish moon.

P.P.P.S. Use the map to find me.

Ema read the letter a few more times, looking for answers, but only finding more questions.

What on earth was this Midnight Guild? Ema had never heard of it, nor anything like it.

Had Alois Blažek been one of Silvie's tutors, then? Silvie had said he'd been a ghost whisperer.

What kind of educational establishment was this?

Her eyes drifted to the second letter, and Ema's hands shook as she unfolded it.

It was a detailed map of the city, but it was also completely bare of any markers.

Use the map to find me.

Ema sniffed it and found the faintest scent of lemon still lingering in the middle. She staggered to her feet, toward the hole in the wall, and pushed aside the ivy. As she held the map up toward the sky, moonlight shone through the thin paper.

Ema leaned in close. Her eyes scanned every inch of the city, until finally—squinting hard—she noticed four small, faint lines on a street not too far from her home in Old Town.

It was, she realized, a door.

In the center of it was a clock, its tiny hands pointed straight upward.

Midnight.

Above the door was an almost circle.

A full-ish moon.

She lowered the map again, looking up at the real full-ish moon hanging heavily in the sky.

A chill ran straight through her, but Ema seized hold of it as she realized what she had to do next.

To find Silvie, she'd first have to find this Midnight Guild.

And she'd have to find it *tonight*.

ABANDON ALL
DOUBT, YE
WHO ENTER
HERE

⫸ 11 ⫷

I n the ever-darkening night, Ema sat on Silvie's laundry-
tub bed and ran each mystifying clue through her mind. If
she was to be of any help to Silvie at all, she'd need to push
past the maelstrom of dread coursing through her. She'd
need to be *curious*.

Firstly, about Silvie herself.

She was an acolyte at the Midnight Guild, whatever *that*
was. This must be where she'd learned all her strange skills.
She spoke of her tutors with fondness, but it was clear that
she had run away from something bad.

Why else would she hide away in a hole like this?

Then there was the fact she would only meet under
the full-ish moon, which—according to Silvie's invitation
from Alois Blažek—was exactly when the Midnight Guild
operated. That couldn't be a coincidence. She *must* have
been trying to avoid bumping into anyone associated with
the guild.

It was this realization that brought back the memory of the hooded figure in the mausoleum and the way Silvie had reacted with trembling terror.

Had she recognized that person?

Was it the guild member who she had been avoiding?

Ema tried to remember details, but other than the second white tulip she'd found on the floor in that person's wake, the only memory she could summon was the silver brooch on their collar. It had been in the shape of a star, just like the stars embossed on the strange letter Silvie had sent her that night, *and* the invitation Silvie had received from Alois Blažek.

It was this part of the puzzle—Silvie's deceased sponsor—that made Ema's insides itch the most, and not *just* because Silvie had said he was a ghost whisperer. He'd died just before Ema had met Silvie—at a young age, under circumstances that clearly left her friend so distraught she'd sought Ema's help to try to contact him beyond the grave.

His death was the center of this mystery.

Had Silvie witnessed his demise? Had she been unable to save him? Is that why she'd wanted to ask his forgiveness? But if so, why had she run away?

The last line of Liliana's misfortune pushed into Ema's mind.

murderer

Had Silvie witnessed Alois's *murder*?

And had she gone back into the graveyard to face his murderer?

Was the Midnight Guild—with all its seemingly peculiar but wondrous teachings—a place where murderers lurked?

With a jolt of terror, Ema climbed off the laundry-tub bed. If Silvie was in that place, then Ema needed to get her out of it . . . immediately.

Trembling with fear and urgency, Ema wrapped herself in Silvie's midnight-blue cloak, tucked the map and her research documents inside it, and scrambled out of the hole in the wall. Once on the waterwheel, she paused and stuck her head back through the ivy.

"I'll find her, Béla," Ema whispered. "I promise."

The night air was warm, and yet Ema still shivered as she rode her boneshaker over the ancient bricks of Charles Bridge, past the lamplit arches of the Klementinum, and through the labyrinthic streets. In Big Old Town Square, people were emerging from restaurants, theaters, and music halls. She tucked her boneshaker in the shadowed front door of her family's house and peered up at the Astronomical Clock.

Midnight was only twenty minutes away.

With the map in hand, she hurried on, under the arched walkway beside the Church of Our Lady before Týn and through a series of winding streets, ducking past the nighttime strollers, until she finally emerged in a small courtyard. Tucking herself beneath a small tree, Ema took out her monocular spyglass and held it up to her eye.

It took her only a few seconds to find the spot that the map had marked. It was an alleyway, barely wide enough for two people to stand side by side in, and so dark it seemed like a black hole. Most people walked past it, but every now and then, someone would part from the crowds and slip quickly into the void. Without exception, each person who did this was dressed not too dissimilarly to Ema — dark cloak and hood drawn up.

Who were they?

And what was down that alley?

Ema pressed the spyglass closer and sharpened the focus. After watching twelve people dart into the alley, she confirmed that none of them was wearing a silver star brooch like the figure from the mausoleum.

As midnight grew closer, Ema grew tenser.

Checking her pocket watch, Ema saw she had five minutes before she'd lose her chance at finding out.

Less worrying, more daring.

As another person disappeared into the alleyway, Ema snapped her spyglass closed and slunk across the courtyard toward it, trying to ignore the urge to run back the way she had come.

It was one thing to sneak out into the dark city with someone else by her side, seeking nothing but adventure,

but quite another thing to sneak out alone, seeking unknown danger. A danger that—if Ema's suspicions were
correct—involved a murder and a kidnapping.

Her feet passed silently over the cobbles as she inched
her way forward. Squinting, she could see that the alley
was almost as short as it was narrow. And despite the
many people she'd seen step into it, it was empty.

There was, however, a door. Although, to call it a door
was almost an exaggeration. The wood was weather-beaten,
its hinges rusted, and despite the darkness, Ema could make
out angrily scrawled words painted in bright red across it:

PRIVATE PROPERTY!
CARTS THAT PARK HERE
WILL BE CHOPPED INTO FIREWOOD!

It looked far from welcoming.

Underneath the warnings, however, was a faint
engraving.

A star.

Ignoring the itching of her bones, Ema opened the
door and stepped through, only to find herself in another
empty alleyway. It stretched out on either side of her, with
no other doors or people in sight.

Ema stood there, frozen with confusion.

The person she'd followed couldn't have disappeared
that quickly. As she reached for the door she'd just come

through, the handle turned, and the door swung toward her.

Ema had just enough time to press herself against the wall as two more cloaked figures stepped through. She waited for them to turn and see her, but instead they both hurried forward, straight into the solid brick wall ahead of them.

Straight *through* it.

They disappeared as quickly as they'd arrived, and Ema stared after them, wondering whether she really had just seen that happen.

As she reached a hand to the wall, an identical hand reached out to touch hers.

Ema swallowed a shriek, realizing it was a reflection. She pushed her hand farther, until it connected with the smooth solid glass of a mirror.

An *angled* mirror — positioned on the edge of a gap in the wall to make it look like there was no gap. She had no time to marvel at the ingenuity of it, however, because the door behind her began to open again. With no other choice, Ema leaped through the gap.

This time, she found herself in a narrow stone tunnel and saw two figures disappearing around a corner ahead of her. Hearing footsteps behind her, Ema pulled Silvie's cloak tighter around her and hurried on, her heart fluttering wildly.

At the end of the short tunnel, she turned a corner and

found a winding staircase. Ema tiptoed down it, her hands running across the cold stone walls on either side to keep her balance. Finally, she reached the bottom and found herself standing on an ancient cobbled street, lit by flaming torches, the sky shut off by a vaulted ceiling of stone and shadow.

There's an entire city hidden beneath your feet, Ema Vašková. If you know where to look.

Silvie's words whispered through her as she hurried onward along a labyrinth of tunnels that wound deeper beneath Prague. She followed the whispered voices ahead of her and tried to keep ahead of the footsteps of those behind her, until—at last—she arrived at another door.

This one was nothing like the first.

Made of dark wood with an arched top, it was twice Ema's height. In each of its four panels was an ornate emblem: a planet, a magician's wand, a brass cog, and a bone-white skull.

Ema twisted the handle and inched it open, seeing nothing but complete darkness beyond. The footsteps behind her grew louder, and Ema realized she had no time to hesitate. She stepped through the door, feeling for a wall to press herself against. As the door opened again beside her, the faint light from behind it cast a brief glow across wherever it was Ema now was, before disappearing as the door clunked closed again. Ema pressed herself harder against the wall, her heart thundering at what she'd just seen.

There were *hundreds* of cloaked figures gathered before her.

Hushed voices merged into one another, reverberating off faraway walls and a faraway ceiling that Ema could not see. But Ema could *feel* the crowd's anticipation—it hummed through the air like a chimed glass. They were waiting for something. But what?

Suddenly a bell tolled, echoing across the vast cavern like an explosion. The shock sucked the air from Ema's lungs, and as another chime boomed around, her heart gave a sharp stutter.

Louder whispers fluttered around her.

"—*it's time*—"

"—*finally*—"

"—*just watch*—"

Another bell tolled, followed swiftly by a high-pitched buzzing noise. Ema pressed herself against the wall as a beam of light burst from high above the crowd. It struck a wall in a perfect circle of yellow, illuminating the ancient stone.

When the next toll struck, the spotlight began to move. It swept down across the people below. Ema watched in frozen horror as the light swooped in all directions— upward, downward, sideways—revealing ever more startling things in its wake: a giant bat, a copper moon, an enormous birdcage, a golden clock, and a rearing bear's skeleton. Everything was so high up and spread out—whatever crypt they were in, it was as big as the inside of a church.

As the final toll of midnight reverberated around her, the light settled on a lone figure standing on a platform high above them. It was a man in a pinstripe tailcoat and a towering top hat. He smiled a dazzling, white-toothed smile and raised his arms.

"WELCOME. WELCOME. WELCOME. WELCOME. WELCOME."

His booming voice echoed around them, and he spoke with an accent Ema couldn't quite identify. The crowd hushed immediately.

"FOR THE NEXT HOUR, YOU WILL BEAR WITNESS TO THE FANTASTICAL, THE UNIMAGINABLE, AND THE DOWNRIGHT FRIGHTFUL. FRIGHTFUL. FRIGHTFUL. FRIGHTFUL. FRIGHTFUL."

He let the last word rattle across the room, setting off a fresh wave of excited whispers in the crowd, and icy dread through Ema. His smile widened even further.

"SO, WITHOUT FURTHER ADO, IT IS MY PLEASURE TO INTRODUCE TONIGHT'S CURATORS. CURATORS. CURATORS. CURATORS. CURATORS."

A heavy clank sounded as another spotlight burst into life, this time illuminating the floating copper moon even farther up in the seemingly endless ceiling. A cloaked figure was sitting casually astride it, pointing a telescope up to the black sky.

"THIBAULT FINKELSTEIN, OUR ASTRONO-MER. ASTRONOMER. ASTRONOMER. ASTRONO-MER. ASTRONOMER."

Another spotlight clanked on, crisscrossing the others to illuminate two more cloaked figures, who were floating cross-legged in the air on the other side of the cavern. Ema gasped along with all the faceless people around her.

"ANINHA AND KAZIMÍR CARVOSA, OUR IL-LUSIONISTS. ILLUSIONISTS. ILLUSIONISTS. ILLUSIONISTS. ILLUSIONISTS."

CLANK. Another crisscrossing light appeared and illuminated another strange, cloaked figure—this time silhouetted in a cloud of steam and sparks halfway up a colossal stone wall.

"ŽOFIE MARKOVA, OUR DREAMER. DREAM-ER. DREAMER. DREAMER. DREAMER."

The next spotlight shone directly down onto the bear skeleton—which was now moving its head and snapping its lower jaw as another cloaked figure glided eerily to stand beside it.

"AND FINALLY, FLORENTINA FALKENBERG,

OUR BONE SCULPTOR. SCULPTOR. SCULPTOR. SCULPTOR. SCULPTOR."

Ema's gaze snapped from one curator to another again and again. She felt a niggling sense that something important was staring her right in the face, but she was too disoriented to see it.

"THERE ARE FOUR DOORS TO CHOOSE FROM. FOUR SPECTACLES TO EXPLORE. BUT YOU ONLY HAVE ONE HOUR. HOUR. HOUR. HOUR. HOUR."

The answer struck her the very same moment that the room flooded with bright light, loud music, and deafening cheers. Shielding her eyes and pressing herself farther still against the wall, Ema shook with the revelation of what she'd just seen: each cloaked figure was wearing a silver star brooch.

It had been a *curator* they'd encountered that night in Alois's mausoleum.

And that curator—whichever one it was—had taken Silvie.

The sudden brightness was followed by a long, chilling cello note. As more instruments joined in with the darkly dulcet tones of a Bohemian waltz, Ema's eyes fluttered open. It was the impossibly high vaulted ceiling she saw first. The Astronomer's copper moon floated beneath the stone arches, tightrope walkers in shimmering sequins sashayed along high wires, and inside the giant birdcage was a human-sized raven—with decidedly human legs—sitting serenely on a perch.

In just those few short seconds of searing light, all five curators and the grinning impresario had miraculously vanished.

Ema's gaze lowered to the glittering marble floor and the twelve-piece orchestra in the middle of it. She hadn't stumbled across the circus she'd once accused Silvie of running away from at all.

Or at least, not quite.

It seemed to be a circus, a ballroom, and a peculiar underground lair all at once.

Beneath her bewilderment at the sight before her, Ema knew that nothing had ever made more sense, or felt more familiar, than what she was seeing right then. Silvie was the very embodiment of this peculiar, wonderful, mysterious Midnight Guild.

Her friend was here, somewhere — she had to be.

Seizing hold of that certainty with everything she had, she turned her attention to the crowd before her, whose excited chatter had merged into one, barely decipherable babble.

"—*any moment*—"

"—*which one*—"

"—*just wait*—"

Their hooded cloaks were now folded over their elbows, revealing their midnight-blue suits and dresses. Their faces, however, were all hidden behind plain black masks. Ema shoved aside any curiosity about who was hiding behind each mask, because it was clear that every masked spectator was an adult.

But there *were* children here too — she'd seen them. Several small figures were weaving through the spectators now, and, unlike the adults around them, these children were dressed in an extraordinary manner.

They weren't spectacle watchers, Ema realized. They were spectacle *makers* — herding guests toward the four colossal doorways that ringed the ballroom floor.

A girl in blue puffed shorts and a ruffle-necked shirt, with impossibly blue pigtails, and wheels attached to the bottoms of her boots, glided across the ballroom floor like a floating wraith. She was herding several spectators toward a square door painted bright gold, with a cog emblem above it.

" —is the best spectacle of all. This way, this door—"

Ema took her spyglass out of her pocket and pressed it to her eye, turning it to the next doorway, which was tall, narrow, and painted purple, with a magician's wand emblem on its open door.

There was a boy standing near it, dressed in black, with a bright red neckerchief and beret, his face painted white, with a small black tear painted beneath each eye. He beckoned spectators toward him with exaggerated gestures, and even though his lips never moved, and even though she was on the other side of the room from him, Ema found herself understanding him entirely.

THIS WAY, MADAM, THIS DOOR HERE, THERE IS MAGIC THIS WAY. IGNORE THE OTHER SPEC-TACLES; THEY DO NOT COMPARE. COME, THIS DOOR HERE.

A girl with long red hair stood beside the door directly across the ballroom, wearing a dark feathered cloak and a long black beak—just like the raven in the birdcage. She seemed entirely unconcerned about herding the crowd, or even acknowledging their existence, and merely stood there, wings crossed and head tilted. Despite this apparent apathy, it was the raven's black-and-silver striped door, with the rearing bear skeleton standing guard, that most of the crowd flocked toward.

Ema turned her scope to the final doorway — a round hole in the wall with a planet emblem illuminated above. In front was a boy dressed as a bat, with leathery wings connecting his arms to his torso, and a tight-fitting cap over his eyes and head, with two large ears protruding from it. Unlike the other three, he didn't seem to be having much luck encouraging patrons toward his door, as everyone whom he approached seemed to shake their head and walk away as soon as he started speaking.

Ema scanned the room again with her spyglass, but there were no other children. She put her spyglass away and tried to ignore her disappointment.

She cast her gaze at the looming doorways, through which much of the masked crowd was now disappearing. *Spectacles*, the impresario had called them. In Ema's experience, wherever there was a spectacle, there was Silvie. She'd just have to search each one. Looking up at the large golden clock, she saw she had just under an hour to do so — the clock's single arm had already begun inching away from the jewel-embellished twelve at the top, toward the jet-black thirteen to its right.

With the ballroom slowly emptying, Ema realized

she needed to stay hidden, so she tucked her shoulders up to her ears and slunk into the swirling throng.

"Actually, let's go to that one—"

"Can't we go to them all?"

"You heard the impresario. There won't be time."

Ema pressed on, sidestepping out of the way of the mime boy, then coming to a halt as the blue-haired girl came speeding in her direction. The boy stumbled over an invisible obstacle, staggering into the girl's path. She swerved to miss him but tangled her wheeled boots together and crashed to the floor, right onto Ema's feet.

"You idiot!" the girl spat at the mime, glaring furiously.

OOPS! The boy's hands came to his cheeks in exaggerated silent shock, but Ema saw the corners of his mouth twitch in a quick smug smile as he gestured again. *I DIDN'T SEE YOU!*

To Ema's relief, they seemed too intent on scowling at each other to notice her tug her feet free and slip around them. She stumbled to the nearest doorway, unsure which one it even was, and let the surging crowd drag her through it.

Wedged tightly together, they crossed the threshold into a wall of cool steam. The music from the ballroom disappeared, replaced with the syncopated rhythm of gears clunking and pipes hissing. Then, as she blinked away the steam, the crowd spread out, and Ema saw they had emerged into another cavern, lit by hundreds of electric lights scattered across the ceiling.

What kind of place was this, to have electricity on this scale? It was . . . extraordinary.

For a heart-stopping moment, Ema was back on the river island with Silvie, looking up at the twinkling lights in the trees, her heart humming like an electric charge.

And then someone bumped into her back, forcing her forward. She staggered to the side of the crowd, against a wall, and sucked in a shaky breath as she took in the sight before her.

If the ballroom had been as big as a church, this room was the size of a cathedral. Its mossy stone walls looked just as ancient as one too.

How could a space like this be hidden under a city?

In the center of the room were three machines: one that looked at first glance like a giant headless bird, its wooden skeleton stretched out as wide as a house, with taut fabric wings and tail, a leather harness dangling from its middle. A second was a small hot-air balloon—midnight blue and speckled with stars, with the grandest gondola Ema had ever seen. And the third was a peculiar contraption that Ema could barely fathom, despite it being right in front of her, which seemed to be part bicycle, part balloon, with fabric wings, a paper tail, and wooden propellers.

Neat rows of long tables formed a symmetrical grid,

upon which was an unending array of gadgets. Along the farthest wall, in bright calligraphy, was a sign:

ŽOFIE'S BAZAAR
Fly into the World of Tomorrow

Under that sign, sitting casually on an oil drum, was a woman with dark skin and glimmering eyes. She wore a beige suit, with a red scarf and red gloves, and had red lips.

The Dreamer.

"Welcome," the curator said, silencing the last of the murmurs. "My name is Žofie Markova, and I am so pleased that tonight you have all—very wisely indeed— chosen to visit the most extraordinary spectacle this guild has to offer."

She hopped off the drum, and the crowd parted for her as if it were made of liquid as she made her way toward the flying machines.

"As an aeronaut, I've seen spectacles that most people cannot even imagine—a bird's-eye view of every wonder this world has to offer."

Žofie Markova climbed onto the ledge of the balloon's gondola, pulled a rope to fire up the burner, and grinned as the balloon lifted several feet into the air, straining at its ropes.

The crowd gasped. Ema turned her head to look around the room for Silvie, but instead her eyes stayed locked on the curator. It was almost impossible to take your eyes off a woman like Žofie Markova. She had the look of someone who refused to believe that even the sky was the limit.

"Tonight, I will do my very best to give you a sweet, delectable taste of what it is like to fly!" She jumped from the gondola onto a table and grabbed hold of a long metal lever. "With modern technology—and a little imagination—nothing is impossible."

She pulled the lever, and there was a loud clunk from up in the impossibly high ceiling. Everyone looked up, including Ema. A large wooden bird appeared from a hidden alcove. It flew out across the ceiling, gliding along a suspended track. Hanging from its harness, wearing a pair of goggles, was a boy.

As the crowd cheered at the display happening above them, Ema found herself turning her attention back to the curator, her teeth itching in unease and uncertainty.

Was this one of Silvie's tutors?

Ema looked up at the silver star brooch that glinted at the base of Žofie Markova's neck.

Or was this Silvie's kidnapper?

With that gut-wrenching reminder of her quest, Ema finally managed to tear her gaze away. It was then that she noticed two more children now standing beside the hot-air balloon: a girl and boy with matching red hair, both dressed as miniature versions of the curator.

Žofie Markova beamed down proudly at them. "My acolytes here have more wonders to share with you too, devices they have designed and built themselves. The imagination of children is unparalleled. One day, they will achieve things that will make my own pursuits pale in comparison."

Ema scanned the room, the ceiling, and the crowd. Silvie was not in this spectacle. Or at least, nowhere obvious.

But as Ema made her way back to the door to the ball-room, a sudden chill, deep in her bones, brought her to a halt. She turned to face the bazaar again, opened her spy-glass, and pressed it to her eye.

"These delights are available for you to buy and take home too," Žofie announced loudly. "You'll find among these stalls gadgets to suit needs you never even knew you had. A dog-powered sewing machine, perhaps. Gives your pet the exercise they need, and you the respite *you* need."

Ema turned her spyglass across the displays of gadgets, then up across every inch of the ceiling, then down across the crowd once more.

What was it she was missing?

There was something important here, she could feel it.

"Or maybe something like this," Žofie shouted. "One of my bestsellers, exclusive to anyone lucky enough to secure an invite to the Midnight Guild."

Ema swiveled her spyglass again. As her lens view passed over the Dreamer, a jolt of shock coursed through her. She lowered her spyglass, every inch of her skeleton shaking, as Žofie Markova lifted a device up to her eye.

"A monocular spyglass."

The noise of the Dreamer's spectacle disappeared behind the ringing in Ema's ears as she turned her
spyglass over in her hand—just like Silvie had done that
night they'd gone goblin hunting—and found the maker's
engraving on the underside:

MARKOVA & CO
1889

Cogs she hadn't even known were misaligned suddenly slammed into place in her mind. Silvie wasn't the
only person in Ema's life who was connected to the Midnight Guild.

Her parents were too. How else could they have possibly bought this for her as a gift?

She thought back to her disastrous interview with

Dagmara Bartoňová. They'd been talking about some sort of curatorship when she'd entered the drawing room, hadn't they? One they'd been disappointed not to get. Their expedition . . . they were trying to become curators *here*. Which meant that even Dagmara Bartoňová knew about this place. It seemed the only person who didn't know was Ema. This realization left a new twisting knot in the pit of her stomach. Ema drew in a breath and tried her best to ignore the stinging hurt. First, she would find Silvie, then she would worry about what other secrets may or may not have been kept from her. Tucking the spyglass back into her pocket, she stepped forward, straight into a moving object.

The impact sent both Ema and her collider sprawling onto the floor. Ema hurried to pull her hood back over her head, then looked at the boy lying on the floor beside her.

He wore the same outfit as the two acolytes standing with Žofie Markova, but his seemed more tattered and covered in oil smears. An array of tools was scattered on the floor all around him.

"Sorry, I didn't see you!"

"Sorry, I didn't see you!"

They spoke at once, in matching tones of quiet breathlessness. Ema helped him gather his tools, shooting subtle glances at him and praying that he wouldn't look up at her and see just how out of place she was, but he avoided eye contact entirely.

Once they were both back on their feet, he looked up at her. Ema held her breath and readied her limbs to run, but the boy just gave her a quick smile and whispered a thank-you.

Then he tucked his shoulders up to his ears and disappeared into the crowd.

Shuddering in relief, Ema tucked her own shoulders up to her ears and hurried through the steam-filled doorway.

Back in the ballroom, the orchestra was playing a lively piece of baroque. Some spectators were gathered around in small groups, talking, drinking, some even dancing. The blue-haired girl was still wheeling through the lingering crowd. The raven was still standing statuelike beside their door, where a line of spectators was waiting impatiently to go in. The mime boy was limping — and Ema spotted what looked suspiciously like wheel marks over his left foot. And the bat boy had a look of desperation on his face as he timidly approached a couple of leftover spectators.

Ema skirted the ballroom wall until she reached the doorway with the magician's wand carved into it. No sooner had she stepped through it than she found herself coming to an abrupt halt.

A hundred different versions of her face spread out in a kaleidoscopic array before her, and it took a moment for her to realize she was looking at a mirror maze.

Carefully, Ema felt her way forward, then sideways, then forward again. A hundred of her arms stretched out in a hundred different directions as she went. After several steps, she wasn't even sure she was walking in the right direction anymore. She spun around, trying to get her bearings, but seeing a hundred versions of herself spin at the same time made her feel unsteady. She lurched forward, and, this time, nothing blocked her way. When she looked up, she saw a theater.

Huge pillars twisted toward a blue-and-gold coffered ceiling, and on the gilded stage were a man and a woman. Before Ema even spotted the silver star brooches beneath their chins, she knew they were the levitating curators the impresario had introduced as the Illusionists.

Once again, Ema felt that uncomfortable realization that these two might be more of Silvie's tutors, or her kidnappers, or both.

The man was standing in a canvas box that covered everything from his toes to his neck, above which he wore a simple black bowler hat and a wickedly mischievous grin. The woman wore a green-and-gold tail jacket over matching trousers, her dark ringletted hair framing her light brown face, and she was holding a bejeweled weapon—halfway between a dagger and a sword—up above her head. She had a decidedly mischievous glint in her blue eyes.

"This here is my grandmother's facão," she announced.

"My most treasured possession from my homeland, Brazil. I have used it to hunt, to fight, and tonight I shall use it to teach every husband in this room an important lesson."

She cast a glance at her partner, whose grin widened.

The crowd laughed.

Ema tiptoed to the last row of seats and crouched behind them.

"Kazimír here insulted my feijoada last night, a recipe my grandmother passed down to me, as her grandmother did before her, and hers before that!"

The crowd oohed!

The male Illusionist made an exaggerated face of apology. "Aninha, my dear wife! I didn't insult it; I merely said it needed a pinch more salt."

With a roar, she sank her weapon straight through the canvas box, right where the man's stomach would be.

"Ooh, that tickles!" he cried, eliciting a rumble of laughter from the crowd. "I promise I shall never question your seasoning ever again!"

As Aninha pulled the blade free again, Ema took her spyglass out of her pocket. She turned it over the crowd, seeing nothing but midnight-blue outfits and plain black masks.

"What about that time you suggested that my bustle was too small?"

"Oh no, I beg you, not again—ahh!"

As the crowd guffawed, Ema lowered her spyglass

and looked frantically around the theater. Then, near the side of the stage, she realized there was another, smaller doorway, above which was written AKADEMIE MAGICKÁ.

Did your tutors teach you to do that?

They teach me the very greatest wonders of this universe, illusion being one of them.

As the Illusionists continued their performance, Ema slunk past the audience and went through the door. It opened into a much smaller cavern, half-full with spectators, who were gathered in two groups.

The closest, smallest group was huddled around a performer juggling flaming torches, the sight of which made Ema come to a startled halt.

The performer was a girl with long black braided hair, who couldn't be much more than a year or so older than her and Silvie. An acolyte, most likely, considering she was allowed to perform to a crowd, rather than simply herding the patrons toward the doorways in the ballroom like the other children Ema had seen.

Ema was jolted out of her reverie by the sound of something flying through the air, followed by the loud thunk of that something hitting a wall. Ema looked up to see a wooden board with a red-and-white painted target, and a throwing knife embedded in the second-most inner ring.

The second performer was hidden behind the larger gathering of patrons.

As Ema approached, another knife flew into the wall, sinking straight into the center of the target. The crowd cheered, and they raised their hands to clap, giving Ema a glimpse at the source of their delight.

It was a girl with a blindfold covering most of her face and a throwing knife clamped between her teeth. The gap disappeared again, obstructing Ema's view, but it had been enough to make Ema come to a heart-shuddering stop.

The girl had been hanging upside down like a bat, her waves of dark auburn curls cascading down to the floor.

Ema stood there, staring in disbelief at what she was seeing, trying to swallow down the sudden lump of hurt building in her throat. It was one thing to know Silvie had lied about leaving the city, but another thing to see it. Had she just grown bored of their Midnight Manifesto? Or had she decided that night in the graveyard that Ema just wasn't cut out for adventuring?

"Silvie!" The sound of Ema's voice was lost in the hubbub. As she elbowed her way through Silvie's audience, ignoring their yelps of surprise, she realized she was angry. Very angry. She tugged the blindfold down from Silvie's face. "How could you—oh."

Bright blue eyes blinked up at her in astonishment, and Ema realized she'd made a huge mistake.

This was not Silvie.

Panic held Ema in its grip as she immediately realized just how careless she'd been. The whole crowd was looking at her now. The girl tilted her upside-down head and narrowed her upside-down, bright blue eyes.

"How could I *what*?"

Ema offered up a small, shaky smile. "How do you do that?" She waved her hand at the target. "I've never seen anything so impressive. Bravo!"

The girl's eyes stayed narrow but held a glint of something that reminded Ema of the sword-wielding curator, as did her light brown skin. And the upward tilt of the corners of her mouth reminded her of the sword-tickled curator. Aside from her hair, she looked nothing like Silvie.

This was the Illusionists' daughter.

Ema suddenly became aware that the knife thrower was not the only one glaring at her interruption. Every masked face gathered around the two of them was now turned toward her, and Ema didn't need to see their faces to know they were less than impressed.

"I . . . I . . . I'm sorry I interrupted," Ema stammered. "I'll leave . . . leave you to it."

She spun around, looking for a way out of the group of spectators. Finally, she spotted a thin gap and leaped toward it.

"Stop!"

Behind her, there was the sound of feet dropping heavily onto the floor. Ema hurried to squeeze past elbows, but a surprisingly strong hand clamped on to her shoulder and pulled her back.

The girl held her tightly in place, then addressed the crowd. "Come back in five minutes and I'll invite one of you to stand in front of the target this time, if you dare." She grinned mischievously, then leveled Ema with a challenging glare. "Unless *you'd* like to have a go now?"

Ema cast a quick, terrified glance at the knife-riddled target. "Um, no, thank you."

"Very well—back in five minutes then, ladies and gentlemen."

The crowd dispersed, and the girl's hand tightened on Ema's shoulder. She leaned in close to Ema's ear, her breath warm but her voice cold.

"You're not supposed to be here."

"Yes . . . yes I am."

The girl ran her gaze up and down Ema's outfit. "Your clothes say otherwise."

"I . . . I was invited."

"By whom?"

"Dagmara Bartoňová."

Ema said the name without hesitation, and it wasn't just her who was surprised to hear it come out of her mouth. And as she watched the girl's eyes widen in shock, she wondered if she'd made a mistake. There was no other choice, however, than to press on.

"She is the headmistress of—"

"I know who Dagmara Bartoňová is," the girl said, moving in even more closely. "Did she send you here to spy? You look like a spy, hidden under that hooded cloak of yours. I should take you to my parents. They'll be furious." She nudged her forward.

"Wait, no!" Ema said, struggling to free herself at the same time as scrambling to remember what Silvie's invitation from Alois had said. "Dagmara, she . . . she sponsored me. She said I had potential for—"

"Espionage?"

"I think I've just disproven that quite spectacularly. What kind of spy walks up to the person they're supposed to spy on and yanks their blindfold off?"

The girl stopped, looked at Ema, then snorted. "That's a good point."

Ema's heart gave a little hiccup of relief, but it was short-lived.

"Although," the girl said, eyes narrowing further, "when my blindfold is on my ears are much sharper. And I didn't hear you approach."

"I—"

The girl shook her head. "You're incredibly peculiar."

Ema didn't know if that was a compliment or an insult or simply a statement of fact—it seemed to be all three at once. So she responded with a knowing nod.

"Yes, I'm aware of that."

"The rules of this guild are strictly enforced. No one— and I mean *no one*—is allowed to venture out of their spectacle area. Not even the curators themselves. Do you even realize how much trouble you're in?"

Ema's heart pounded painfully. Silvie needed her, and Ema had let herself fail at the one thing she was supposed to be good at—being unnoticed. Could she do nothing right?

"I didn't know I wasn't allowed in here," she said softly. "I'm new. No one has told me the rules yet."

The girl stared long and hard at her, then rolled her eyes and tugged Ema along. "Come."

"Please—"

"Quiet."

Ema snapped her mouth closed and had no choice but

to let herself be hauled back out into the theater. The Illusionists were still on the stage — Aninha sheathing her blade, while her husband Kazimír's seemingly decapitated head was still pleading for forgiveness.

Would the girl stop their show? Would she drag Ema on that stage and reveal her misdemeanor to the entire room?

Ema trembled at the thought, but the girl marched her up the length of the theater and back into the mirror maze. She moved quickly and deftly through it, tugging Ema along, without so much as brushing against the glass. Ema watched a hundred versions of her own frightened face blink at her; then the mirrors were gone, and they were back in the ballroom.

The orchestra was playing a mournful waltz, and there were more spectators in here than when Ema had last walked through. And yet, it seemed that it was only the line to the raven's doorway that was growing. Even the raven in the birdcage seemed to be staring downward in a daydream. The other children all looked lost and frustrated. As Ema was hauled across the ballroom floor, the mime boy looked up and gasped.

"Oh, hello, Matylda!"

"Mimes shouldn't speak," Matylda admonished, and despite the toothy grin she gave him, the boy nodded in deference and gave a short bow.

SORRY.

Ema tried to swallow, but her throat felt like it was coated in cobwebs. "Where are you taking me?"

Matylda didn't respond. She steered Ema toward the hapless boy in the bat costume, who was trailing after a couple of entirely uninterested spectators.

As Matylda tapped him on the shoulder and cleared her throat, Ema glanced up at the golden clock and saw that half an hour had already passed.

The bat boy turned with an excited grin, then his eyes widened. "Oh—"

"I found a wayward scientist. Which means she belongs to *you*, bat boy," Matylda said, giving Ema a little nudge toward him. "Looks like you could do with the help, though she could do with a thorough lesson on our rules."

The boy blinked at Matylda, then at Ema, then back again.

"Hank-tat ou-yat!"

"Excuse me?"

"I said thank you," the boy said. "In bat latin, my new language, based on pig latin but modified slightly. You see, what I do is move the first letter of a word to the end of the word and then add *-at* to the end. Thank you becomes hank-tat ou-yat, see?"

"Not really, it just sounds like you're vomiting random sounds."

The boy shrugged. "Yes, well, it takes a while to get used to an entirely new language."

"Speaking of new things," Matylda said, tilting her chin at Ema. "Make sure to take her *straight* to Herr Finkelstein."

Ema detected some sort of subtle emphasis in Matylda's command. The boy glanced behind him, at the moon-shaped doorway he was assigned to, and a small smile twitched at the corner of his mouth. Ema's bones began to itch uncomfortably.

"I will," the boy said. "Ood-gat ye-bat!"

Matylda glowered at him, shook her head, then spun on her heel and marched away.

Ema had been slowly inching away and was about to make a run for it when a leathery-winged arm hooked itself around her arm, and the bat boy grinned up at her.

"You're incredibly late, but never mind that now, this way, isn't this doorway wondrous? I love how you step through it and it feels like you're walking in space, but really it's just a lot of black paint and some cleverly arranged lights. Oh! I probably shouldn't have told you that . . . but you'll learn soon enough!"

The boy spoke at a million miles an hour, with breath control to rival that of a hundred flutists.

"Stop tugging," he said as he dragged Ema forward. "You needn't be worried—it's just an illusion. Just through these hidden curtains and . . . ta-da! We made it to the moon."

Ema finally stopped struggling. Instead, she gawked at the sight before her in astonishment. "This is supposed to look like the moon?"

"Yes, the moon, home to the *homovespertilio*, otherwise known as man-bats. See, there are waterfalls and beaches. Those bison and unicorns are just models, of course, but the goats are real. Mind that gray one over there, he's a headbutter. Ow—see? Let's walk quicker, this way."

It was a spectacle for certain, but not in a good way.

It was preposterous.

There were barely a dozen spectators in this room, and a single man-bat lurked behind them with a tray of wine and cheese in his hand. It took Ema less than three steps to see that Silvie was not here, and another three to realize that her predicament was about to become worse than she could have ever imagined.

"Ah, there's Herr Finkelstein and Mr. Rivers. Let's go and introduce you to them."

Ema's limbs felt like noodles, and it was all she could do to stay upright as she was led toward both the Astronomer and the impresario. They were standing beside a broken mechanical unicorn sculpture, deep in conversation. And as she and the boy came to a halt behind them,

Ema realized that now there really was no escape.

"Perhaps Žofie can fix—"

"You know she won't agree to work with another curator, Ephraim. Not after last time—"

"Excuse me," the boy announced loudly. "Dobrý večer!"

Both men turned, both men frowned, and it was only the impresario who finally offered a smile.

"Yes, Valentýn?"

Valentýn grinned back, then nudged Ema forward.

"Master of the Universe, Mr. Impresario, allow me to introduce the girl scientist who can't tell the time. I believe you are expecting her."

As both men turned their gazes to her, Ema quickly dropped hers to the floor.

A chill coursed through her so suddenly it made her gasp, and she clasped on to Valentýn's arm to steady herself.

Beneath the Astronomer's feet was a very dark shadow.

"No, Valentýn," he said gruffly. "I was expecting no such girl."

For the first time in Ema's life, she wished she truly was invisible. Lifting her gaze from the Astronomer's dark shadow, up to his almost-black eyes, she felt a bone-deep certainty that this was *not* one of Silvie's tutors. There was no mischief, no curiosity, no warmth in his demeanor — in fact, he had the look of someone who hadn't smiled in a very long time, if ever.

Ema had never knowingly met a kidnapper before, but she suspected they were all of an unsmiling, somber disposition. And his shadow . . . despite no longer looking at it, Ema could still feel its cold, heavy, dark presence, filling her with overwhelming sadness and regret. It was then that she noticed the mourning ring on his left pinky finger — a silver band with tightly plaited human hair embedded around its circumference. It took all her resolve not to shudder.

"Well," said the impresario, startling her. "Looks like we have an enigma on our hands. How does an unexpected girl turn up here so unexpectedly?"

Despite the shudder that ran down her at the mention of the word "enigma," Ema was grateful for the excuse to look away from the curator, and even more grateful when she was greeted by a friendly, crinkle-eyed smile.

"Dagmara Bartoňová."

His eyebrows shot upward. "Dagmara Bartoňová is your sponsor? You must be truly remarkable. She hasn't sponsored anyone in years. May we see your letter of recommendation?"

Ema could feel the Astronomer's glare as her mind scrambled for an excuse. Dagmara Bartoňová had seen straight through Ema's feigned interest in rock formations, and Ema had no doubt that these two men were equally as astute. The only person she knew who had been any good at trickery was Silvie. But Silvie had never really *lied*. She'd just been very selective with the truth.

"She didn't give me a letter," Ema said, rummaging in her cloak pocket. "All I have is this map. I didn't even know what I would find here tonight—let alone that I had been 'sponsored.'"

"Ooh, the mystery deepens twofold," the impresario said, taking the map from Ema and holding it up to the light. "I never thought I'd see the day that Dagmara

Bartoňová developed such a mischievously playful streak. Tell me, child, what is your name?"

"'Em—'" she started, then stopped herself, hastily snatching the first name that came to her. "Liliana."

"Emiliana?"

Blink. Nod.

"Delighted to meet you, Emiliana. My name is Ephraim Rivers, this is Thibault Finkelstein, and our ears are all yours. We'd love to hear all about your no-doubt wondrous academic accomplishments. How is it you came to impress the indomitable Dagmara Bartoňová so much that she sent you to us?"

The two men stared. Valentýn gave her a grin of encouragement beneath his wonky bat mask. Ema took a shaky breath and tried to be grateful that at least her parents weren't here to see this next bit.

"Well, I know the periodic table by heart, I can navigate a chemistry laboratory with minimal catastrophe, my math is middling to fair, and I can describe every type of rock in Bohemia if you'd be inclined to hear it. The truth is, however, that I really haven't found my scientific calling, though I know it's in me somewhere."

The Astronomer's eyes narrowed. "Is she trying to mock me?"

Ema gasped in panic. "No, I would never—"

"Not *you*, the headmistress. Why would she send me

such a pupil? We take the best of the best, not the most lost of the lost."

The impresario shot him a look Ema couldn't quite translate. "Thibault—"

"Actually, Mr. Rivers, I share Herr Finkelstein's confusion. I can think of no reason why she would send me here either. In fact, I disappoint her greatly. The only thing I know for certain is that the headmistress is as mystifying as the universe itself."

Ephraim Rivers let out a short laugh. "Well, you're certainly right about that. Tell us what you know about this mystifying universe, Emiliana."

"Well, for starters, the moon is made of rock and looks *nothing* like this," Ema said, waving an arm about the room. "There are no unicorns, no waterfalls, no man-bats, and certainly no goats. That was all a ridiculous sham made up by New World newspapermen decades ago. I'm surprised you would present such a hoax—"

Ema snapped her mouth shut, realizing she wasn't being as selective with the truth as she probably should. She was surprised, however, when the impresario started laughing.

"I merely provide the theater and pomp I was told these patrons expect," Herr Finkelstein said, frowning up at the patronless room. "I never claim all this is real."

"Well, at least the girl is up-front," Ephraim Rivers

said. "Saints know we could do with more of that around here. Welcome to the guild, Emiliana. I hope we can help you find your calling. This is a most unusual scenario . . . but then we do rather run on the unusual. Perhaps you could start by helping Valentýn find some more patrons. Valentýn, suit her up and explain how things work around here, would you?"

They all turned to the bat boy beside her, whose mask was continuing to slip farther down his face. He pushed it up a bit, revealing a nervous, hopeful grin.

"I swear I will not let her out of my orbit," he said. "But first, if you'll excuse my impertinence, I have something to ask of Herr Finkelstein."

The Astronomer frowned. "What is it, Valentýn?"

"Now that we have Emiliana here to help in the ballroom, would you consider allowing me the chance to show you what I've been working on? I'm ready to be an acolyte."

Valentýn's eyes were full of pleading and his smile full of hope. Ema wondered whether this was why he'd been so thrilled at her arrival, and her heart gave a beat of pity for him.

"Show me tomorrow night, Valentýn," the Astronomer said, turning away from the children and back to the impresario. "I'll be writing to Dagmara to get her explanation of all this."

Ema let a visibly disappointed Valentýn lead her away again. She consoled herself by thinking that by the time Dagmara received his letter, Ema would not only be long gone, never to return, but she'd have Silvie too.

A few minutes later, Ema found herself dressed as a man-bat, staring out across the near-empty ballroom. Her heart pounded in time to the frenetic prestissimo of the orchestra's rendition of "In the Hall of the Mountain King" as she looked up to see that the golden arrow was now just a few minutes shy of the thirteenth hour.

She may have managed to bluff her way out of trouble just now, but she couldn't find relief in it, as it had cost her precious time. She had but a few minutes to get into the final spectacle area — where Silvie must surely be.

Time was not her only adversary, however. The weight of hostile eyes had her teeth itching as she realized any powers of stealth she might once have had were firmly gone now.

The blue-haired wheeler wheeled past with a furious glare. Across the ballroom, the mime boy was fixing her with an exaggeratedly wicked smirk. The raven too had turned their beaked face Ema's way, and Ema could feel their hollow eyes bore into her as they cocked their head. Even the one up in the birdcage was looking in her direction now. And Valentýn seemed to be holding true to his word that he would not let her out of his orbit. His bat wing remained firmly linked with hers, and he had not stopped chattering since they'd left the Astronomer and impresario.

There was no way that she could sneak away now.

"Emiliana?"

Ema felt dizzy with dread.

"Emiliana?"

She'd come all this way, just to let Silvie down.

There was a sharp tug on her bat wing. "Emiliana!"

Ema turned to Valentýn, who was looking at her expectantly.

"Oh, um, yes?"

"Have you been listening to anything I've said?"

"Of course," Ema lied. "Every word of it."

He narrowed his eyes, then raised an eyebrow. "Why don't you recap, then?"

Ema cleared her throat. She'd only heard fragments of his chattering, but she realized now that Silvie had told her so much about this place, without actually *telling* her. The missing bits, she'd figured out for herself.

"This Midnight Guild is one of many spread out across the world. Each is a secret society run by an impresario, who gathers four of the greatest minds in their city and offers them a curatorship. Those curators put on spectacles and have three nights every full-ish moon to impress the spectators and secure patronage for whatever endeavor it is they need to finance. Those spectators hide their identities so as not to encourage favoritism, so there is no knowing who they might be—perhaps a famous explorer, or maybe even the king of Bohemia himself. Acolytes are like apprentices and must prove themselves a worthy addition to their designated spectacle—it's a much-coveted position, and rarely handed out. And the bottom of the pack are children like us—the herders—whose sole job is to encourage patrons toward our spectacle. We are not permitted to enter any spectacle other than our own, because the curators all hate each other and fear being spied on by one another. The acolytes are forbidden from mingling, and us herders are encouraged to make our loyalties clear by any means necessary—namely, making the other herders' lives miserable. It is only the patrons who are free to roam as they please, but they only have an hour each night to do so."

"Very good!" Valentýn beamed. "You know, I was on the verge of becoming an acolyte under my previous curator. Vendula was far less gloomy than Herr Finkelstein, and—just between you and me—it was much easier to encourage patrons into her spectacle area. Her underground garden was very popular. I wish you could have seen it, Emiliana. Only a botanist as brilliant as Vendula Beranová could grow such a spectacular underground garden. I hope she returns from her expedition soon. Botany is more exciting and dangerous than you might expect. I even miss the thorns and stings and constant scratches, though I'm saving a small fortune on bandages. I'm not sure how Herr Finkelstein will take to bat latin, but I don't see what other way I can showcase my skill with languages in a spectacle like his. Oh, I wouldn't walk that way, if I were you. Stay as close to this door as you can if you value your feet."

Ema had been inching sideways, waiting for Valentýn to look away. She'd been thinking that, if she ran quickly enough, perhaps the raven girl wouldn't be able to stop her from barging through that door. Perhaps she'd even be able to find Silvie before she was caught. But as the golden arrow clicked again, now just a fraction away from thirteen, Ema realized that plan was futile.

Ema bit the inside of her cheek to stop herself from crying. She needed to do something, and quickly—but what? Every inch of her skeleton was screaming that Silvie was here, somewhere.

"Nearly time to go home; my parents will be waiting up. I expect yours will be too," Valentýn said. "Any questions?"

As the music began to build up toward its final crescendo, Ema's gaze settled on the orchestra in the middle of the room, and an inexplicable chill coursed through her.

A question burst from her lips before she had the chance to stop it.

"How did Alois Blažek die?"

Valentýn's gasp of shock was barely covered by the crashing of a cymbal. "How could you possibly know about—"

"Dagmara Bartoňová," Ema said quickly. "I only know his name. I . . . I'm curious to know how he died, though. It must have been awful—everyone seems to know everyone very well down here."

Valentýn glanced nervously around the room, then sighed. "Yes, I suppose if I were you, I'd also like to know about the death of a curator. Especially one who had the most lucrative and successful spectacle." He sidled up closer, bent his head toward her ear, and whispered, "You needn't worry, though. Mr. Rivers conducted a thorough investigation. He concluded that it was but an unfortunate accident."

Ema's spine shuddered, and Liliana's misfortune pushed itself to her mind.

Murderer.

"What kind of unfortunate accident?"

Valentýn's gaze flicked up to the vaulted ceiling, to where the Astronomer's moon, the impresario's podium, and the birdcage were still dangling far above.

"Something fell from the ceiling."

"What kind of something?"

"A whale skeleton."

Ema blinked at him, wondering if she'd heard him correctly. "Pardon?"

"It was hanging from the ceiling on a contraption that made it appear to be swimming. The contraption's safety chain was seemingly not sturdy enough, however, and the whole thing came down, right onto Alois Blažek, who was performing underneath. Luckily, this was during a rehearsal and so there were no spectators or orchestra down there. And Mr. Rivers, the other curators, and two acolytes who were present at the time were all thankfully out of the way."

Ema looked up at the impossibly high ceiling and shuddered.

"It was Herr Finkelstein's first night as curator," Valentýn whispered. "I wonder if that's why he's so reluctant to let me be his acolyte. You see, it was *Alois's* acolyte's whale skeleton that killed him. Can you imagine that? Accidentally killing your own curator!"

Ema grimaced and nodded. "Who was this acolyte?"

Valentýn looked toward the raven's doorway, his expression turning grim.

"Her name is Florentina Falkenberg."

Another shudder ran through Ema as she remembered both the ominous figure in the mausoleum and the equally ominous curator who had made a bear skeleton dance earlier that night. Were they the same person?

"The Bone Sculptor? She was an acolyte?"

"Yes."

"And now she's a curator in her own right? Isn't that a little . . . suspicious?"

But Ema's voice was drowned out by a thundering chime from the clock. With a series of loud clunks, the entire ballroom plunged into darkness, the music came to an abrupt halt, and Valentýn's hand clamped down on her own.

"The hour is over," he said. "Come now. If we're quick we might avoid getting tripped over or wheeled on."

"No, I can't leave yet — "

"Ah, I know. It's all so exciting, isn't it? I didn't want to leave on my first night either! But leave you must. We cannot stay beyond the hour."

By the time the third chime sounded, they were surrounded — elbow to elbow — by patrons. Light arched out of the main tunnel doorway as it groaned open. As Valentýn urged her through it, Ema's mind scrambled for a plan. She couldn't leave without Silvie. Not now that she knew that Alois Blažek really had died under suspicious circumstances. Silvie's disappearance was somehow connected. How could it not be?

The fourth chime rang out, and Ema stopped trying to struggle free of Valentýn.

"I can see myself out from here," she said, though she

had no intention of going quite so easily as all that. Then quickly added: "Thank you for tonight."

"You are most welcome." He gave her a bright smile. Then, on the fifth chime, he let go, looking about the crowd as if trying to spot someone. "See you tomorrow, Emiliana."

As soon as he was out of sight, Ema pushed herself to the edge of the moving crowd, pressed herself against the stone wall, then inched her way back toward the ballroom. The chimes kept coming, as did the patrons.

As the thirteenth chime echoed away, Ema waited a moment longer in the darkness while the last of the patrons spilled into the tunnel. Then, as the door began to creak closed again, Ema ran back toward it. Her fingertips just brushed the handle as the door shut heavily.

The distinctive clunk of the lock followed a heartbeat later and shot through Ema like a physical blow.

There was no reaching Silvie now.

The murder hypothesis

≋ 16 ≋

Ema woke the next day with her arms in a leathery tangle and her bat mask covering one eye. Once again, echoes of her nightmares rang in her ears: the flapping of bat wings above her, the yowling of some wretched creature in the distance, and her own voice crying Silvie's name. But as she sat up and looked around the sunspeckled room, Ema could see that all was still and serene.

This was the complete opposite of the churning tumult of shame and despair coursing through her as she remembered the strange events of the previous night. She'd found the Midnight Guild, she'd avoided trouble by the skin of her teeth, but she'd failed to rescue Silvie — or even get close to it.

The attic room breeze ruffled her eyelashes, and, with a yelp, Ema ducked under her blankets. She stayed there until her tears had dried and her growling stomach had her lifting the corner of her blanket to peer through. Josef had left her a single apricot kolache and a half glass of milk on her bedside table. She rationalized that she couldn't come up with a decent plan of what to do next on an empty stomach.

She reached an arm through the gap, grabbed the kolache, and pulled it quickly under the covers. The first bite was hard to swallow as she thought back to all the children she'd met the previous night. That was the only thing that didn't make sense about the guild, where Silvie was concerned: the hostility—no matter how much she tried, she could never imagine Silvie behaving like those children had last night. Certainly not like Matylda, anyway.

Beyond the blankets, the breeze picked up. Ema ignored it and took another tentative nibble, chewing slowly as she wondered where Silvie was at that moment, and whether her friend was hungry or scared or both. What had Ema been thinking, marching up to Matylda like that without making doubly—or even triply—sure that it was Silvie? Would Silvie be safe with her now, if Ema had just been more careful?

As a hot tear snaked down Ema's cheek, the attic room windows rattled noisily.

Ema threw her blankets aside.

"I know!" she said, rubbing the tear away. "I know I failed her."

The breeze stopped, and Ema looked down at her pastry, wondering if she was so deliriously hungry it was making her talk to things that weren't there. She couldn't face another bite, however. Instead, she climbed wearily out of bed and gathered Silvie's trinket box into her lap, ignoring the breeze as it picked up around her again.

"I don't care if the impresario thinks Alois's death was an accident; I know it wasn't."

Again, the breeze stopped.

"Okay, good, we agree on that, then?"

A soft gust blew the tips of her hair. Ema swatted it aside and took another reluctant bite of her breakfast as she opened the trinket box and stared down at its contents, willing it to reveal the answers to all her problems. No such luck. She shut the box's lid again and got to her feet, swaying ever so slightly.

"I should tell Josef everything. He can help me go to the police."

The breeze blew around her.

"I can't do this alone," Ema said, pretending she was talking to herself, because talking to the wind was odd even for her. "I'm out of my depth, and it's too dangerous."

The breeze whistled.

"I'll write down everything I know about Alois's death. A murder investigation is no different, really, from a science investigation: you ask a question, form a hypothesis, and then study the data. There must be something the impresario missed. If I can identify that something, the police will know what to do."

As she reached for the Ema Enigma documents, the windows began to rattle again.

"Stop it!"

The breeze stilled.

Ema took a deep breath, closed her eyes, and brought the all-important question to her lips.

"So. Who killed Alois Blažek?"

An hour later, after sifting through every bewildering thing she'd observed the night before and all those nights with Silvie, Ema finally opened her eyes and began to write.

The Murder Hypothesis

Question: Who killed Alois Blažek?

Data

Victim: Alois Blažek

– A self-proclaimed ghost whisperer and curator of the most successful and lucrative spectacle within the Midnight Guild

– Silvie's sponsor

– Killed during a rehearsal several months ago, crushed beneath a whale skeleton that fell from the ceiling

– His death was ruled an unfortunate accident

Ema looked at the list, and, happy that it didn't contain anything that wasn't objectively true, she moved on. She tried hard to remember any other detail about the hooded figure in the mausoleum, but nothing came to mind other than that silver star brooch. This meant that there were five suspects for who had taken Silvie and, most likely, killed Alois.

The warring curators.

Suspect 1: Žofie Markova
- *An aeronaut and engineer, curator of Žofie's Bazaar, where she sells and demonstrates all sorts of newfangled technologies*
- *Wears a star brooch*
- *Spectacle was just over half-full*
- *Present during the fall of the whale skeleton*
- *Most likely up in the ceiling near to where it fell from*
- *Known hostility toward all other curators/spectacles*
- *Motive: get Alois out of the way so that her spectacle would draw bigger crowds*

Ema's pencil scratched across the paper.

Suspects 2 & 3: Aninha and Kazimír Carvosa
- *Illusionists from Brazil and curators of a spectacle filled with trickery and daredevilry*
- *Aninha smiles with delight as she plunges swords into people's bellies*

- Kazimir smiles with delight whilst having a sword plunged into his
  belly
- Both wear a star brooch
- Both were present during the fall of the whale skeleton
- Both were most likely floating up in the ceiling when the whale fell
- Spectacle was less than half-full
- Known hostility toward all other curators/spectacles
- Motive: get Alois out of the way so that more patrons would come to
  their spectacle

Shivering, Ema wrapped her blanket around her shoulders and tried her best to ignore the unease settling into her skeleton as she pressed on.

Suspect 4: Thibault Finkelstein
- A so-called astronomer who curates a ludicrous spectacle
  that suggests the moon is filled with waterfalls, rivers, goats,
  and man-bats
- Spectacle barely had any patrons
- Wears a star brooch
- Was present during the fall of the whale skeleton
- Most likely up on his floating moon when the whale fell
- Permanently gloomy demeanor and dark shadow
- My bones were itching most uncomfortably when I met him
- Known hostility toward all other curators/spectacles
- Motive: get Alois out of the way so that his spectacle might attract
  more patrons

With a flick of paper and a fresh pencil, she began the final list.

Suspect 5: Florentina Falkenberg
- *Alois's acolyte at the time of his death, sculpting animal bones for his spectacle*
- *Was given Alois's curatorship upon his demise*
- *Wears a star brooch*
- *Known hostility toward all other curators/spectacles*
- *Attracts the most patrons to her spectacle*
- *Was present during the fall of her whale skeleton*
- *Physical location when whale fell is unknown*
- *Motive: get Alois out of the way so that she could become curator*

For the next hour, Ema read and reread every sentence. Every time she picked up her pencil to write down what was surely the most logical hypothesis—that Florentina Falkenberg was the murderer—she stopped again.

It made the most sense, but that didn't mean it was true.

All she had to go on was her intuition, but Ema knew that was not how science worked.

Moreover, *each* curator had a motive, *each* curator was there at the time of his death, but there wasn't a single shred of empirical evidence that could tie any one of them to the crime. In fact, the only thing that even suggested it wasn't an accident, as the impresario had concluded, was the fact that Ema felt, in her very bones, that it had been murder.

"A perfect murder," Ema whispered, "as there's seemingly no evidence that there was one. I can't take this to the police, can I? They'll dismiss it just like Mr. Rivers did, and that won't help me get Silvie back."

Her eyelashes ruffled in the breeze. Ema shivered, looking up at the wallpapered wall.

Find her.

"I know! I'm trying! Just . . . leave me alone."

The breeze stopped, and the attic room door opened. Ema hurriedly stashed her papers away and slipped under her bed covers as Josef rushed in. He looked wretched, worry lines across his forehead and a helpless look of desperation in his eyes as they scanned the room, then settled on Ema.

"Ferkel?"

"No, I'm Ema."

"Is Ferkel not here? Who were you just talking to, if it wasn't her?"

"Myself," Ema said, not knowing if she was lying or not. "Still no sign of Ferkel?"

He shook his head. "I've checked every laundry basket within a mile radius, looked under every cart from here to the castle, and spent the morning baking a hundred of those kolache in anticipation of someone coming round to let me know Ferkel has ruined a priceless heirloom or eaten their favorite stockings. Nothing. It's like she's disappeared off the face of the earth."

"I'm sure she'll turn up," Ema said. "She *has* to."

Josef looked at her then, and his frown deepened. "I hate to say this, beruška, but you look awful. Your hair looks like it's been attacked by a flock of angry pigeons, and those dark circles under your eyes are large enough to have their own gravitational field. Did you have another bad night?"

"It was awful," Ema said half-truthfully, thinking back to the bewildering splendor of the Midnight Guild, her devastating failure to find Silvie before it ended, and the useless investigation she'd just shoved under her pillow. "I feel more wretched than I've ever felt before."

"Oh, beruška, you poor thing. Worry will do that to you, but you're right . . . Ferkel *will* turn up." He gave her a little, awkward pat on the head. "You get some more sleep. I'm going to make some reward posters and put them up around the city. Whatever trouble Ferkel has gotten herself into, there will no doubt be a path of destruction in her wake. I just need to follow that path to find her."

"Wait, Josef . . ."

"What is it?"

Her uncle studied her carefully as he waited for her to continue. Ema's fingers twitched, ready to grab her murder research lists. She could tell him everything. She could ask for his advice. Then she wouldn't be alone in this. All she had to do was say the words. The breeze started up again, and Josef stared at her in weary confusion.

"Good luck," she said finally.

"Thank you, beruška."

And then he was gone again, as was the breeze.

"Herr Finkelstein's letter won't have reached Dagmara Bartoňová yet," Ema whispered, feeling her decision settle over her like a blanket made of knives. "I'll go back tonight, I'll search Florentina Falkenberg's spectacle for Silvie, but if Silvie isn't out of that place with me *tonight*, then I'm asking for help. Do you understand?"

The breeze stayed still.

"Good, that's settled, then."

Ema slept through the rest of the afternoon and evening. It was the attic room breeze that woke her a little after eleven o'clock. She dressed in her man-bat costume, making sure every strand of her shimmery hair was carefully hidden, and then carefully tucked another outfit under her wing — Silvie's dark blue cloak and a simple black mask. She might be much shorter than the patrons, but at least this outfit would offer Silvie some disguise. Especially if she was hidden deep within the crowd.

When Ema looked up into the duck-foot mirror, she could see fear written all over her face. It wasn't the thought of sneaking into the guild that terrified her the most; it was the fact that the answers she had gotten the previous night had only opened more questions. The most confusing of which was how had Silvie had so many tutors? Žofie's flying machines, Aninha and Kazimír's magic tricks, the botanist who was a curator before Herr Finkelstein's arrival . . . Silvie had told her that she'd had tutors teach her these things, and Ema knew she hadn't been lying about that.

But how was that possible if it was against the rules to visit another spectacle?

Ema felt more confused now than before she'd arrived at the guild. Confusion and fear were a terrible combination for a would-be rescuer. It took every atom of willpower she had to make her legs move.

She found Josef asleep in a chair in the workshop, clutching a bowl filled with Ferkel's favorite meats and pastries. She quietly gathered a selection of tools, tucking them into her belt, then slipped out the door, running from shadow to shadow.

Toward Silvie.

Toward a murderer.

I t was a quarter to midnight when Ema stepped through the invisible door in the alleyway. Her skeleton itched in a way that she had never felt before; there was a heavy sense of dread and warning, but also a steady thrum of certainty that, so long as she stuck to her plan, she *would* find Silvie tonight.

It was this feeling she clung to as she wove through the blue-clad patrons already lining up along the entire length of the lamplit tunnel. First, she had to find Valentýn and question him about the guild's other exits. When she finally approached the end of the tunnel and spotted Valentýn, however, she came to a halt.

He wasn't alone.

Gathered on either side of the ballroom door were two groups of children. To the left were the acolytes, standing in silent seriousness. To the right, gathered around the terrified-looking bat boy, were the herders.

And Matylda.

The knife thrower was wearing a black-and-white baggy suit, a painted red nose, and a sardonic smile as she loomed over Valentýn. She'd positioned herself between him and the others—like a lioness claiming first dibs on her prey, snarling at anyone who tried to take a bite before she was done.

Ema pressed herself in between a group of patrons, her heart thundering. She'd hoped to be able to question Valentýn before the door opened, so that she could slip on her disguise before the ballroom lights turned on.

That clearly wasn't an option anymore.

Less worrying, more daring.

Trying not to trip over her own wobbly legs, Ema wove through the patrons, toward the doorway. She cleared her throat.

"Hello, Valentýn."

The children all jumped. After a few blinks, their scowls returned.

"Emiliana," Matylda said, smiling unpleasantly. "Valentýn has been regaling us with details of your impressive interview last night. Apparently, your branch of science is so unusual and so secret that Dagmara Bartoňová would not reveal it in writing. Care to share it with us?"

"I wasn't regaling anyone with anything," Valentýn insisted, looking panicked and apologetic. "I was being interrogated."

Matylda had a glint of something in her eyes that Ema couldn't quite read, and she wondered if there were any knives hidden in that clown outfit of hers. But as the knife thrower stepped toward her, Ema realized with surprise that she wasn't scared.

"It's nice to see you again, Matylda," she said politely, ignoring the question. "I love your outfit. It suits you perfectly."

The corner of Matylda's mouth twitched upward, and, once again, a flash of something unreadable glinted in her blue eyes.

"You're not one of those scientists who tries to reanimate dead frogs, are you?" asked the blue-haired wheeler.

"Nah, she looks more like the sort who studies rocks," said the raven, speaking from behind a beaked mask. "I'd say she's about as harmless as a wet sock."

Matylda took another step toward Ema. "It's the harmless-looking ones you need to be most wary of. Isn't that right, Ambrož?"

As quick as one of her knife throws, Matylda's eyes hardened, and Ema felt a flash of panic. Then the knife thrower looked up over Ema's shoulder, directing that dagger-sharp gaze toward the group of acolytes. Ema looked behind her, and after a few confused blinks she noticed someone standing in the shadows. It was the boy from Žofie's Bazaar, the one she'd slammed into last night. Ambrož glared at Matylda, then looked away again.

"So, Emiliana. Just what is this mysterious science of yours?"

Ema turned back to find Matylda staring directly at her again.

"You made it quite clear to me that sharing secrets among spectacles is against the rules. Why should I give you mine?"

Matylda smirked. "I've earned the right to break a few rules now and again."

"Is that why you are dressed like a clown tonight? And why you're here, instead of with the other acolytes? Did you break a rule?" Ema was shocked by her own brazenness, but felt herself standing a little straighter and smiling a little brighter nonetheless. Again, the corner of Matylda's mouth twitched upward, and she gave a nonchalant shrug.

The raven girl laughed. "At least once a week Matylda gets into trouble and finds herself banished to the ballroom. What was it this time, Matylda?"

"I gave one of my fellow acolytes a haircut she apparently didn't want. Although she shouldn't have been standing so close to my performance, should she? It's so easy to miss my target in the heat of the moment."

Ema scoffed. "I doubt you ever miss your target."

Matylda grinned.

"Well, um," said Valentýn, "if you'd kindly excuse me, I should really be briefing Emiliana on her duties for tonight. I have my acolyte interview with Herr Finkelstein shortly, after all."

He tried to step around the mime boy, who stuck his foot out. Valentýn collided, face-first, into the back of Matylda.

"Sorry," Valentýn said. "I didn't mean to—"

Matylda opened her mouth to respond, but there was a loud click from the ballroom door.

"Aha!" Ema said, grabbing Valentýn's arm and pulling him away. "The door's unlocked."

As she tugged Valentýn toward the pitch-dark ballroom, Ema swallowed down a bubble of rage. She was more determined than ever to get Silvie out of this horrible place, full of horrible children.

As soon as they were through the door, Valentýn linked their bat wings and started steering her through the dark ballroom.

"Hat-tat as-wat rilliant-bat," he whispered.

"Excuse me?"

"Sorry, I was practicing my bat latin. I said, that was brilliant. Facing up to Matylda and the others like that. You're so fearless. Now, come, I know a safe spot where we can stand until the lights come on. The others have never found me there, so we needn't worry about them bothering us."

Behind them, Ema could hear hundreds of shuffling feet and excited whispers. As the first chime of midnight echoed through the room, Valentýn tugged her to a halt. Ema had no idea where in the ballroom they were, but every hair on her arms and neck suddenly stood on end. Shuddering, she took a deep breath and tried to ignore her itching bones.

"Valentýn?" Ema whispered into the darkness.

"Yes, Emiliana?" Valentýn whispered back from the darkness.

The second chime rang out, and, with a heavy clunk, the spotlight burst into life above them—illuminating the giant birdcage with its giant bird inside. Ema shuddered again.

"I have a tiny question, if I may?" Ema said, trying to sound nonchalant.

"Ou-yat ay-mat."

"Did you just say *you may*?"

Though she couldn't see him, Ema sensed a delighted grin spread across Valentýn's cheeks. "Very good. What's your tiny question?"

Ema waited for the third chime to quiet, watching the spotlight swirl across the ceiling, then down across the crowd.

"It occurred to me last night that, should there be another unfortunate accident like the whale skeleton incident, I should know where the emergency exits are. Surely that door we came through isn't the only way in and out?"

The spotlight swept right across her face, and Ema

yelped in surprise, blinking away the bright spots.

"You needn't worry about accidents, Emiliana. The impresario has put strict new rules in place about the size of things that can be hung from the ceiling."

The spotlight arced across the ceiling once more, revealing the terrifying silhouettes of the curators high above them.

"Yes, but what about a fire? Surely, as herders, we must also know where to show the patrons to if need be."

"The curators will take charge. Or the impresario. They know where all the exits are and will make sure people get out safely. Now be quiet, please, or you'll give our hiding spot away."

Ema opened her mouth to press him further, but the chimes were reverberating through her already trembling skeleton, and it was all she could do not to curl into a ball on the floor.

Then, as the spotlight swooped back down again, Ema realized just where it was Valentýn had positioned them. They were standing right by the orchestra, in the middle of a dark, ominous shadow. Was this the exact spot where Alois Blažek had been killed?

Perhaps these shadows you see are the dead kind.

Ema squeezed her eyes shut. Light burns from the spotlight swayed behind her eyelids, merging into the undulating form of a whale skeleton, swimming across the dark sky above her head.

And then the skeleton fell.

Ema's eyes snapped open again, but the image of the falling skeleton wouldn't leave her.

"Why are you shaking?" Valentýn whispered. "You're not ill, are you?"

Ema couldn't form words. As the final chime sounded and the spotlight settled on the impresario, every bone in Ema's body felt electrically charged.

"WELCOME. WELCOME. WELCOME. WELCOME. WELCOME."

It wasn't the Midnight Guild that Ema was seeing or hearing now, though, it was Silvie that night in the graveyard: the white tulip, the eyeball necklace, the look of despair, and her desperate plea for Ema to help.

As light burst out to fill the room and the orchestra began to play, Ema was pulled back from her memories to find Valentýn looking at her in concern.

"You look like you've seen a ghost."

"I'd just really like to know where those exits are, Valentýn. Do you really not know where they are?"

"No, I don't."

Ema saw the tiniest twitch between his eyebrows and knew he was lying. "Valentýn —"

"I need to go now, Emiliana. I've been waiting for an opportunity to show my bat latin to Herr Finkelstein for months now, so I can't be late. All you need to do is tell people how wonderful the Astronomer's spectacle is and nudge them through the door."

"But—"

"You'll be fine. There won't be any fires or accidents, and I won't be more than fifteen minutes."

And just like that, he was gone—as was Ema's chance at realizing the first part of her rescue plan.

A cymbal crashed behind her and sent Ema hurrying away from that horrible dark shadow. She wandered aimlessly through the crowd, willing her nerves to settle so that she could think more clearly.

Just because she hadn't gotten an answer from Valentýn didn't mean her plan was doomed. There clearly *were* other exits. There must be—all Ema had to do was find them. Despite her ridiculous costume, none of the patrons had seemed to notice her existence tonight. For the first time, Ema felt a bubble of pride at her unusual skill.

It meant that the second part of her plan—sneaking into Florentina Falkenberg's spectacle unseen—was one she could surely count on getting right, at least. For once, her accidental stealth felt like a warm comforting blanket wrapped around her.

Feeling a renewed sense of purpose and hope, Ema tucked her shoulders up to her ears and made her way across the ballroom. The wheeler did not even blink as

Ema passed her, heading toward the towering doorway through which most of the patrons were heading.

As she crept closer still, the raven beside that door did not turn their beaked mask her way, and Ema felt a small, triumphant smile tug at her mouth. But as she reached for the cloak beneath her bat wing, an uncomfortable shudder ran right down her spine.

Ema turned, her teeth itching, and scanned the ballroom, feeling increasingly confused and uneasy, until finally settling on the source of her discomfort.

Across the room, Matylda was staring right at her.

The Moonlight Garden

≋ 18 ≋

Ema watched helplessly as the second part of her plan unraveled before her very eyes. Everything about the way Matylda was glaring at her was clearly meant to intimidate. And yet, just like in the tunnel, Ema felt a perplexing sense of mischief bubble up inside her. The more Matylda glared, the more Ema grew determined not to let a knife-throwing clown stand in the way of her completing her mission.

She summoned her brightest smile and wiggled her fingers in a friendly wave, then grinned when Matylda's scowl deepened.

Why was she trying to rile a girl who threw knives for a living?

Matylda mouthed the words: *What are you doing?*

Ema pretended to look very confused.

Matylda crossed her arms and shook her head.

Ema pretended to look even more confused.

Matylda nodded pointedly at Ema's herding spot across the room.

Ema pretended to look flabbergasted that she wasn't in that very spot.

Matylda blinked.

Ema thanked her with pressed palms and a deep bow.

Matylda rolled her eyes.

Ema blew her a kiss.

Matylda gagged, squeezing her eyes closed in mock disgust.

And that was all the time Ema needed to throw the cloak over her head and shoulders and dart quickly into the throng of patrons.

As the crowd shuffled forward, Ema peeked through her hood to find Matylda looking out across the ballroom in confusion.

The mischievous delight Ema felt lasted only another second. If Matylda had seen her, did that mean her stealth was failing? And if it was failing, how on earth was she supposed to sneak Silvie out of the guild without being seen? Especially since Matylda would soon realize exactly where Ema had snuck off to.

Panic fluttered in her chest.

With the first two parts of her plan now compromised, it was surely best to revert to plan B: abandon her mission and seek help. Instead, she put her head down and shuffled along, her heart thundering and her palms itching as she got closer to the doorway. The raven did not reach out to grab her, though. And a moment later, Ema found herself over the threshold and in a corridor. A new panic set in as the crowd crept forward.

What kind of horror would await in the Bone Sculptor's spectacle?

An imposing iron gate loomed ahead, and Ema risked pulling her hood back slightly to get a better look at the metal lettering above it: THE MOONLIGHT GARDEN.

Ema's panic morphed into bewilderment as she passed through the iron gates into the most spectacular garden she'd ever seen. Beneath the vaulted stone ceilings hung a luminescent moon, casting a silvery glow across a wild tangle of greenery that filled the vast room. Rising up above the botany were gleaming white marble sculptures of every animal imaginable, wrapped in curling vines.

Ema was swept down some mossy stone steps, partly by the awestruck patrons around her, partly by the fact that she was too confused to do anything else.

I wish you could have seen it, Emiliana. Only a botanist as brilliant as Vendula Beranová could grow such a spectacular underground garden.

Had she somehow come through the wrong doorway? Was the botanist back from her expedition?

At the bottom of the steps, there was a black brick

path that forked three ways. Not knowing which way to turn, Ema let herself be swept to the left by a woman with a dreamy smile beneath her mask.

The moment they stepped beneath the arch, a towering plant beside them began to shudder and move. Both Ema and the woman gasped as the plant twisted itself into the form of a girl. The leaves on her costume trembled as she moved, and a painted green face appeared, with startling green eyes blinking open.

Those green eyes stared right through Ema, however. The plant girl smiled as she extended a thin, green arm right past Ema's face, holding a single white flower up to the woman beside her.

"Welcome to the Moonlight Garden," said the plant girl in a voice like rustling leaves. "May you find peace and beauty in that which terrifies us all."

As the woman took the delicate white flower, a shiver ran from the base of Ema's spine right to the top of her scalp. It was no flower at all; in the center of its delicately carved white petals was a tiny rodent skull. Ema stifled a yelp and staggered on along the path.

This was, without a doubt, the Bone Sculptor's spectacle.

Everywhere she looked, she found more evidence.

In the peach tree next to her was a small nest made of twig-like bones. Perched within that nest were two lovebirds. Their skeletons nestled lovingly together in an eternal embrace. There was something strangely beautiful about the way the birds had been arranged, but that didn't stop Ema from shuddering.

She turned quickly away again, looking instead to the many patrons who were ambling past in a dreamlike manner. Even with the masks covering their eyes, Ema could see the serenity on their faces.

Ema felt anything but serene as she hurried down the canopied tunnel. The only thing that mattered now was finding Silvie and getting as far away from this place as possible. But first, Ema had to get as far away from all these bones as possible.

So she ran.

Down path after path she went, feeling more and more unsettled. It was like a labyrinth—and far bigger than the previous spectacle spaces. Finally, she found a large stone rising out from a cluster of ferns, climbed up onto it, took out her spyglass, and pressed it to her eye. But after a few minutes of scanning the gardens, Ema snapped the spyglass closed in frustration.

It would take her hours to search this place for Silvie.

But it wasn't the lack of time, nor the discomfort of the skeletons that made Ema realize that step three of her plan was going as disastrously wrong as the first two.

She could feel—in her *own* very bones—that Silvie was not in this garden.

Neither, it seemed, was Florentina Falkenberg.

Ema squinted at the group gathered around the wall again, trying to ignore the voice at the back of her mind telling her that her plan was futile, and it was time to admit defeat.

Matylda could well have sounded the alarm by now.

Valentýn would be back from his interview at any minute.

Either way, she was in trouble.

So, she might as well continue.

Once again, her heart gave a little flutter.

Climbing down, Ema tucked her shoulders up to her ears and made her way over to the wall. She crept, unnoticed, to the front of the crowd, where a very tall, very thin, and very angry woman in a long shroud was squaring up to the archway guard.

"We were next," the woman was saying. "We were next the last few times too. This is unacceptable."

"Agáta, is it really worth all this?" the woman's companion said grumpily.

"Yes, Oskar, it is. She's even more gifted than he was, from what I hear." She tapped impatiently on the wing of a raven-boy standing guard in front of the arch. "I demand you tell me when Frau Falkenberg will see us."

The raven tilted his head in a birdlike manner. "She is otherwise engaged. You will have to wait."

As the woman drew herself even taller, ready to launch into another tirade, Ema seized the moment and slipped

behind the raven, through the archway, and into the shadowy tunnel beyond.

"Do you even know who I am?"

"No, paní, that is the point—"

"Well, I'll tell you—"

The darkness swallowed her whole.

Ema hurried down a stone tunnel, around a sharp corner, and onward to a curtain door halfway down. Fingers
trembling, Ema nudged a corner of the curtain aside, until
there was just enough space to press one eye to the gap.
The room beyond was almost as dark as the corridor itself, save for the single flickering lightbulb that dangled
from the middle of the ceiling. Directly beneath it was a
round table, draped in a blood-red tablecloth; three figures sat around it, holding hands.

Two were patrons—a man and a woman—their hoods
down and their faces covered with thin black masks. The
other was a young woman in a high-necked, puffed-sleeve
mourning dress. The light caught the delicate contours of
her face, and Ema could see her eyes darting beneath her
closed lids. At the base of her collar was the silver star
brooch. When the Bone Sculptor spoke, it was in a soft
and melodic whisper.

"Aleks . . . are you there?"

Silence.

Ema squinted, trying to see if Silvie was anywhere in
the room—or where a prisoner-shaped hiding place might

be—but it was too dark to tell. She could only just make out the rough outlines of cabinets and crates beyond the ring of light on the table.

Her gaze was drawn back to the Bone Sculptor.

Florentina frowned slightly, then she gasped. "Oh! I heard something!"

"What?" said the man. "What did he say?"

"It's hard to decipher. Is Aleks English?"

"No."

"Swedish?"

"No. Aleks is Czech just like the rest of us. Are you sure you have the correct ghost?"

"Absolutely," Florentina said quickly. "It's definitely him. I can feel it."

Ema thought she heard a flicker of panic in the Bone Sculptor's voice.

"Aleks, we just want to know if you are happy where you are," Florentina called out. "One knock for no, two knocks for yes."

A loud and hollow knock sounded from the ceiling, making the light flicker.

A charge of fear coursed through Ema, but she forced herself to keep watching. Her heart was pulsating so much she could feel it moving the front of her cloak, but her eyes were locked on the scene before her.

After several long slow heartbeats, another knock

sounded—this time from near one of the shadow-drenched cabinets.

One of the mourners let out a small sigh. "Oh, thank goodness."

"If there's anything else, please give us a sign," Florentina said softly. "Any sign at all—"

There was a rattling noise from the table that made the two mourners gasp and pull their hands away. Then, as Florentina reached for them again, the rattling intensified. Several items on the table bounced around, and Ema watched in horror as the séance table began to lift from the floor.

The mourners' cries of shock were drowned out as the table slammed heavily back down again. Several candlesticks toppled over, and something small slid from the table. It hit the carpet with a dull thud and rolled toward Ema.

Ema felt as if she'd been plunged into the icy depths of the Vltava River as she stared at it.

It stared straight back at her.

Silvie's eyeball necklace.

≈ 19 ≈

Ema stared unblinkingly at the proof she'd been looking for, and that proof stared unblinkingly straight back at her. The eyeball was just as unsettling as the first time she'd seen it.

It *had* been Florentina Falkenberg in the graveyard that night.

It *was* Florentina Falkenberg who had taken Silvie.

Although she'd come to suspect as much, Ema now felt the truth of those two facts as deeply as she felt the horrified disbelief of what she'd just witnessed.

Florentina Falkenberg had summoned a ghost, and that ghost had lifted a heavy table straight off the floor.

It was impossible.

And yet, it had happened.

As her mind scrambled to comprehend the gravity of what she'd just seen, she realized Florentina was now on her feet, gently stilling all the wobbling objects on the table. The two mourners had pushed their chairs back from the table and were clutching their hands to their chests. Ema's own heart was beating so hard her chest was still fluttering visibly through her cloak.

"That was a good sign," Florentina said reassuringly. "I realize it might seem alarming, but Aleks clearly wanted to let you feel his presence one last time."

Ema couldn't see their faces beneath the masks, but she saw their shoulders shaking with emotion.

"Come," Florentina said, guiding them toward the door. "I am so happy to have been able to help you tonight. If I can ever do anything else, please let me know."

Ema had just enough time to press herself flat against the wall when the curtain opened, and they stepped out into the corridor.

"Thank you, Frau Falkenberg," said the woman. "You have brought us great peace."

"I'm just sorry my predecessor wasn't able to do this for you sooner," Florentina said. "Did you ever visit him?"

"No, we were never able . . ." Their footsteps and their voices faded away as they rounded the corner.

The curtain was wide open now, and Ema stared into the room with overwhelming terror. With just that single bulb above the table, most of the room was still drenched in shadow.

Perhaps these shadows you see are the dead kind.

Ema didn't want to go in, but she needed to. "Silvie?"

she whispered, then drew in a deep breath and stepped forward.

Every bone in her body itched, and the moment she crossed the threshold she was certain the temperature dropped all around her.

"Silvie?"

Her voice was hoarse and barely more than a whisper, but in the silent room it felt uncomfortably loud.

"Silvie? Are you in here?"

The continued silence was deafening. Ema forced herself to keep inching forward into the room, only coming to a halt when she reached Silvie's necklace.

As her fingers curled over the eyeball, the very same shudder ran up her arm as it had done that night in Alois's mausoleum. Once again, she had the uncomfortable feeling that she was now being watched.

Ema spun round.

"Silvie? Are you here?"

Aside from her and the furniture, though, the room was empty. Ema made a slow circle. As she faced the wall behind her, she stifled a shriek—long, dark shadowy tendrils snaked out across the entirety of it, as if they were all reaching toward her. What was casting such shadows?

With a shudder, Ema turned away from them.

Still that feeling of being watched persisted.

Gripping the eyeball tightly, Ema hurried over to the nearest cabinet and threw the doors open.

Shelves of hollow-eyed animal skulls stared back at her. She swallowed a scream and shut the doors again, moving to the next cabinet, then the next. The more she looked, the more she realized there was no room to hide a child anywhere; everything was packed full of bones and other monstrous curiosities.

Ema bit back a growl of frustration as a new sense of certainty crept over her, and she angrily rubbed a hot tear away as it snaked down her cheek.

Silvie wasn't here.

Why did this keep happening?

What was she missing?

As Ema drew herself up and began to make her way back to the door, her fists clenched tightly in frustration. The eyeball necklace dug into her left palm.

Ema stopped.

One by one, the hairs on the back of her neck began to rise.

Whoever was watching her was behind her.

She turned slowly, her pale gray eyes meeting a pair of hazel eyes. They belonged to a man with long brown hair, an ostentatiously ruffled collar, and a stare of such somber seriousness it could rival Herr Finkelstein's. Though she had never set eyes on this man before, she knew in an instant exactly who he was.

Alois Blažek.

His portrait hung on the wall in a gilded frame. As she

approached him slowly, those painted amber eyes remained fixed on her, as did the perfectly human-looking eyeball dangling around his neck.

"Where is she?"

Alois Blažek did not respond.

Just like in the Astronomer's spectacle, Ema felt a prickling sense of unease. Despite this, Ema reached out and touched the painting.

An electric shock shot up her arm.

She yelped and pulled it away again.

Footsteps sounded in the corridor.

Ema looked around her in a panic. There was only one hiding place in the entire room, and the thought of even touching it filled Ema with horror.

The ghostly levitating table.

"Come," Florentina was saying loudly. "This way."

Feeling sick to her stomach, Ema lifted a corner of the tablecloth and peered underneath, then gasped in astonishment.

There were levers and pulleys attached to the underside of the table and what looked like a pedal-controlled contraption under the table's legs.

The knocking sounds . . . the levitation . . . it hadn't been real at all! Florentina wasn't just a kidnapper and murderer. She was also a complete fraud.

It was anger that gripped Ema this time, but she ducked under the table, just as the footsteps turned into the room and the curtain swished closed once more. Ema put a hand to her racing heart, only to find the fluttering was in her cloak pocket, something *lumpy*. The lump wriggled. Ema peered inside and found Béla blinking up at her.

Ema blinked back down at him in astonishment.

Had he been in there ever since she'd taken Silvie's cloak?

And had it been him flapping around her room at night, causing those strange dreams?

"Please tell me you found something?" came Florentina's voice.

"Nothing at all," said another voice, one that Ema recognized immediately. "I'm sorry."

The Astronomer.

Putting one hand gently over Béla to keep him still, Ema peered under the edge of the tablecloth. Herr Finkelstein was standing by the doorway, looking as gloomy as ever, wearing a blue cloak and a black mask. Even with his face hidden, Ema would recognize the Astronomer's darkened shadow anywhere, and that unsettling mourning ring glinting on his left hand.

He wasn't supposed to be out of his spectacle area.

What on earth was he doing here? And in disguise, no less.

He was holding a leather journal in his hand, which he held out. "Here, you should take this back and keep it hidden. You really don't want it falling into the wrong hands."

The Bone Sculptor groaned as she took it from him, then began pacing the room, pinching the bridge of her nose. The calm serenity she'd shown with the two mourners was now gone. Ema didn't need to use her twitchology skills to see that she was extremely stressed.

"I need those names, Thibault," the Bone Sculptor said. "Without them, I have nothing."

"Perhaps your spy will have more luck than me?"

Ema was starting to feel increasingly uneasy—rivalry, spies, murders. It was all too much. Despite being an enchanting place on the face of it, this guild really did seem to be hiding a dark and dangerous side. And Silvie was somehow caught up in it all.

"Perhaps, but I can't keep this up for much longer. It doesn't matter that the contraptions you built are working better than expected. One way or another, Ephraim will find out what I've been doing. I'm surprised I've got as far as I have, for as long as I have."

"There is still time, Florentina. Vendula will respond soon, I'm sure of it."

"We've both written to her three times, with no response."

"Mail isn't reliable in that part of the world. You just need to be patient."

"No, Thibault. Tomorrow night, for better or worse, I'll have this finished."

"What do you mean?"

Florentina stopped pacing and looked up at Alois Blažek's portrait, her expression grim. Ema's skin prickled with unease.

"All these months and I haven't got nearly enough . . ." Florentina said with a bite of frustration in her voice. "But I'll cut my losses and run, if I have to. My spy and I already have plans in place, to implement at a moment's notice. It'll be my last resort, but I'll destroy *everything*. There will be no evidence left behind."

Ema flinched as the Bone Sculptor's evident fury crackled through the air. What, exactly, was she after? What had led her to lie, steal, cheat, kidnap . . . even murder? And what was this evidence that she was willing to destroy? The contraptions under the table? The journal in her hands? Something else?

Florentina walked over to Alois's portrait with the journal tucked in her armpit and lifted the painting to reveal a hidden safe behind it. Ema watched her turn the safe's dial three times, her teeth itching increasingly as it turned left to one, then right to two, and then left to twelve.

The safe opened, and Florentina shoved the journal between what looked like stacks of banknotes. Then she turned back to the Astronomer and sighed. "I must prepare for my next clients, and you'd better get back before anyone notices you are gone."

"Let me know if you need anything else."

"You've done *plenty*," she said with a grim smile. "Thank you."

He gave her a small, somber nod, then disappeared through the curtain.

Ema watched as Florentina Falkenberg closed the safe, returned the portrait to its position, then bent forward and rested her forehead on the wall.

Ema realized it was now or never.

With one hand on Béla, she shuffled silently out from under the table. She inched backward toward the curtain, holding her breath until she was on the other side of it.

It was then that she realized she was still clutching the eyeball necklace.

Florentina would surely notice its absence.

Reluctantly, Ema reached for the curtain again, inching it open ever so slightly, ready to throw the necklace back onto the carpet where she'd found it.

But she hesitated.

It was Silvie's. As unsettling as it was, it clearly meant a lot to her friend, and the thought of putting it back in the hands of her kidnapper filled Ema with a fiery rage she'd never felt before.

Ema glared silently but furiously at the Bone Sculptor's back.

Florentina turned with a gasp.

Their eyes locked.

≈ 20 ≈

For the second time that night, Ema found herself staring into a pair of eyes that should not have been staring back at her. She hadn't made a sound, so how had Florentina Falkenberg sensed she was there? Her stealth had never failed like this before, even when she'd *tried* to make it fail.

The Bone Sculptor blinked, and Ema swiftly dropped the end of the curtain. As her heart thundered and Béla wriggled furiously beneath her hand, she began to stagger backward. She almost tripped over her own feet as she turned and ran around the corner, back toward the Moonlight Garden. Behind her, the curtains scraped loudly apart.

"Who's there?" the Bone Sculptor called out in a voice hitched with panic. "Show yourself."

At the corridor's end, the raven acolyte was still trying to keep the tall woman in the shroud from barging through uninvited. Ema slipped under the raven's wing and leaped behind the nearest bush, peering through some ferns to see the Bone Sculptor appear beside the raven, her face ashen and her eyes darting.

"Did someone just come out of here?" Florentina asked.

Ema felt a fresh surge of panic. Béla was still trying to wriggle free.

"No, Frau Falkenberg," said the raven in bemusement. "Not since your last customer left."

"Are you certain? I saw a pale face with ghostly gray eyes—"

"Well, I should hope so," said the waiting woman. "Seeing spirits is your job, after all. Speaking of which, it is our turn now. I have a bone to pick with Aunt Wibke about the will she wrote me out of. Come, Oskar." She grabbed her companion and elbowed her way past both the raven and the startled-looking curator.

Florentina cast one last confused glance around her spectacle, then turned back into the dark corridor and disappeared.

Ema waited a few more moments for her pulse to slow down enough that it no longer made her dizzy, before lifting her hood and stepping out from her hiding place. It was then that she realized she was still clutching the eyeball necklace, and her panic spiked up again. Soon,

Florentina would realize it was gone and know for sure that someone had been in her room.

"We need to leave," Ema whispered to the bat. "We're out of time and out of places to search. I've failed. Again."

She stumbled down the nearest path, weaving unsteadily through the patrons. Never in her life had her bones trembled so.

"I don't understand, Béla. I've searched everywhere in this guild for her and found nothing. And yet"—Ema shuddered—"she is here. I can feel it." Béla wriggled his face free, blinking up at Ema accusingly. "I promise I'll let you go when we're safely out of here—" Another shudder ran through her, bringing her to a halt. As she tried to soothe the squirming bat, Ema looked around her uncertainly. She needed help; that much was certain. But what wasn't certain was whether anyone would take her seriously if she asked for it. So now what?

Finally, she looked back down at Béla.

"You want to find her too, don't you?"

The bat blinked.

"All right. We'll try it your way."

Giving his head one more soothing stroke, she opened her hand and watched him soar up into the air.

"Find her."

Béla swooped upward. The first shriek of surprise from a spectator sounded just a few moments later. More shrieks followed, then morphed into oohs and aahs as Béla zigzagged across the underground night sky, past the shining moon, and then out through the main doorway toward the ballroom.

With her midnight-blue cloak flowing behind her, Ema raced down the garden path after him, up the mossy stone steps to the doorway, and out of the Bone Sculptor's spectacle.

The orchestra was in the middle of Wagner's "Ride of the Valkyries," a small group of patrons was dancing, the Astronomer's moon was spinning gently, and the giant bird in the birdcage was slumped sleepily against the bars, dangling its human feet out above the ballroom floor.

The raven was adjusting the bear skeleton's top hat and paid no attention as Ema staggered breathlessly out of Florentina's spectacle area, casting her blue cloak aside so that she was back in her bat costume. The wheeler girl was spinning idly in circles. And the mime boy was examining his fingernails.

Across the ballroom, however, Matylda and Valentýn were both looking at Ema in astonishment.

Her plan to rescue Silvie unnoticed might be in tatters, but she wasn't ready to give up just yet. Béla would find Silvie eventually; she just had to keep him in sight — even if that meant following him through every corner of the guild.

Ema glanced up at the large clock above the tunnel door.

The end of the midnight hour was just a few minutes away.

A scream sounded from the crowd of dancers as Béla swooped and flapped right through the center of the room, over the heads of the musicians. A violin screeched, a cymbal was knocked to the floor, and a cellist ducked behind his instrument. And then the bat swoop-dived through the doorway into Žofie Markova's bazaar.

Ema ran after him, adrenaline vibrating every atom of her being.

She was skirting around the orchestra's dark shadow when Valentýn and Matylda rounded the other side and blocked her route. Ema only just avoided colliding with them.

"What on earth has gotten into you?" the bat boy asked, his eyes wide with outrage and awe. "Did you really just do what I think you did? Did you just come out of the Bone Sculptor's spectacle?"

"She definitely did," Matylda said. "And how did a bat get in here?"

"Can't chat right now," Ema said, darting around them. She paused on the doorway's threshold and grinned at the two of them. "Don't worry about the bat, though — I'll make sure to chase it out."

And then she sprang through the doorway, into the steam-filled corridor beyond.

"Emiliana!" Valentýn called out after her. "You can't go in there!"

"What do you mean you didn't notice her?" Ema heard Matylda yell. "She ran right past you. Perhaps you should stop spinning and—"

The noise of the ballroom disappeared between hissing steam and clunking gears. And then Ema was in Žofie's Bazaar once again. The room was abuzz with excited activity, and Ema's bones thrummed as her eyes darted around the room.

Béla was flying in chaotic circles high above the patrons.

"You shouldn't be in here."

Ema leaped out of her skin, turning to find the boy she'd collided with the night before standing right beside her. Just like the previous night, she hadn't noticed him approach. And how could he see her?

"Hello, um, Ambrož, is it?"

Ambrož stared at her, his brows pinched and his eyes skeptical. "Why are you here?"

"I'm just trying to chase the bat," Ema said truthfully. "It's causing all sorts of mayhem."

"Emiliana!" hissed a voice behind her.

She and Ambrož both turned to find Valentýn and Matylda standing in the doorway.

Ambrož scowled at the two of them, then turned back to Ema. "That bat isn't the only one causing mayhem, it seems." He nodded across the room to Žofie Markova, who was watching Béla disrupt her spectacle. His expression turned grimmer, as did his tone. "You do realize what will happen if she catches you?"

Ema swallowed, then looked at Ambrož again, expecting to find a furious scowl the likes of which he kept throwing at Matylda. But he just looked worried and weary.

"Yes, I realize I'm going to get into huge trouble, but I need to chase that bat."

"Well, you're not going to catch it just by staring at it from all the way over here. Let me grab a net. Stay there."

He slunk into the crowd, weaving through it invisibly.

Ema cast another look at Valentýn and Matylda.

"She's your responsibility," Matylda said, giving him a little shove. "You make her leave."

"I can't!"

"You must!"

"I'm back," said Ambrož, once again appearing next to Ema so suddenly she gasped. Was this how other people felt around her? It really was unnerving. The boy was wielding a net and scanning the room with a frown. "Where did the bat go?"

Valentýn screamed and ducked under his bat wing as Béla swooped over the two of them, back through the doorway and out of sight. Ema chased after him, just as Matylda began scolding Valentýn.

"Leave him alone," Ema hissed at Matylda as she ran past them. "Find someone else to bother."

"Are you offering?" Matylda called back.

Ema pressed on, once again emerging breathlessly in the ballroom.

Béla swooped past the clock.

Closing time was less than a minute away, and the bat still hadn't led her to Silvie. Ema felt sick with dread as she waited to see which spectacle he would fly into next.

The other three children appeared beside her, Ambrož with his net.

"Give that here," Matylda said, grabbing the net from Ambrož. "You're useless at catching things."

Ambrož held firm, and the two of them wrestled. Neither seemed to notice the bat fly right past them and then onward, out of reach.

"It's too late," Valentýn said. "Look."

The four of them watched Béla flap his way up into the ceiling, passing the Astronomer's moon, then the birdcage, then the impresario's floating podium, before finally disappearing into the dark recesses above.

But as the others continued to bicker about who let the bat get away, Ema was frozen to the spot. Her heart seemed to have come to a complete standstill as she processed what she'd just seen: a thin arm, stretching through the bars of the birdcage, reaching out longingly to Béla as he flew past.

She'd found Silvie.

In a cage.

Fifty meters in the air.

Entirely unreachable.

As the final minute of the midnight hour began, Ema stared up at Silvie. Her friend had climbed the bars of her cage, right to the top, and was frantically searching the ceiling for Béla. Ema felt a deep sense of helplessness close in around her.

"I think the bat is gone, Emiliana," Matylda said in a voice that seemed far away.

"You can stop staring now."

"Is she all right? She isn't blinking," said another voice, which Ema would have recognized as Valentýn's, had she tried to.

Even if she were to scream at the top of her lungs, it was doubtful Silvie would be able to hear her over the music.

"My cat does the very same thing sometimes," said another voice at the edge of Ema's consciousness. *"Even when I wave my hand in front of its face. Look—see, no response."*

"*Well then, Ambrož, do you have any suggestions for how we get her out of this weird trance?*"

Ema needed to find help, but to whom should she turn?

The impresario was the most logical person to ask. And yet, Ema felt a shuddering certainty that it was too risky. Not only because she'd lied and cheated her way into his guild, but because of Florentina Falkenberg's furious declaration: *My spy and I already have plans in place, to implement at a moment's notice . . . I'll destroy everything.*

As Ema stared up at Silvie, another unwanted image crept into her mind. Only this time it wasn't a whale skeleton that fell from the ceiling . . . it was Silvie's birdcage.

Was her friend's life Florentina's "last resort"?

If Ema went to the impresario now, would she be able to convince him in time to get Silvie down from that cage? What if Florentina's spy was watching him, ready to raise the alarm? It was too much of a risk to assume otherwise.

"*We need to do something, Matylda. The patrons are starting to stare at her.*"

Ema could sneak out now and head straight to Josef. But as far as she knew, he had no idea this place existed. It would take too long to explain it, let alone convince him it was real.

Her parents? They *did* know about this place, and they were due back any day now. But if the guild only ran for three nights a month, and they weren't back by tomorrow, they'd have to wait another month. Silvie might not have that long.

"If you two aren't going to do anything, I'm going to poke her. With a knife, if need be! Oh, for saints' sake, that was a joke, Valentýn. Why are you looking so horrified? Oh wow, I've never seen Florentina look so angry. Emiliana, what did you do in there?"

Ema jolted, and the ballroom music went from sounding like a faraway dream to an earsplitting cacophony. Her gaze snapped toward the raven doorway as Florentina Falkenberg stepped out of it, looking furious.

Murderous, even.

The eyeball necklace suddenly felt heavy in Ema's pocket. By taking it, Ema had ensured that Florentina would know that someone had likely overheard everything she'd said to the Astronomer.

"Well, Emiliana," Matylda said. "Now that you're back on Earth, it would be a brilliant time to start explaining yourself."

Ema pulled her attention to the three children, studying them as they studied her. They stood shoulder to shoulder, staring at her with such identical expressions of suspicion that Ema had to do a double take. She needed to make a quick decision about how to help Silvie, but the one she settled on in that moment surprised even her.

"My name isn't Emiliana, it's Ema."

Matylda blinked. "You — "

"Lied, yes," Ema said. "About a lot more than you realize. Dagmara Bartoňová hasn't sponsored me. She won't even let me into her school."

They stared at her in wide-eyed astonishment, and, suddenly, the three of them made much more sense to her.

"That's not even the worst of it, though," she continued, sidling up closer to them. "The reason Florentina is over there looking like she wants to murder someone is my fault too. I stole something from her séance room. I found proof that she's a complete fraud, a kidnapper, and quite probably a murderer too."

If Ema hadn't been so filled with urgency, she might have been delighted at the way she'd left them completely awestruck.

"What kind of trickster are you?" Matylda asked, scowling hard.

"No more of a trickster than you are. I'll admit, up until a few moments ago you had me convinced your sole ambition in life was to torment poor Valentýn to the end of his days. You do an excellent impression of a bully — but you're protecting him from the others, aren't you? That's why you always get yourself into trouble, so that you can be out here with him."

Matylda's scowl twitched.

"And I'll hazard a guess that Ambrož was once a part of your forbidden little gang too, weren't you? You'd meet in secret, share your skills, and go on adventures."

Valentýn gasped. "How could you possibly know—"

"Be quiet, Val," Matylda said bitingly, but Ema saw the brief glint of panic in the knife thrower's eyes.

"But how could she know that?" Valentýn insisted. "It's impossible—"

"Nothing is impossible," the knife thrower snapped.

"With a little imagination?" Ema finished, and Matylda barely contained her surprise. "We need to talk. In private. Right now."

"No." Ambrož shook his head. "We need to take you to the impresario—"

"You'll do no such thing."

"Oh, really? And why is that?"

"Because if you do that, then you risk the one person I think all four of us care very deeply about."

"And who would that be?" asked Valentýn.

"Silvie."

A loud chime cut through the air, the music came to an abrupt halt, and Ema only caught a split-second glance at their shocked faces before the lights clunked out.

"Meet me at the western end of Charles Bridge in ten minutes," Ema whispered into the darkness. "I'll explain everything."

The night air was stiflingly muggy as Ema hurried past the looming statues of saints toward the gate tower, but she felt a glimmer of optimism. She had found Silvie's friends.

The curators weren't Silvie's peculiar tutors.

Those three bickering, loyal, remarkable children were. And she knew that it was they who would help her get her friend back safely.

She just needed to convince them of that fact. If they turned up, that was — without bringing the impresario with them. Or worse — Florentina Falkenberg.

Just in case, Ema buried herself in the shadows, peeking carefully around the stone wall to watch and wait. A few minutes later, she heard footsteps.

Walking side by side along the deserted bridge were the silhouettes of a bat boy and a clown with a top hat.

"She said to meet her here," Valentýn whispered. "Where is she?"

Ema stepped out from the shadows. "I'm here. Where's Ambrož?"

Valentýn shrieked. Matylda didn't.

"Ambrož won't be coming," Matylda said angrily. "He'll be too scared of losing his precious place as an acolyte. Even though his curator barely acknowledges his existence."

"What did he do to upset you so much?"

"Ema," said Valentýn. "I think it should be us asking the questions. We may not have turned you in just yet, but that doesn't mean we won't. What did you mean about

Silvie being in danger? And how do you even know her?"

"Perhaps we should wait a few more minutes to see if Ambrož comes."

"Tell us about Silvie right now, or we'll turn around."

Ema cast another nervous glance down the length of the deserted bridge, then nodded. "I met Silvie in December, when she was dangling upside down from a rafter trying to befriend a colony of bats. That bat I was chasing tonight is called Béla. Silvie found him in a puddle and then gave him a safe place to roost over the winter. We would meet at midnight, and Silvie would teach me all sorts of peculiar things."

"You're lying," Matylda said.

"I'm not!"

The knife thrower crossed her arms. "Yes, you are. Silvie left Prague in *November*."

"The night of Alois's death?"

Instead of softening, both Matylda's and Valentýn's frowns deepened.

"She went home to grieve," Valentýn said. "To Brno, on the other side of the country."

"Who told you that?"

"Florentina."

"Well, Florentina lied. Silvie never left Prague. I met her when I said I met her, we hunted goblins, trawled treasures from the river, and did a thousand other brilliantly ludicrous things."

Matylda was darkly silent, her face unreadable.

It was Valentýn who finally broke the silence. "That does sound like Silvie—"

"That doesn't mean it's true," Matylda said. "Ema has admitted to lying through her teeth already; why should we believe her now? Silvie is at home, mourning. She wouldn't have stayed here without telling us."

Ema saw the hurt flash in the knife thrower's eyes.

"Silvie kept things from me too," Ema said. "I don't think she wanted to lie, nor do I think she didn't trust us. I think she was just very scared."

"Silvie's not scared of anything," Matylda said. "You're not the first to go sneaking unwelcomed into spectacles. I chased Silvie out with my throwing knives several times—" She snapped her mouth closed, as if she'd said more than she'd intended.

Ema smiled. "Is that how you became friends?"

"It's how we became mortal enemies. Especially when she insinuated that I wasn't even that good an aim."

"And you wanted to prove her wrong, didn't you?" Ema said. "She knows exactly which buttons to press, doesn't she?"

Matylda stared at Ema in stubborn silence, until Valentýn nudged her.

"We agreed to meet after the guild ended," Matylda sighed. "I would demonstrate that I could cut an apple from a hundred paces away. The next night she made me try it from two hundred paces. And then she insisted on making me dizzy first. Night after night, she kept finding more targets that she claimed I could never hit, and then taunted me until I proved her wrong. This went on for weeks before I realized I no longer wanted to throw knives at her."

Ema stifled a smile and turned to Valentýn. "Did Silvie trick you into being her friend too?"

"No," Valentýn said. "She rescued me from one of Vendula's new exhibits—a corpse flower. The smell knocked me out. I woke up to find myself being dragged out of the bushes I'd fainted in. Silvie's face appeared, asking if I was all right. Then she saw the small scratches on my hand from my earlier wrestling with a wayward rose-bush and demanded that I let her take me to a hospital. It took me ten minutes to convince her I was fine. And another ten minutes to convince her that I had no intention of revealing her skullduggery to Vendula or the impresario. Before I knew it, *she* had convinced *me* that it would be a brilliant idea to take a small cutting of the flower." He grinned. "We dangled it under Matylda's nose later that night as she tried to hit a blueberry balanced on a gatepost fifty paces away."

"I still made the shot."

"And then you vomited on my shoes."

"What about Ambrož?" Ema asked. "How did Silvie convince him to join you?"

"More wicked trickery," Valentýn said, grinning. "She found him tinkering with one of his little mechanical animals and started asking him questions, forgetting she was supposed to stay hidden. When he began marching her to Žofie Markova, she started bombarding him with endless questions, and the next thing he knew, he'd agreed to teach her how to make a mechanical—"

"Raven?" Ema finished.

Valentýn blinked, then nodded.

"Look," Matylda said. "You may have been right about me and Valentýn being friends with Silvie, but you're wrong about Ambrož. He is not her friend. Silvie was wrong to think he ever could be."

"But—"

"If Ambrož comes tonight, he'll be bringing Žofie Markova with him. I doubt that's something you want to hang around for, is it?"

Ema peered out of their hiding spot and looked up along the length of Charles Bridge. She still felt a prickle of unease that they were being watched, but there was no one in sight. "All right," she said finally. "Let's go somewhere we can talk safely. Follow me. Discreetly." She looked at their outfits. "Well, as discreetly as you can."

Kampa Island was fast asleep. Ema led the way, darting from shadow to shadow, toward the little bridge that overlooked the soapery's waterwheel. Once there, she tugged

Matylda and Valentýn down behind the bridge wall and held a finger to her lips in warning.

Valentýn's eyes widened.

Matylda's eyes narrowed.

Ema peered over the edge of the wall, squinting into the gloom. There was no sign of anyone, but she still felt like invisible eyes were watching.

She ducked back down again. 'You'll have to follow me inside one by one.'

'Inside where?' Matylda asked dubiously.

Without further explanation, Ema leaped over the bridge and onto the waterwheel's giant paddles. They creaked beneath her weight. Behind her, she heard them both suck in a startled gasp as she pushed the ivy aside and climbed in through the hole in the wall. As Ema scrambled to light a lantern, she heard a small scuffle outside, then the sound of someone jumping onto the waterwheel.

"I'll go first," Matylda whispered loudly. "I'm the one with knives. If she's luring us in there to try to drown us in laundry tubs, I'll, oh—"

Matylda's clown-painted face appeared through the ivy, looking almost comically disbelieving as she took in the sight. Finally, Matylda's gaze settled on the laundry-tub bed and the collection of items Ema had tipped out of Silvie's trinket box. She bounded through the hole and staggered over, picking up the deck of cards and turning it in her hand.

"She's been living here," Ema said softly. "Alone, for months."

"Well, is it safe?" Valentýn called. He made a small hole in the ivy and peered through with one eye. Ema watched as that one eye made the same disbelieving sweep of Silvie's hidden room. Valentýn scrambled through the hole, getting his foot caught in his wing and tumbling down in a tangle.

Both Ema and Matylda sprang forward to catch him, elbowing each other as they each tried to untangle him from himself.

"Stop fussing!" Valentýn said, struggling to right his bat mask. When his face finally emerged, he waved a winged arm around the room. "Now please explain *everything*."

Ema gestured to the laundry-tub bed. "There's a lot to tell you, so you better sit down."

They sat.

They stared.

Ema took off her bat mask, shook out her hair, and began to talk. "I met Silvie, as I told you, at the stroke of midnight, as she was dangling upside down from the rafters of an abandoned house. I thought she was a ghost. She thought I was one too."

Matylda snorted. "I can see why—"

"Just let her talk," Valentýn interrupted, giving Matylda a less-than-intimidating glare that somehow worked.

Matylda waved her hand for Ema to continue.

Ema described every detail of her adventures with Silvie—the toffee-sealed invitations, walking the plank and watching goblin effigies appear from the depths of the Vltava, the Midnight Manifesto, and the lessons Silvie had passed on from her beloved, but peculiar, tutors.

Matylda and Valentýn continued to sit and stare as Ema finished describing their penultimate adventure on the Hunger Wall. They only blinked when Ema's wistful smile dropped from her face.

"Last week Silvie asked to meet me at a graveyard."

Ema described the night in the mausoleum in detail—the mausoleum, the white tulips, the eyeball necklace, Silvie's desperation to say sorry to the man in the tomb, being interrupted by the brooch-wearing curator, escaping through the graveyard, Silvie's insistence that they should both go straight home, and Ema's later realization that Silvie had done the exact opposite of that.

"Then she sent me a letter that made no sense."

Ema explained about her unease and the ensuing search that led her first to the soapery, then to the Midnight Guild. When she'd finished explaining what she'd just seen in the Bone Sculptor's séance room, and *who* she'd just seen in the birdcage, she stopped.

"Silvie wouldn't have returned without telling us," Valentýn insisted. "She wouldn't do that, would she, Matylda?"

"Not without good reason." Matylda frowned at Ema. "Are you suggesting—"

"That Alois's death wasn't an accident? Yes."

Valentýn gaped. "And you think—"

"That he was murdered? Also yes."

Matylda and Valentýn looked at each other, and a wordless conversation played out between them.

"What is it?" Ema asked. "If there's something you're not telling me, now would be—"

Ema heard the faintest *creeeeak* of a wooden paddle bearing an unwanted weight and the tiniest rustle of leaves. She looked up at the hole in the wall and saw a pair of blue-green eyes peering through the ivy.

Ema leaped toward the hole, reached through it, and caught hold of a wrist. She tugged it sharply, and the body attached to the wrist tumbled in through the hole, landing with a thud by Ema's feet.

Ambrož.

He *had* been on the bridge, after all.

As he started to push himself up off the floor, a foot appeared and pushed him back down again.

"Matylda, don't—"

But it wasn't Matylda.

"*He's* the reason Silvie ran away," Valentýn said, glaring angrily down at Ambrož. "And *he's* the one who is responsible for Alois's death."

A mbrož staggered to his feet and brushed dirt from his knees, glaring at Matylda and Valentýn.

"What aren't you telling me?" Ema demanded of all three of them.

Matylda opened her mouth, but Ambrož got in there first.

"*I'll* explain," he said. "The night before Alois died, Matylda, Valentýn, Silvie, and I were discussing the opportunity I'd been given to work on the closing spectacle. Žofie had selected me to test the safety chain that would hold Florentina Falkenberg's whale skeleton—"

"Only because her *darling* twins were ill," Matylda interrupted. "She'd never have chosen you otherwise."

Ambrož glowered at her. "That might be so, but it's entirely beside the point." He turned back to Ema. "It was the first time she'd ever given me an honor like this."

Ema watched his expression flitter between shame and

desperation. If she were to hazard a guess, it would be the same expression she wore every time she wanted her parents to acknowledge her. All he wanted—more than anything—was to prove himself.

She gave him a small smile of encouragement.

He cleared his throat and continued. "I had checked each chain link a hundred times and wanted to go back to the guild to check them again, just in case. Silvie could see how important it was to me to get this one job right. So she suggested we all sneak into the guild to see how the chain was holding up. I should never have agreed to it."

Matylda scoffed. "Or it was your plan all along, so that you could pin the blame for your mistakes on someone else, should you need to. And it turns out you *did* need to, didn't you?"

Ema felt suddenly chilled again. "What do you mean?"

"We snuck in the next morning before the curators and impresario were due to arrive," Ambrož continued, so quietly Ema had to lean closer to hear him. "When we got in, we saw that the whale skeleton hadn't fallen during the night. Still, I wanted to make sure. It's one thing having it remain in place while it's completely still, but the mechanism Florentina and Žofie had created to make it swim would put extra strain on the chain."

"They were working *together*?" Ema asked, confused. "I thought they were rivals?"

"Florentina is as good at tricking people into being her friend as Silvie is," Matylda said coldly. "Except— unlike Silvie—she clearly does it for her own benefit. She did it with Vendula too, didn't she, Val?"

Ema thought back to what she'd seen earlier that night. "And Herr Finkelstein," she said. "They've been working together too."

At this, all three of them looked to her with matching expressions of shock and disbelief.

"I'll explain it once Ambrož is finished with *his* explanation," Ema said. "You were telling me about the whale skeleton?"

Ambrož nodded. "Silvie and I hoisted ourselves up to the impresario's podium. From there, Silvie helped me up to the top of the ceiling. I checked *every single* link again. When I was satisfied that they were all in perfect condition, I signaled to Matylda and Valentýn to begin operating the crank. The whale began to swim, and the chain not only held, but barely even groaned under the tension."

He paused here, and Ema could picture the entire scene in her head. If she hadn't known what was to come, the very image of it would have filled her with delight.

"Silvie was delighted," Ambrož said proudly. "She said I should be more confident in my work, and I said that I was so confident in the strength of that chain that

I'd happily send a bear to dance along the whale's spine."

He stopped again, glancing furtively toward Matylda and Valentýn.

"I shouldn't have said it," Ambrož whispered. "I knew Silvie well enough to know she'd take my words as a challenge. Before I could stop her, she'd rappeled down the length of the chain until she was standing on the whale's spine. And then she danced."

Ema didn't know whether to shudder in horror, or shiver in awe. All she did know was that it was exactly the kind of ludicrous thing that Silvie would do.

"What happened?" Ema asked nervously.

"Nothing," Ambrož said. "The chain was as reliable as I knew it would be."

"But clearly, you were wrong." Valentýn seethed. "As the whole thing came tumbling down on top of Alois just a few hours later."

"Yes, but—"

This time it was Matylda who stepped forward, tears welling up in the corners of her eyes. "Look what you did, Ambrož! She's been living here, thinking she killed her own curator! She trusted you. You promised that chain was strong enough."

"It was!" Ambrož cried. "I am just as certain today as I was then that the chain was perfectly sound."

"Stop lying!"

Ema put a hand on Matylda's shoulder. Ambrož's face was a picture of anguish, and she knew, in her very bones, that he meant what he said.

"He's not lying," Ema said.

"How would you even know that?" Matylda snapped, rubbing at her eyes. "Your secret science?"

"Actually, yes, but also because what he's saying just confirms my suspicions. Think about it. Even with Silvie's added weight, the chain held just fine. And the whale was still up there hours later when they began their rehearsal."

"Silvie's weight weakened the chain link he failed to inspect properly," Matylda said. "And yet, afterward, Ambrož had the gall to keep insisting it wasn't his fault. If he hadn't taken up all my time arguing about it, I could have found Silvie before she left. I could have convinced her it wasn't her fault—persuaded her to stay. But she was gone before I could do that."

"It *wasn't* her fault," Ambrož said, reaching into his pocket. "And it wasn't mine." He held out a warped chain link. "I begged the impresario to let me have this. And I've spent every single day trying to work out how I could have missed such an obvious flaw. Even Žofie was as flummoxed as I was, but she accepted Mr. Rivers's conclusion and even offered to resign."

Ema took the chain link and turned it over in her hands. "This was found in the debris?"

Ambrož nodded. "The way it's twisted . . . I'm certain

it's one of the links that Žofie discarded when she was working on the chain. That work took place in the ballroom itself. Anyone could have picked it up without her noticing. Over the past few months, I've slowly come to the same conclusion Ema did. I think someone cut the chain with bolt-cutters while the lights were off."

Valentýn shook his head. "The impresario would have found a cut link. He'd have known then it was no accident. Stop trying to exonerate yourself."

"If I had wanted to divert the blame—as you keep insisting—then I could have gone to the impresario that very night and told him what Silvie had done. But I didn't, did I?! I would never do that! And Žofie has kept me hidden away, like some useless pet she can't get rid of, ever since."

"Let's just focus on the evidence we have at hand," Ema said, holding up the chain link. "Could someone have swapped the cut chain link for this one before Mr. Rivers had a chance to get down from his podium? Ambrož, who was down on the ballroom floor when the whale fell?"

"Me, Alois, Kazimír, and Florentina. I was so stunned after watching it come crashing down, and so terrified of what I'd see next, that it took me a few minutes to switch the lights back on. There was plenty of time for someone to swap the cut link for this warped one after the whale fell." He looked pointedly at Matylda.

Matylda's nostrils flared. "Are you suggesting my parents did it?"

"They *hated* Alois."

"The exact same could be said of your precious Žofie. Perhaps you even helped her, hoping to get her to finally notice you properly."

"You don't really think he's capable of that," Ema said, studying every inch of Matylda's face. "You don't even really blame him for any of this—you're just worried about Silvie."

"Whatever it is you're doing, please stop," Matylda said. "It's creepy."

Ema flinched. "All right, let's think about this rationally. Both Florentina and Kazimír would have been within reach of the links to swap them out. That leaves the curators up in the ceiling, all within reach to cut the chain. It could have been Aninha—"

"Or Žofie," Matylda cut in, turning her glare back to Ambrož before softening again as she turned to Valentýn. "Or . . . Vendula?"

"No, it was Herr Finkelstein's first night, remember?" said Valentýn. "Vendula had just left for her expedition. Everyone was expecting her to be replaced by a couple of well-respected but oddball scientists from the city—"

"Oddball?!" But Ema realized now wasn't the time for her to reveal that it had been her very own parents who were after that curatorship. "What I mean is," she said, "isn't it odd that they would hire Herr Finkelstein instead, then?"

"You said he was working with Florentina," Ambrož said. "Is that what you saw when you were sneaking around her spectacle?"

"Yes," said Ema. "He arrived at her séance room disguised as a patron. He handed her a journal and told her to keep it hidden, so that it wouldn't fall into the wrong hands. They're clearly up to something, but I don't know what exactly. And there's something about his shadow—" Ema stopped, realizing Matylda was frowning at her again. "There's just something about him that makes me feel uneasy."

"Other than his permanently gloomy demeanor?" Matylda offered. "I don't think I've ever seen him smile."

"I think he's grieving," Ema said, again before she could stop herself. "He wears a mourning ring," she added quickly. "It has strands of red hair in it plaited with threads of black hair."

"I don't know what Mr. Rivers was thinking when he hired him," Valentýn mused. "Although, come to think of it, it was Alois who brought him to the guild in the first place. I heard Vendula ask about a séance that Herr Finkelstein attended with Alois, but Herr Finkelstein didn't want to discuss it."

"So, Herr Finkelstein was also up in the ceiling that night?" Ema asked.

Valentýn nodded.

"Let's imagine, for a moment, that it was Herr Finkelstein who cut the chain," Ema said. "And that Florentina was ready to swap the chain links. It was the perfect murder, and it gave Florentina a very lucrative spectacle to run. But what would have been in it for him?"

"Perhaps Florentina persuaded Alois to convince Mr. Rivers to hire Thibault, in exchange for him helping her get Alois's curatorship?" Matylda offered. "That way, they both stand to raise not only their prestige, but their wallets too."

"Very well," Ema said. "That makes some sense, at least. If we ignore the fact that Herr Finkelstein seems to be doing a rather rubbish job of bringing in patronage. But why, then, would Florentina imprison Silvie in full sight of the entire guild?"

The question hung heavily in the air for several moments, until Ema herself attempted to answer it.

"Neither of them knew about Silvie's escapades earlier that day," she said. "Or that she blamed herself for what happened. That night in the graveyard, Silvie was so desperate to get things off her chest — I think she went back to the mausoleum after I left. I think she begged Florentina to forgive her. They were both Alois's acolytes, after all. But Silvie would have had no idea she was confessing a sin she hadn't committed, to the very person who *had* committed it."

Ema paused, feeling both certain of her own hypothesis and wary of it.

"We need to go to the impresario right now," Ambrož said.

"No!" Ema and Matylda both shouted.

Ambrož frowned. "Why *on earth* not?"

"Did you not hear Ema say that Florentina has both a spy and a plan in place to get rid of the evidence? She'll kill Silvie before we can get to her."

"We need to think this through first," Ema said. "We need to work out all the variables, identify all the risks—"

"This isn't a science experiment!"

"You're right, it isn't a science experiment. We have only *one chance* at getting this right, or we risk putting Silvie in even more danger. We can't afford any mistakes."

"I have a question," Valentýn said. "If Silvie told Florentina what she and Ambrož did that day, why wouldn't Florentina take her straight to Mr. Rivers to confess? Surely that would solve all her issues, by shifting any remaining doubt away from her?"

Once again, the room fell silent.

Ema scratched her stomach, again thinking back to what she'd heard from Florentina's own lips earlier.

I need those names, Thibault. Without them, I have nothing.

"Because of the three of you," she said, ignoring their confused expressions. "Frau Falkenberg said, 'Without those names, I have nothing.' What if she was talking about you? What if Silvie is *refusing* to confess to the impresario because it means implicating you as well?"

"That does make sense," Matylda said. "She would never give us up."

"But why the cage?" Ambrož said. "Why hide her in plain sight like that?"

"To torment her?" Valentýn offered. "She is dangling from the very same place that the whale skeleton was — forcing her to look down at the very spot where Alois met his end. It's an evilly clever tactic."

"All the more reason for us to take this to Mr. Rivers," said Ambrož. "It's his job to investigate everything that happens in the guild — "

Matylda scoffed. "And what a brilliant job he's done of that so far. What exactly is it, Ambrož, that makes you think he'll be any help whatsoever? He'll refuse to believe any such horror could occur in his guild. He's convinced it was an accident!"

"That's because the evidence *pointed* to it being an accident. No one suspected it was murder, not even you. At least he's trying to bring the guild together. He's got them putting on a spectacle together tomorrow night. Perhaps he's not as useless as you think."

"It won't work. Mark my words."

"Silvie brought *us* together."

"Silvie is different. Ema, why are you scratching your stomach like that? You don't have fleas, do you? And Valentýn, you look like you're in pain. Is everything all right?"

Matylda put her hand to Valentýn's forehead, and Ema forced herself to stop scratching.

Valentýn slapped Matylda's hand away. "Get off, I was just thinking."

"We're missing something important," Ema said.

"Yes," said Ambrož. "Common sense. We need to get to Silvie today."

"We don't know where she is kept during the day," said Ema. "The only time we can be certain of her location is at midnight."

"But it'll be too late by then," Matylda said. "She'll already be in the cage! Maybe Ambrož is right. We should go to Mr. Rivers."

"No," Ema said firmly. "Florentina might have her spy watching Mr. Rivers very closely. It might give her cause to silence Silvie *before* the closing ceremony. Florentina will have her squirreled away somewhere by now."

"Well, what do you suggest, then?"

Ema was silent for a few moments as a plan began to take shape in her mind.

"We need to find whatever evidence Florentina is hiding in that safe, so that Silvie cannot be framed for what happened. Then we need to present this evidence to the impresario *and* get Silvie out of that cage . . . at the very same time."

"That's impossible," Matylda said.

"No, it isn't," Ema continued. "Tonight, I'll sneak into the séance room again before the closing ceremony, while Valentýn distracts Florentina—"

"What?" Valentýn cried. "I can't—"

"You *must*! She nearly caught me tonight. Once we have the evidence from the safe, you will keep hold of it. You said the impresario is insisting that all closing ceremonies be performed on the ground, to avoid another accident, right?"

"Yes, but—"

"Excellent, then that's when I'll get Silvie out of the cage."

"But everyone will be in the ballroom by that point!" Matylda said.

"Exactly, and they'll all be watching the spectacle, not looking up. Even Florentina will be distracted. Ambrož can hoist me up to the cage. And the moment I have her, Valentýn could take the evidence to the impresario. Florentina won't have a chance even to realize she's been caught."

"Am I supposed to just stand around and let the three of you do everything?" Matylda asked.

"No, you make sure no one looks up."

"How am I supposed to stop *hundreds* of people from looking up?"

"I'm sure you can think of something."

Valentýn blew out a long breath, then held his hand out in front of them all. "Well, I can't think of a better plan."

"This is just the kind of ludicrous plan Silvie would come up with," Ambrož said, placing his hand on top of Valentýn's. "Which means it'll either go spectacularly well, or spectacularly wrong."

With a groan of resignation, Matylda put her hand on top of Ambrož's.

They all looked at Ema expectantly.

But she was too busy scratching her stomach, trying to work out why she still felt so unsettled.

"It's *your* plan," Matylda said. "Don't tell me you're too scared?"

With great effort, Ema added her hand to the pile.

Ema woke late the next morning, spitting and blowing and scraping desperately at her tongue, only to find there was nothing in her mouth. She took a few deep breaths as she blinked into the late-morning sun streaming in through the attic room windows.

After days of having the same nightmare over and over, she'd finally had a new one.

The never-ending darkness had gone, replaced by the glittering lights of the ballroom. There were no more bats swooping down and clawing at her hair. And this time she was no longer searching for Silvie but able to see her friend quite clearly, dangling high up in a golden birdcage above the ballroom floor. But each time Ema tried to call out to her, all that came out her mouth was a woeful yowl and a mouthful of white tulip petals.

Ema could still feel the faint traces of them on her tongue.

She washed them away with a guzzle of spiced milk that Josef had set on her bedside table, then hurried to get dressed as the attic room breeze whistled impishly around her.

"I found her," Ema said, unsure if she was talking to the breeze or just herself.

Either way, she explained the previous evening's events as she pulled back the wallpaper above her bed and studied the misfortune. There had to be something that might explain the incessant itching in her bones. After reading each of the scrawled words over and over, however, Ema was still none the wiser.

"I don't understand what it is I'm missing."

The breeze picked up. Ema turned away from the wall and looked down at the floor, where the wilting white petals were chasing each other in a spiral dance.

"Stop," Ema whispered. "You're not being helpful at all."

The petals continued their swirling dance.

Ema's head grew steadily dizzier.

"Please?"

The breeze stopped.

The petals twitched, then fell still.

"I need to clear my head, or I'll be no use tonight."

With that, she hurried out of the room and down the stairs.

Her uncle was in his workshop, hidden behind the

bustled form of Frau Kraus. The white bicycle was balanced against the worktop, but the paintwork looked like it had been attacked by a cat-beast . . . or scraped across a cobbled street.

"You cannot keep trying to buy my forgiveness with baked goods, Herr Kozar. And certainly not ones that look as awful as these."

"I may have accidentally sat on them," Josef said in a weary tone. "But they're probably still edible."

"You can keep your pastries, and you can keep that useless contraption."

With a final tut, she turned, found Ema standing right behind her, and screamed.

"Dobrý den," Ema said, offering her a weak smile.

The woman ran her gaze up and down Ema, shaking her head in dismay. Then she reached into her handbag and rummaged around. "Here," she said, handing Ema a business card. "Take this and at least I'll feel like my trips here weren't a complete waste of time." She tutted, then she click-clacked down the hallway and out the door.

Ema looked down at the card. NEW TOWN HAIR GROOMING SERVICES. She patted at her tangled hair as she and Josef faced each other. He looked as tired as Ema felt. Ema looked at the white bicycle. "I take it she wasn't happy with our work?"

"Not especially."

"I'm sorry."

"Please don't be; it isn't your fault. Your calculations were splendid. I rode that bicycle myself and felt no more than a little saddle tickle when cycling over the cobbles. She was asking for the impossible. When your parents arrive tomorrow, we'll show them what a brilliant job you've done."

Ema jolted. "They're coming back tomorrow?"

"Didn't I tell you? I'm sorry—" He wobbled on his feet.

Ema steered him into the chair. "Still no sign of Ferkel?"

"I thought I heard her last night," Josef said, yawning. "Just before midnight. I was woken up by a noise at the door."

Ema froze. "Oh?"

"I ran outside, of course. I thought I saw something moving in the shadows up ahead. Managed to follow it to Charles Bridge before I lost it again."

The mug fell from Ema's fingers and smashed on the floor. Josef gave a little shriek, then looked up at her in concern.

He'd seen her sneaking out. Or *nearly* seen her, anyway.

"Are you al—"

"I'm fine," Ema squeaked, dropping to her knees to collect the pieces. She picked up the biggest shard with shaky fingers. "Did you, um, find anything?"

"Nothing. It was when I thought I saw a clown in a top hat climbing the steps from Kampa Island that I realized how sleep deprived I must be, so I gave up and went home. But there were several ivy leaves in the hallway when I got back. It was most peculiar."

Ema managed to swallow her gasp. He must have returned just minutes after she'd gotten home. She dropped her gaze again, busying herself with the last of the broken pieces of mug. "Perhaps they blew in when you opened the door?"

Josef sighed heavily. "Yes, you're probably right. Ema, what's wrong? You've turned pale."

Ema was staring down in horror at the pieces of broken porcelain she'd collected.

All *twelve* of them.

With great effort, she cleared her throat. "I'm fine," she said. "Just tired."

"Are you sure?"

"Most certainly."

"You can tell me if there's something bothering you."

"I know."

"I've noticed that there have been no invitations recently. Have you and Silvie had an argument?"

"No!"

Josef flinched.

Ema winced. "I'm sorry. Perhaps we should consider today canceled. So that you don't sit in any more pastries, and I don't make any more customers scream."

Josef got up, wobbled slightly, then took the business card from the worktop. "I could go and get my hair seen to. There's always plenty of gossip at these places. Perhaps someone will have a story of a crazed wild cat roaming the city."

Ema took the card from him. "No, you should sleep."

"But—"

"It will be all right," Ema said, trying to quell her own rising despair for *her* missing loved one, as she nudged him out of the workshop and up the stairs. "I promise. We'll have Silvie back safe and sound soon."

"Silvie?"

"I mean Ferkel."

He looked at her then, eyes narrowed and penetrating behind his spectacles. Ema tried—and failed—to hide the worry she knew was all over her face.

"You should sleep too, Ema," Josef said finally.

"Yes, I *should*," Ema said, leaving out the fact that she wouldn't.

To her relief, he didn't press her further—allowing her to lead him all the way up to the second floor, before staggering into his bedroom to go to sleep.

Ema, meanwhile, hurried upstairs. Later, she would

have to push herself to her limits—as far as her fear of heights went—if she was to pull off her own plan to get Silvie out of that birdcage.

Fifty meters in the air.

And so, as darkness fell, Ema made her way to the very spot where she and Silvie had first locked eyes on each other. She pushed the round window open, letting the breeze gust around her as she peered down at the street far below, then up again to the empty attic room just across from her.

Less worrying, more daring.

Holding the image of a ghostly girl dangling from the rafters like a bat in her mind's eye, Ema climbed onto the ledge and let her feet dangle above the abyss.

Just like that first night, the world seemed to sway around her, and bile tried to crawl its way up her throat. Ema held herself firm, though, leaning ever so slightly farther forward, feeling her cheeks stretch into a grin despite the churning, spinning, dizzying fear that coursed through her.

She stayed on that window ledge until the world stopped spinning and moonlight kissed the tips of her toes.

When the time to get ready finally arrived, she climbed back into the attic room, changed into her bat costume, and stared at herself in the mirror.

The bags under her eyes were enormous, and the bone-itching unease left her shaking visibly. But there was something different now too. It glinted in her candle-smoke eyes the same way that starlight had always glinted in Silvie's.

The attic room breeze blew gently against her cheek.

"I'll do my best," Ema whispered.

And then she crept down the stairs. When she got to Josef's room, she stopped, pressing her ear against the door. Relief swept over her as she heard his gentle snoring, and she pushed away again.

The floorboard creaked underneath her.

Ema stared down at it—and her own foot—in astonishment. The floorboards had *never* creaked beneath her.

Tentatively, she took another step.

This time, the floorboard groaned.

On the other side of the door, she heard Josef grunt. Without waiting to see if she'd woken him, she flew down the rest of the stairs and out the door, wincing at each noisy step she took.

She'd deal with the consequences after she got Silvie safely out of that birdcage.

E ma was a bag of nerves when she arrived at the ball-room doorway. The children were gathered just like the night before. Except now Matylda was back in her knife thrower's costume, standing at the head of the group of acolytes, glaring daggers at anyone who met her eye. It took Ema a moment longer to spot Ambrož—he was stand-ing at the back, in the shadows, looking at nothing and speaking to no one.

Valentýn was standing on the other side of the door, using one wing to shield himself from an onslaught of fly-ing apple pieces that the mime boy was biting off, then spitting his way.

Ema sidled up next to Valentýn and faced his tormen-tor. "Leave him," she said sternly, summoning her most Matylda-esque glare. "Or you'll be joining all those dead frogs I like to experiment on."

The mime boy glowered at her.

Ema glowered harder back at him.

Finally, he blinked, turning his attention to the blue-haired girl instead, who didn't appear much bothered by his nonsense. Valentýn gave Ema a grateful smile, but Ema was too on edge to return it. She stared at the door, wanting to get this all over and done with. Feeling eyes watching her, she peered to the side to find Matylda staring.

Matylda raised an eyebrow. "Are those fleas bothering you again, bat girl?"

Ema stopped scratching her stomach.

With a heavy clunk, the door finally opened. Ema grabbed Valentýn and raced through, letting him steer her through the darkness. When they came to a halt, she took Silvie's cloak out from under her wing and draped it around both their shoulders.

"Ready?" she whispered.

"I think so," he whispered back. "Are you sure Herr Finkelstein won't notice our absence?"

"It's not like he'll be expecting an onslaught of patrons," Ema said. "Just do exactly what we planned, and it will probably be all right."

"Probably?"

"Yes, probably."

They huddled there together as the room filled with shuffling feet and excited murmurs. As the spotlight began its nightly dance, Ema looked up. Her heart gave a shudder of relief when she saw Silvie's feathery silhouette in the birdcage. That relief, however, was short-lived.

There was so much that could go wrong.

The light settled on the impresario.

"WELCOME. WELCOME. WELCOME. WEL-COME. WELCOME."

Ema shuddered. Valentýn's arm linked with hers, giving it a gentle squeeze.

"YOUR FINAL NIGHT HAS ARRIVED, AND I AS-SURE YOU IT WILL BE THE MOST SPLENDID ONE OF ALL. OF ALL. OF ALL. OF ALL. OF ALL."

She squeezed his arm back, then used her other arm to lift the hood over both their heads.

"MAKE SURE YOU ARE BACK HERE IN THIS BALLROOM BEFORE THE MIDNIGHT HOUR ENDS, TO WITNESS A SPECTACLE UNLIKE ANYTHING YOU'LL HAVE SEEN BEFORE. BE-FORE. BEFORE. BEFORE. BEFORE."

The impresario stamped his cane against his podium.

Light and music erupted around them.

"Remember: shoulders up and head down," Ema whispered. "Pretend you want the floor to swallow you whole."

"I don't need to pretend that."

"Good."

She nudged him into the crowd of patrons. It took

them a few fumbling steps and a few precarious wobbles before they found a way to walk together beneath Silvie's cloak.

Ema cast one last glance up at her caged friend as they slipped past the unsuspecting raven and into the Moonlight Garden.

"Valentýn, mind my feet!"

"Sorry, I just . . . I don't think I fully believed you when you told me about this place. This garden really is Vendula's work. Florentina must have tricked her well to get her to agree to this."

He was peering out from under their hood in disbelief. Ema had to nudge him down the mossy steps toward the path. A few steps in, he stopped, his eyes wide.

"Is that — ?"

"A skeleton, yes. Valentýn, we need to hurry. Come on."

She tugged him along the path as he continued to gawk. As they neared the arched doorway, Ema nodded toward the raven guard. "Are you sure you can do this?"

"Of course I can. Silvie needs me to do it."

"I just don't want to get you into trouble."

"Well, that's not your choice. I'm not as hapless as I look." He shrugged his arm free and gave her a bright smile. "Just watch, you'll see."

With that, he nudged Ema out of the cloak.

She ducked behind a bush and watched helplessly as he sauntered confidently toward the waiting crowd, barely reaching up to their shoulders.

"Excuse me," he said loudly, skirting around patrons. "Let me through please, important guild business. Thank you! Excuse me."

Ema tiptoed around the crowd, toward the side of the arch, using Valentýn's distraction to slip past them unnoticed. She arrived at another bush the same moment he elbowed his way to the front of the crowd.

"Dobrý večer," Valentýn said to the raven.

The moment he let his hood drop, the raven growled and seized him by the collar. "You shouldn't be in here."

Ema's fingers twitched to reach out and yank Valentýn back again. Instead, she settled for glowering from her hiding spot.

"Let me go!" Valentýn squeaked. "Herr Finkelstein sent me! Tell Frau Falkenberg that I need to see her urgently."

"I will do no such thing!"

"But—"

The raven lifted Valentýn higher, so that he was on his tiptoes. Ema's fists clenched. The raven turned his beaked face her way, and Ema ducked down farther.

"What is going on here?" Florentina Falkenberg was standing in the archway.

"I caught a trespasser," the raven said. "Should I take him to the impresario?"

"Yes, you should!" she said, glaring at Valentýn in furious disbelief.

"Wait, um, m'lady!" Valentýn said. "I'm here to deliver a very important message to you, that's all. From Herr Finkelstein!"

"Shut up, bat boy," the raven hissed.

"But it's urgent!"

"I said—"

"Stop," said Florentina, eyeing Valentýn suspiciously. She looked up at the line of patrons and plastered on a smile. "Excuse me for just a few short moments." Then, more quietly: "Pass him here. I'll take care of him."

Florentina put an arm around Valentýn's shoulders and led him into the dark hallway. As the raven turned back to the disgruntled patrons, Ema slipped in through the arch.

She followed silently behind the two of them as Florentina nudged Valentýn into the séance room. Her friend disappeared behind the curtain and let out a small yelp.

"For saints' sake, Valentýn, get up off the floor and tell me what it is Herr Finkelstein wanted you to tell me."

Ema made a small gap and peered in. Valentýn had dropped to his knees at the Bone Sculptor's feet. He'd also positioned himself so that Florentina was facing away from the doorway. Ema pushed the curtain open wider. The moment she stepped in, that unsettling feeling of being watched crept over her skin. Static hummed in her ears, and the smell of burned flowers clung to her nostrils. The wall behind her still had those long tendril-like shadows that made Ema want to crawl out of her own skin, for reasons she couldn't explain.

Valentýn wrapped his winged arms around Florentina's legs. "Please, m'lady, I'm only here because I was told to come. Please don't punish me."

Ema inched her way quickly and quietly toward Alois's portrait, the dead curator's painted eyes watching her the entire time.

"Stop calling me m'lady. I'm not that much older than you," Florentina said, grabbing his arms and lifting him from the floor. "I'm not going to punish you."

"But you said—"

"I know what I said," Florentina said in a tone that seemed more exasperated than angry. "And I might well follow through with it if you don't pass on Herr Finkelstein's message right now."

Ema froze as Florentina made to turn toward the séance table. Valentýn jumped forward and wrapped his arms around her again, this time in a hug.

"Oh, thank goodness," Valentýn said, making a motion behind Florentina's back with his hand for Ema to hurry. "I'll make sure to tell Herr Finkelstein how kind you have been."

"Valentýn —"

"Yes, of course!" Valentýn let go but kept her in place with a hand on each of her arms. "He said it was incredibly urgent and important."

"You'd better get on with it, then, hadn't you?"

"Yes," Valentýn said pointedly. "Getting on with it is a brilliant idea."

Ema shook herself and turned back to the portrait, trying to ignore the uncomfortable feeling in her bones as she moved it aside, as Florentina had, to reveal the safe behind. She began to turn the dial the way she'd seen Florentina do it — one, two, twelve — as Valentýn spoke.

"Now, it was hard to hear him as he was whispering, but he said something about some names."

Ema felt the lock release. She gave a nervous glance behind her, then pried the safe door open. The journal was right where Florentina had put it the previous night, as were the many stacks of banknotes. Ema grabbed the journal and tucked it under her wing.

"What names?" There was a slight pitch to Florentina's voice now. "Did he tell you them?"

"No, but he said something about having a new lead. And that you should, um . . . Oh, what was it now?"

Ema was about to close the safe but stopped. Now was

the only chance she'd ever get to make sure Florentina wasn't hiding something else in there—something that could help cement their case against her. Quickly and quietly, Ema reached her arm in as far as she could and began to feel around behind the banknotes.

"Oh," Valentýn said. "He said that you should wait."

"Wait for what?"

"He said you were planning something, but that it should wait."

Ema continued patting, but she couldn't see or feel anything else.

"Thank you, Valentýn. I appreciate you coming to tell me this on his behalf. But I really must get back to work now. As should you."

"Yes," Valentýn said, again pointedly. "Yes, it really is time to leave. But—"

"But what?"

"Well . . ."

Ema ran her hands down the back of the safe one last time. As soon as her fingers brushed the bottom, a sharp jolt of static ran right up her arm.

A tiny gasp left her lips.

Florentina began to turn.

"I must tell you how wonderful your garden is," Valentýn said. "I've not seen anything quite as magical and peaceful. Even with all the skeletons."

"Yes, well, Vendula really is a wonder. I couldn't have done it without her help."

"She must really like you."

Ema watched Florentina stiffen slightly at Valentýn's words. Then, reluctantly, she closed the safe, replaced the portrait, and began to tiptoe back to the curtain.

"I miss her."

"I'm sure you do, but, Valentýn—"

Ema reached the curtain and slipped through.

"Do you know when she'll be back? Do you think she's found any new plant species? Oh, have you heard from her—"

"Enough, Valentýn! Get out—now!"

Ema peered through the curtain, feeling a hot surge of anger as she watched Valentýn shrink away from the Bone Sculptor's outburst.

Florentina spun and stared directly into Ema's eyes.

Florentina's wide-eyed gaze held Ema rigidly in place. She couldn't even blink. How had the Bone Sculptor sensed her there? *Again.*

"Alois?"

The name left Florentina's lips in a raspy whisper. She reached out and grabbed Valentýn's arm. "Tell me you see those strange eyes, Valentýn."

Valentýn squinted right at Ema. "What strange eyes?"

"You don't see them?"

Florentina turned to him, giving Ema the moment she needed to stagger back down the corridor. As she rounded the corner, she heard the curtains screech open.

Ema slipped past the raven and huddled shakily in the bush. A moment later, Valentýn elbowed his way out through the arch and hurried toward her. She slipped under the cloak as he passed, and the two of them made their way back down the path.

"I can't believe that worked," Valentýn whispered. "I'm not sure if I'm about to faint or laugh."

"Perhaps start with not stepping on my feet. Quick, this way." She nudged him toward a tangle of ferns, ducking under branches and foliage until they reached a small white structure in the shape of a tiny house.

Valentýn made a strange noise. "Is that made of . . . teeth?"

"It appears so."

Ignoring her own shudder of disgust, Ema climbed through the tiny entrance, tugging Valentýn in behind her. It was a tight squeeze inside the little house. Ema peered through each of the small windows, checking there wasn't anyone within hearing distance. Finally certain they weren't being spied on, she sat back down and took the journal out from under her wing.

"Is that her diary?" Valentýn asked. "The diary of a murderess would be perfect evidence."

Ema took a deep but wobbly breath as she opened the journal and flicked through the first few pages.

"It's not a diary," she said. "It's a science investigation."

Valentýn blinked. "What? Why would Florentina be conducting a science investigation? She sculpts bones and summons ghosts — she's not experimenting with anything."

Ema ran a finger over the page. It was the same handwriting as Silvie's invitation in her trinket box.

"'This is Alois's journal, not hers. And look at these dates. He wrote this shortly before his death." She flicked through more pages, her eyes skimming over hypotheses, data, equipment lists, various methods of experimentation. "Alois was trying to get his critics—the other curators—to stop seeing his ghost whispering as a fraud. He was trying to find scientific proof that ghosts are real."

"How on earth was he trying to do that?"

Ema kept reading.

"It looks like he started small," she said. "With ancient artifacts and the usual paraphernalia that mediums use—asking his collaborators if they too could sense any sort of spiritual connection when they used them. But this doesn't seem to have worked. He then reflects on how his ability came to him after a near drowning and posits that something extreme is needed to forge a connection between the medium and the spirit realm."

Valentýn paled. "Like a near-death experience."

Ema shuddered, as did Valentýn.

"Yes," Ema rasped. "It says here in his methodology that the test subjects would need to be brought to the brink of death, in order to see whether their powers emerged afterward."

"How—"

Ema flicked through more pages, until she finally found the answer. "Electrotherapy," she whispered, thinking back to the static in the séance room.

"He was testing this all out on himself?" Valentýn's eyes bulged behind the holes in his bat mask.

"No. He needed test subjects who didn't already have his ability. More importantly, he needed test subjects who were *skeptical*. That would have been the only way to ensure that any results were taken seriously. Who better to try to convince than one of the very people who said his claims were impossible?"

"The other curators?"

Ema tried to make sense of it all.

"It would be risky involving any of them," she said. "If they found out about this research before there was verifiable proof of his claims, they might use it against him. They could say it proved nothing more than his fraud. They could shut his spectacle down and be rid of him. He'd have had to think very carefully about which of them to approach. He gave them an opportunity to be the one to prove him wrong, should no results appear. Anyway, it seems it was a gamble that paid off. According to the notes here, whoever the test subjects were, they started to believe. They met in secret while the guild was in progress, to avoid arousing suspicion from the others, while they gathered the data they needed."

Ema felt there was truth in her analysis. But she also felt an uncomfortable twinge—there was still something missing.

"Does it say who?" Valentýn asked.

"No, he seems to have been careful not to name them."

"Them?"

"It seems there were two. See, look here. Each experiment refers to a 'he' and a 'she.'"

Valentýn leaned in closer to peer at the page in her lap. "But that could be *anyone*."

Ema looked up at him. "It *could* be Frau Falkenberg and Herr Finkelstein. They are the ones keeping this journal secret, after all."

"But Herr Finkelstein is a man of *science*," Valentýn said. "Not this kind of science—*real* science."

"He's also grieving someone," Ema said. "That gives him even more motive to at least give *this* kind of science a try. And you're right—scientists are notoriously skeptical. It's their job to be. He would have been the perfect test subject. If Alois was able to convince an actual scientist to believe in the existence of ghosts, then his experiments would be more likely to be taken seriously. And it looks like that's exactly what happened. Here, look." She flipped back to one of the earlier pages in the journal. "Alois writes that *he*—meaning, let's assume, Herr Finkelstein—reported feeling a presence in the room, shortly after receiving a small electric shock from the light switch." She flicked to the next page. "He purposely shocked himself again and reported the same result. *He* is the one who pushed for the electrotherapy, not Alois. In fact, Alois seems to have been the only one who was hesitant to test his own hypothesis." She kept flicking, until she came to the last few pages. "Look, he writes here that he wanted to stop the experiments, as he was worried it was getting too dangerous. The other two wanted to push it even further. Alois refused."

"Would that really make them want to kill him, though?"

"It might, if something went wrong and he had threatened to reveal their dangerous methods to the rest of the guild."

"But they're both unhurt. In fact, the only person who isn't is Alois, and it wasn't electrotherapy that killed him. Did you find anything else in the safe?"

Ema thought about the static shock she'd felt while searching the safe, and the strange sense that there was something else inside there. She didn't think that's what Valentýn was asking about, though.

"No, just this."

"But how does this help us?" Valentýn asked. "Was it all a waste of time? Did I just hug a murderess for absolutely no reason?"

"Alois died because of this research," Ema said. "I've never been more certain of anything in my life. Imagine the prestige that would be given to whomever was able to prove something like this—that ghosts are real, and can be contacted? Imagine the fame, the money."

"But—"

"It might not be an undeniable piece of incriminating evidence, but it's more than we had before, and frankly we have no choice but to stick to our plan. Florentina will learn soon enough that Herr Finkelstein never sent you to her. And Silvie is still in that birdcage. We have this journal, and we can tell Mr. Rivers about the levers under the table. This should plant enough doubt in the impresario's mind to at least get them arrested. Let the impresario figure out all the details. Let him solve the missing pieces. You must show him the bit about Alois's misgivings. It's clear that his refusal to continue with the electrotherapy caused a rift."

She handed him the journal, which he tucked under his own wing.

"We're really doing this?" Valentýn said.

"We have to. For Silvie."

They emerged into the ballroom, wedged between a small group of patrons. Valentýn slipped out from under their cloak and hurried back to his post. Ema bundled the cloak more tightly around herself, peering up at the birdcage above her. Silvie was watching a group of patrons huddled outside the doorway to Žofie Markova's bazaar. Then, with one final glance at her friend, Ema slipped through the Illusionists' doorway and into the mirror maze.

When Ema finally made it through and emerged in the baroque theater, Aninha Carvosa was levitating above her husband's head. As Ema watched the Illusionist ascend slowly up toward the ceiling, Matylda's hand clamped down on her arm, tugging her to the side.

"There you are!"

Ema swallowed a yelp, blinking at the knife thrower in astonishment. "How did you know it was me?"

"Your stomach scratching gave you away; plus I've been waiting for you for ages. What took you so long? Did you get the evidence? Is Valentýn all right? Florentina didn't hurt him, did she?"

"He's fine, Matylda. My arm isn't, though."

Matylda loosened her grip . . . slightly. "Follow me."

They skirted the back of the theater, toward one of the paneled walls. As the crowd clapped, Matylda nudged the panel open, revealing a dark tunnel beyond. Then she nudged Ema into it. The panel closed behind them, sealing them in complete darkness, and Matylda did some more nudging. Ema explained about Alois's journal as she inched her way forward, arms extended, heart pounding, and skeleton itching, until Matylda finally told her to halt.

"It's enough to have that spectacle shut down, at the very least," Matylda said, and Ema could hear the smile in her voice. "It's about time the guild was rid of that ridiculous place — it's immoral to allow such trickery, if you ask me. Lift your arms."

Ema did as she was bid, and Matylda began tightening a harness around her waist.

"But is it enough to get the two of them locked away?" Ema said. "What if it isn't, and they come after Silvie . . . all of us . . . in revenge? What about her spy? We still don't know who that is. Maybe they'll be the one to come after us."

"What you told Valentýn was right," Matylda said. "It's the only option we have. All that matters now is getting Silvie out of that cage. We can worry about the rest later. You can lower your arms now."

Ema was silent. It felt like the darkness was constricting her.

"I can hear you scratching again," Matylda said. "Are you sure you're up to this?"

"I'm fine," Ema lied. "Just tell me the plan."

Matylda took her by the shoulders and turned her round, lifting her hands. "This ladder will take you all the way to the top of the ballroom ceiling. When you reach the last rung, just reach up and you'll find a hatch. Your harness has a latch here." She tugged Ema's middle. "Ambrož has arranged three different wires to get you to the cage and back again. The first one will get you to Herr Finkelstein's moon. Once you're there, you'll need to swap to the next wire, which will get you to the impresario's podium. The final wire will help you descend down to the birdcage. You'll have to strap Silvie into this spare harness, then make your way back the same way. You'll have to go one at a time, though, because Ambrož will have the other end of the wire to hoist you back up."

Ema felt dizzy. "All right."

"Are you sure? If you don't follow those instructions precisely, he can't guarantee you won't plummet."

Ema shuddered.

Matylda was silent for a long moment.

"Look, I don't know what this secret science of yours is, Ema, but I do know that whatever it is, Silvie clearly thinks it's remarkable — she thinks that *you're* remarkable. If Silvie believes in you, then so do I. You can do this."

Her words made the itching in Ema's bones ever so slightly more bearable.

"Thank you, Matylda."

"Just bring Silvie back."

"I will."

And with that, Ema began to climb.

⪻ 26 ⪼

Climbing a seemingly never-ending ladder in pitch-black darkness was even worse than she'd imagined. Although Ema couldn't see how high she was, her sinking stomach still seemed to be able to sense that it was *too* high. And yet, miraculously, she kept climbing.

Her palms were slick with sweat by the time she realized she had run out of ladder. And as she reached around for the hatch's handle, her stomach had run out of patience. Ema swallowed an entire mouthful of acidic bile as her fingers finally found a metal latch. She pushed the hatch open, and—despite her window ledge antics earlier that day—the world began to swirl around her.

It was worse than anything Silvie had ever made her climb—three times as high as the Hunger Wall, at least. The ballroom looked tiny from this height, and the masked crowd looked minuscule as they all congregated around the stage.

Another bubble of bile climbed up her throat, but Ema gulped it down again.

Everyone was gathered below. The impresario stood in the center by the orchestra. The curators were all framed by their own doorways. The ballroom floor was packed, with everybody wedged in elbow to elbow. Ema spotted Valentýn standing by a wall with his bat wings wrapped around the journal, and Matylda standing beside the mirror-maze doorway with her arms crossed. Across from Ema, less high but still far above the crowd, was another hatch. Ambrož's face was peering over the edge of it at her. And in the birdcage, Silvie was looking down, completely unaware of Ema's woozy, vomit-swallowing presence above her.

This was the closest she had been to her friend in days, though. Just the thought of getting close enough to touch her was enough to stop the world from spinning. Ema focused on the birdcage as she pushed herself onto the ledge and swung her legs out over the void.

The lights dimmed.

A spotlight beamed down onto the impresario, standing in the center of the ballroom.

"WE WILL FINISH THIS MIDNIGHT HOUR AS WE DO EVERY FULL MOON. MOON. MOON. MOON. MOON," Ephraim Rivers announced, his booming voice spreading an instant ripple of silence over the crowd. "WITH A PERFORMANCE THAT WILL

LEAVE YOU DREAMING OF THIS PLACE UNTIL YOUR NEXT VISIT. VISIT. VISIT. VISIT. VISIT."

He raised his arms, and each of the four looming doorways creaked open. The curators all stepped forward, and Ema watched as—one by one—each empty doorway was filled by the curators' spectacle contribution. A shining, metal solar system from the round door; an array of colored lights from the brass door; a wall of tiny, angled mirrors from the purple door; and the towering, dancing bear skeleton from the raven door.

A single piano note sounded, then began to repeat. By the third note, each doorway contraption started to move. The solar system spun—lights bursting across the room and bouncing off the wall of mirrors, then reflecting in a hundred different directions– and the bear skeleton started to dance.

Ema was transfixed by it all.

It was only when the final *twelfth* note rang out that she blinked herself back to attention.

"I GIVE YOU . . . 'LA DANSE MACABRE.' MACABRE. MACABRE. MACABRE. MACABRE," the impresario shouted.

The cellos began a deep and low pizzicato, the violinist struck a long bone-jarring series of notes, and Ema reached for Ambrož's first wire. With a sharp click, she latched the clip onto her belt and nodded to Ambrož, who nodded back.

Grabbing the wire with both hands, she threw herself forward.

Ema swooped through the air in a long, wide arc. As the rushing air caught her wings and stung her eyes, she made one of the most regretful decisions of her life: she looked down.

Her stomach felt like it had turned inside out.

The crowd was dancing to the music, weaving in and out of one another, making Ema feel even more disoriented. It was then that her feet collided with something hard, sending her into a spin. Ema reached out an arm, her fingers brushing the Astronomer's moon, before seizing hold of empty air. The violin began its main theme, and Ema clung to the wire as she was sent hurtling back the way she'd come.

This time, as she began to swoop and spin toward the moon again, she closed her eyes. The moment she felt her momentum slow, she snapped them open and grabbed the edge of the moon with both hands, gripping on with all her strength. She heaved herself onto it, feeling a dizzying alchemic mix of terror, exhilaration, and disbelief at what she'd just done.

Ema clipped the new wire onto her belt and unlatched the first one, wrapping it around the moon so she and Silvie could use it again to get back. Then, keeping her gaze firmly on the impresario's podium, she swung herself forward again.

The air rushed sickeningly fast around her, her stomach flip-flopped, but this time her feet were ready. She aimed them up over the bars of the podium and landed on the platform in a crouch, her heart hammering and adrenaline coursing through her like an electrical storm.

She had no choice but to look down now.

Leaning over the edge, she could see the top of Silvie's head, as her friend peered down at the spectacle below. Ema's eyes darted to Ambrož, who was staring up at her with an expression that pleaded for her to hurry up.

Ema clipped herself onto the final wire, tugged it to make sure it was secure, then nodded to Ambrož.

Ambrož nodded back.

Ema inched herself off the edge, swaying slightly as she dangled over the void. The wire gave a small jolt, then she started to descend smoothly. Ema kept her gaze fixed on Silvie. Her feet were almost touching the top of the birdcage when the wire gave another jolt, bringing her to a sudden stop. Her legs flailed beneath her, wedging one foot between the iron bars.

The next thing she knew, she was upside down.

Her torso collided with the side of the cage, and as she gripped on to the bars, Silvie's dark hair whipped round and her eyes locked with Ema's.

The music rose, and Silvie screamed.

Despite the predicament she was in, and despite the terror in Silvie's eyes, finally being within reach of her friend had Ema grinning so widely her cheeks instantly ached. She tugged her mask off, letting her spider-silk hair cascade down toward the ballroom.

"Hello, Silvie."

Silvie's eyes and mouth widened. She shook her head and blinked, then took off her own mask. "Ema?"

"Yep."

"What are you . . . How are . . . What?"

Ema's blood was now rushing to her head, and she tried to blink away the dizziness. Silvie's face wavered closer, until they were almost nose to nose.

"I'm . . . here to rescue you."

Silvie blinked. "Rescue me?"

"Yes, rescue you from Florentina. You're safe now. Almost, anyway. And don't worry—we've got plans for Florentina too."

"We?" Silvie followed Ema's gaze and saw Ambrož waving from his hatch. But when she looked back at Ema, it was not with a look of relief—but one of panic. "Oh, Ema, what have you done?"

Every bone in Ema's skeleton began to hum with dread and confusion, and her grin faltered. "I . . . I found you," she whispered. "After Florentina kidnapped you . . ."

Ema's vision began to blur, but she could still see the horror that crept across her friend's face. "Florentina didn't kidnap me, Ema," Silvie said. "I'm her spy."

≋ 27 ≋

"**I** think the blood rushing to my head is making me delirious," Ema said. "Because what you just said made no sense."

Silvie's blurry face disappeared. Ema felt something clamp down on her wedged foot and shove it, and then it was free. Over the music, she heard the creaking of hinges. The world spun, and then she was sitting in the cage, with Silvie's face in front of her again, slowly returning into sharp focus.

"At least I didn't wet myself," Ema said, blinking away the last of her dizziness. "That would have had unfortunate consequences, seeing as I—"

"Ema," Silvie repeated. "What did you do?"

Silvie was still staring at her in a way that made every bone in Ema's skeleton feel like it had been struck like a tuning fork.

Of all the reactions she'd expected from Silvie, this

wide-eyed unhappiness was the last thing on the list.

"What did I *do*?" Ema said. "What I did was realize you were lying to me. Turns out I can spot your lies even in a letter."

"I should have known that you'd see straight through it," Silvie said, with a small smile that quickly turned into a wince. "Oh, Ema, I didn't *want* to lie—"

"I know you didn't. And I'm not angry. I've been *terrified*. Especially after I found out you'd been living alone in a damp storage room beneath a soapery."

"'How—"

"The soap packets and Béla. Where is Béla anyway? Did he find you? Actually, never mind that now—I found all your things, including the blank map. And then I found myself in this place. I also found myself in trouble, several times. But that didn't stop me from trying to find you, night after night, no matter how many more terrifying things I uncovered, like the fact Alois was killed by a falling whale skeleton. I found Matylda and Valentýn and Ambrož. It took me a little while to find the signs that *they* were your tutors, not the curators. And then I found you imprisoned in a giant birdcage, dangling from the ceiling."

"But, Ema, I'm not imprisoned—"

"And despite all these impossible things, I now find you in complete denial! I don't know what Florentina said to make you trust her. She seems to have a special knack for that. She's tricked several curators into helping her, I even watched her convince her patrons she could communicate with the dead, when really she's using trickery and taking their money." Ema reached into her collar and pulled the eyeball necklace free. "When I realized it was her that was in the mausoleum that night, and when I learned she's been working secretly with Herr Finkelstein, I realized I needed help getting you as far away from her as possible, as quickly as possible. Ambrož is waiting for us to get out of here; Matylda and Valentýn are also helping. You need to trust me on this. And you need to let me get you out of this cage before the song ends."

"Ema—"

"Florentina's not who you think she is, Silvie. She's a fraud, a liar, and a murderer."

Silvie lifted her gaze from the necklace and looked at Ema with that unflinching dismay. "No, Florentina's not who *you* think she is. And I can tell by the way you're scratching your stomach that you're doubting your own words."

Ema stopped scratching and shook her head. "It's the only theory that makes any sense."

"I can see why you'd think that," said Silvie. "And you're right about one thing. Alois *was* murdered that night. For months, I thought his death was my fault, but when you found that other tulip . . . I had to find out why

Florentina had left it there. That's why I went back. But *she* didn't leave it, Ema. Someone else was feeling guilty about his death. Florentina is certain that someone murdered him, and she's desperate to find out who is responsible."

"Silvie, she's a fraud. I've seen it with my own eyes."

"Yes, I know, but—it's the only way she can stay in a position of power, so that she can use it to find the names of those who Alois was working with—those who *killed* him. She doesn't like lying any more than I do. Alois was involved in something dangerous. Some illicit research that he kept hidden from everyone. Florentina is convinced that if she can find out who he was working with, it'll lead her to his killers. The only thing we know is that one of his partners—a patron no less—had a bandaged hand. Florentina saw that much, and even though it's a flimsy clue . . . it's all we have. That's why I'm up in this cage. I'm looking for that patron."

Ema stared at Silvie, as her mind scrambled to make sense of this new information. The dizziness came back.

"It wasn't her and Herr Finkelstein that pushed Alois to do electrotherapy?"

Panic tore across her friend's face, and Ema wilted under the realization that perhaps she hadn't been helping her friend all this time. Perhaps she'd just made things worse.

What had she done?

Silvie frowned. "You've seen the journal?"

Ema nodded solemnly. "I took it from her safe not long ago."

"Where is that journal, Ema?"

"Valentýn has it. He's going to give it to Ephraim any moment now. Before the song ends."

Silvie leaned over the edge of the cage to peer down, and Ema followed her gaze. The music was building up to its final crescendo, and through the dancing crowd, the small bat-like form of Valentýn was ducking, diving, and tripping his way over to the impresario.

"Oh, Ema! This can't be happening!"

For the first time since she'd known Silvie, Ema saw pure terror on her friend's face.

"We haven't got the names of Alois's partners yet. After everything we've done to try to find out what really happened, Florentina is going to be blamed for it all."

"I . . . I'm sorry."

"We need to get down there and stop him!"

Silvie threw her legs over the edge of the birdcage, then beckoned Ema over.

Ema started to unclip the wire, but Silvie shook her head. "We'll go together. Now."

"But Ambrož said we have to go one at a time—"

"There's no time for that." Silvie wrapped her arms around Ema's neck. "Jump, Ema."

"What?!"

"I said jump."

"But we need to go up!"

"No, we need to go down. Right now."

"But—"

Then once again, the world tilted and Ema found herself airborne. Silvie's legs wrapped around her middle, and Ema clung to her friend with every ounce of strength she could muster as they began to plummet.

Ema peered down.

Several masked faces peered up.

Then with a jolt that nearly sent Silvie tumbling out of her grasp, they stopped falling.

As she and Silvie dangled and swayed, Ema's own terrified gaze locked with Matylda's.

The knife thrower gave her a small, uneasy nod, then drew a blade and angled it upward, aiming toward one of the spotlights.

As soon as the light hit the knife's steel edge, it bounced off and scattered in a hundred different directions, hitting more reflective surfaces—carefully angled mirrors in the stone walls, Ema realized with a brief flutter of awe.

A crisscrossed web of light formed around Ema's middle, and if it weren't for the fact that their legs were dangling below it as they swung from side to side, she might have found herself in awe of Matylda's ingenious distraction.

"Silvie, stop wriggling! Ambrož won't be able to hold

us for long, and I don't want to drop you—"

Silvie's arms kept moving behind her. "No! Down, Ambrož. Take us down!"

Just when Ema thought her arms were finally about to give up, she and Silvie started to descend again—more slowly this time, but still swaying and spinning. The music got louder and more frenetic. The number of masked faces peering up at them increased, and a ripple of gasps and shrieks joined in with the orchestra's finale.

It was directly into the orchestra that the two of them swung, barely missing the string section to land in a tangled heap of feathers, wings, and spider-silk hair.

The golden clock struck thirteen.

The music stopped.

The lights clunked off.

The ringing in Ema's ears was so loud it hurt.

And then the now-invisible crowd erupted in applause.

"Are you hurt?" Silvie whispered.

The clapping continued, as did the shuffling of hundreds of feet.

Ema pushed herself up off the floor. "I'll have some bruises, I suspect. But I don't think anything is broken. How about you?"

"You broke my fall."

"Glad to be of service."

"Ema, we need to hurry—"

"Yes, come on."

But as Ema started to hoist her friend up off the floor, a hand clamped down on her shoulder. The voice that spoke to her through the darkness sent the world spinning around her once more.

"Do not move," said Dagmara Bartoňová. "Either of you."

As the sounds of scuffling feet made their way toward the tunnel door, Ema didn't dare move. Neither, it seemed, did Silvie, who held her hand in a tight squeeze, her palm warm and sweaty.

After several agonizingly long minutes, the door slammed shut with a heavy clunk, and the lights snapped on with a whir and a clank, which echoed around the now nearly empty ballroom. Ema blinked at the brightness, but she could *feel* many eyes watching her. It took a few rapid blinks before she could see those watchful eyes.

The first face that Ema saw as the world swam into bright, clear focus was the grinning skeleton bear. Then five more figures stepped forward, blocking out the brightness. The curators all peered down at Ema and Silvie, their silver star brooches glinting and their anger palpable — she could *feel* it radiating toward her, filling the ballroom.

For the third time in as many nights, Ema and Florentina locked eyes. She watched as the Bone Sculptor's expression morphed from shock, to recognition, then fury. Dagmara still had her hand clamped on Ema's shoulder. And Ema could feel more eyes watching her from behind, though she didn't dare look.

As the silence rang on, Žofie Markova was the first to speak.

"Well?" said Žofie curtly. "Now would be a fabulous time for you two to explain yourselves."

Ema opened her mouth, but no words came out. Beside her, she watched Silvie do the same.

"Silvie," said Kazimír Carvosa, tugging the bird mask off the top of Silvie's head. "Matylda said you'd gone home."

"I sponsored her to come back," Florentina said quickly. "I must have forgotten to tell you."

Kazimír gave his fellow curator an indignant huff, followed swiftly by a sneer. "Forgetful as well as fraudulent, why doesn't that surprise me?"

Florentina's nose twitched, but she leveled the Illusionist with a hard stare. Ema's small reprieve was lost, however, when all ten eyes flicked, dagger quick, back to her.

"And who are you?" Aninha asked, nodding toward Ema with the same sharp tilt of the chin that Matylda used to demand answers. "Given the outfit, I take it she's one of yours, Herr Finkelstein?"

"It would seem so," Thibault Finkelstein said, his almost-black eyes inscrutable. "An unexpected gift from the headmistress."

"Yes, that's exactly why I've come tonight," Dagmara said above her. "You shouldn't be here."

Finally, Ema summoned the willpower to turn her head to look up at the headmistress. "I know, but—"

Dagmara wasn't looking at her, however, but behind her—to the eyes that Ema could still feel boring into her. Slowly, Ema turned—the dread coursing through her veins making her head swim with dizziness.

There were three patrons standing in front of the tunnel's door, and they all reached up to lower their hoods and remove their plain black masks.

Ema's mother's face appeared first—her expression twitching chaotically between shock, dismay, and tenderness. Her father's face appeared next—his confusion arranged neatly and fixedly across his face. But when the third face revealed itself, Ema sucked in a sharp breath of surprise.

Františka was the only one who was grinning. "I hitched a ride with Máma and Táta tonight to surprise you in the morning," she said, with a small shake of her head. "But looks like you beat me to the surprising."

Ema blinked at the three of them. "You're *here*? But you weren't due back until tomorrow!"

It was then that Ema noticed her mother clutching a

bundle of research documents and realized they'd come back early for the guild, not for her. Before her parents could respond, another voice piped up.

"I should probably declare myself *here* too," said Josef. "Although I'm still struggling to comprehend exactly what *here* is."

Everyone turned to the six-foot-tall man-bat standing beside the Astronomer's doorway. He reached up a leathery wing-arm and tugged at the mask on his head.

"When I saw Ema sneaking out of the house earlier, I thought perhaps she was trying to find Ferkel for me," he said. "I hurried out to help her — as well as scold her, of course — but she was too quick. By the time I had followed her through that alleyway door, and then followed some other people through a seemingly solid wall, I realized I wasn't really chasing my niece through the underparts of the city . . . I was having a very strange dream. This was confirmed by" — he waved an arm around the ballroom and the glaring curators — "all this."

Ema swallowed. "Uncle, I—"

"Bear with me," Josef said, holding up a hand to silence her. "I haven't got to the weirdest part of the dream yet." He looked sheepishly down at his costume and shook his head before continuing. "I hurried in through this doorway here, as it looked nice and quiet and empty — but oh was I wrong when I saw what was on the other side of it. Then someone started questioning me — rather rudely — about who I was and why I wasn't dressed appropriately. I think I must have mumbled something about bat costumes and nieces, because the next thing I know I've been jostled into this outfit and bitten three times by a goat. Now, we all know you can't feel pain in dreams . . . which was confusing. And then, back here in the ballroom, my feet kept getting assaulted by a ferocious girl with blue hair and wheels on her feet, inflicting more pain and confusion. And then finally I witness my niece tumble through the air with a giant raven." He leveled Ema with the same look he gave Ferkel each time the cat-beast caused mayhem — resigned bemusement. "This isn't a ridiculous dream, is it?"

"The ridiculous part is right, at least," said Dagmara Bartoňová. "And as touching as this family reunion is, I'm afraid we need to address Ema's skullduggery. I'll not have *anyone* using my name and reputation for their own purposes."

Ema saw the precise moment her parents' expressions turned from shock to horror.

"You didn't sponsor her?" Karel asked.

"I have not sponsored anyone since securing Františka's acolyteship at the Vienna guild all those years ago," Dagmara said. "It seems your youngest daughter has found her true calling: she has perfected the art of sneaking into places she ought not be, faking identities, and causing havoc in the process."

"What?" Ema's parents shrieked in unison. "Ema!"

"Did you think this would impress me?" Dagmara pressed, her glare cutting straight through Ema. "Or make me reconsider my decision not to let you into my school?"

"No, I—"

"Is this some new field of study of yours? Mischief-ology, perhaps?"

Unable to bear the pressing weight of Dagmara's angry glare and her parents' looks of disappointment, Ema turned to the other figures still looming behind her. The curators were all looking at her as if she were some sort of distasteful anomaly.

After a lifetime of wanting to be noticed, Ema had finally gotten her wish. Now, however, she wanted nothing more than for the ground to open and swallow her whole. Her fingers reached out for Silvie's, but her friend was no longer beside her. Silvie was whispering into Florentina Falkenberg's ear, and Ema had never felt more alone.

"I'll admit, you've piqued my curiosity, Ema Vašková," Dagmara continued. "But I'm not yet convinced I'll be impressed by your explanations. So please, convince me."

"Allow me to do that on her behalf," said a new voice.

Ephraim Rivers strode forward, with Valentýn, Ambrož, and Matylda at his heels. His face was a tangled knot of different frowns: outraged, disbelieving, but calmly determined all at once.

As everyone turned their attention sharply toward the impresario, Ema felt their gazes lift from her as if they'd been a physical heavy weight. She sucked in a sharp breath of relief, only to let it shakily out again when she saw the panic on Silvie's face.

"Our little intruder here is quite the enigma," he said, looking first at Ema, then up at her parents and sister — who had come to stand around her. "Knowing now this is one of your daughters, I'm not surprised she has achieved such an astonishing feat."

Dagmara tutted. "You call breaking rules an astonishing feat?"

"Sometimes we must all break the rules in order to pursue vital work," Ephraim Rivers said, his gaze just as cutting as the headmistress's. "You should know that more than anyone, Dagmara — how many times did you ignore those who said women and girls could not and should not become academics? I daresay Ema here has done something equally as tenacious and miraculous."

Dagmara narrowed her eyes but remained silent.

Ema stared up at the impresario with a thundering heart and itchy palms.

"The girl, it seems, has been up to much more than you realize," the impresario said, shaking his head slightly. "In fact, her transgressions pale in comparison to the shocking discovery she has uncovered within these very walls." His voice hardened and cracked. "Within *my* guild, no less."

He pulled Alois's journal out from behind his back.

"Where did you get that?" Florentina asked.

Ephraim's frowns tightened. "Are you saying it's yours?"

Florentina opened her mouth, then snapped it shut again. The muscle under her left eye gave a tiny twitch.

"What's going on?" Aninha interjected. "Is a single question going to be answered this evening, or are we supposed to figure out each new mystery ourselves?"

Ephraim Rivers was staring at Ema now, and one by one everyone else in the room followed suit, until Ema was once again nearly crushed by the weight of it. She wasn't sure what was worse: the baffled disappointment in her parents' eyes, or the pleading desperation in Silvie's.

"Do you understand the significance of what you children have presented me with tonight, Ema?" Ephraim asked.

Ema swallowed, unable to meet Silvie's gaze as she nodded.

"You realize, then, that this evidence of yours — should it prove what you imply it proves — will uncover the most serious crime of all . . . murder."

Again, Ema nodded solemnly.

"The misfortune . . ." Josef said. "It's true then?"

Ema's mother gasped. "Misfortune? Josef, I told you not to fill her mind with that nonsense."

"I did not fill her mind with anything but bicycle-making nonsense; she found the misfortune herself—"

Ephraim shot them a silencing look. Then he turned back to Ema. "Just to be perfectly clear, you understand that there are consequences for providing false evidence or testimony? And, therefore, you must answer my next questions simply and plainly with the truth?"

Again, Ema nodded.

"Mr. Rivers," Silvie said, running to stand between them. "You can ask me these questions. Ema—she doesn't know this place, or these people—except for me. It's my fault she snuck in here . . . it's been so confusing for her. Let me explain everything."

"The children have filled me in on where you've been," the impresario said, his face softening. "I'm so sorry you felt responsible for what happened, Silvie. And I can't imagine how confusing it's been for you. Especially having no one but Florentina to talk to about all this—"

"What are you implying?" Florentina cut in.

Ephraim Rivers's face hardened again. "We'll get to what I'm *implying* in a minute." He turned his glare to Herr Finkelstein. "No one interrupt me again, understand?"

The Astronomer's permanently gloomy expression convulsed—confusion pinching between his brows. When everyone was silent — as instructed — the impresario turned back to Ema.

Ephraim gave her a small, but kind smile. "First question, Ema. I understand the reason you came to this guild was to find Silvie, after a series of unusual events — which we won't get into just now — led you to believe she was in danger. Is that correct?"

Ema nodded. "Yes."

"And you knew that danger surrounded the death of Alois Blažek, which you suspected — after your first visit here — to have been falsely declared an accident?"

Again, Ema nodded. "That's correct."

There was a collective rumble of gasps, but Ema could not tear her eyes from the impresario — his stern but encouraging gaze was the only thing keeping her from trembling. She dreaded to think how her family, Dagmara, or worse, Silvie would be looking at her right now.

"Murder?" Aninha asked. "It *was* an accident! Ephraim — you yourself determined that."

"That I did," Ephraim said gravely. "But sometimes it takes an outsider's eye to see that which the rest of us would rather not. Now, Ema, I'm going to move swiftly on to the troubling evidence you have collected over the past few nights. When and where did you find this journal?"

Beside her, Silvie bristled. Ema's mind scrambled for any scrap of information she'd missed — any clue that

Silvie's proclamation about Florentina's innocence was right. When she tried to sift through every detail and clue, however, it all collided in her mind.

"Just answer truthfully," Ephraim pressed.

"I found it in the séance room," Ema said quietly. "In a safe hidden behind Alois's portrait, less than an hour ago."

"And how did you know about the safe?"

"I was hiding under the séance table as she opened it to put that journal inside."

"She?"

"Frau Falkenberg."

"And who gave her the journal?"

Again, Ema opened her mouth to respond but found herself having to swallow down a heavy lump of unease. Despite not being able to see Silvie, she could *feel* her friend's despair.

"Who gave her the journal, Ema?"

Ema turned to the line of curators and forced herself to look the Astronomer in the eye.

"Herr Finkelstein," Ema croaked out. "He disguised himself as a patron and snuck into the séance room to give it to her."

The Astronomer flinched—his jaw tightening—but he remained silent. As did Florentina, though the Bone Sculptor's carefully curated demeanor was no longer as steadfast. She suddenly looked *so* young, and *so* frightened.

"I've only had a brief read of this," Ephraim Rivers said, nodding to the journal. "But what I saw was hugely disturbing. Research as dangerous and contentious as this should have never taken place within this guild without everyone's approval."

"What dangerous and contentious research?" Žofie Markova asked.

"Research so dangerous and contentious Alois was silenced to make sure it never came to light."

This time, when the impresario turned to Ema, his questions became faster and angrier.

"Is it true that you heard Thibault and Florentina discuss destroying evidence and keeping their misdeeds hidden from me?"

Ema swallowed. "Yes, but —"

"And is it also true that you found levers and pulleys beneath the séance table, which Florentina used to make the table levitate?"

Ema nodded. "Ye —"

"It's not what it looks like!" Silvie bit out.

"I'll be the judge of what it does and doesn't look like." The impresario paused for a moment, and Ema noticed a slight shake of his head. "It is my responsibility, not just to the guild but also to Alois himself, to make sure every piece of evidence, every witness statement, and indeed any accusation of wrongdoing is taken seriously."

The room fell silent.

They all watched the impresario as he pinched the bridge of his nose. When he looked back up at them all, Ema could see the glistening of unshed tears in the corners of his eyes.

"They didn't kill him," Silvie cried. "And they weren't the ones working with him on those experiments! They were working together to find his real killer."

The impresario was glaring at Florentina. "Alois *begged* me to hire Thibault—"

"Yes," said Florentina. "Because they were *friends* . . . and because Thibault needed the chance—"

"To contact his lost loved one?" Mr. Rivers said, nodding to the mourning ring on the Astronomer's finger. "That was, in hindsight, rather convenient. And let's not forget that *you* begged me to hire you, before Alois was even laid to rest. The two of you have fared quite well since his demise."

"I would never hurt him," Florentina seethed. "I want *justice* for him."

The impresario glowered. "As do I. And it seems Ema Vašková here has been the one to see that happen." He turned to her parents. "You should be proud of your daughter. She is shrewd, brave, and determined—exactly what it takes to be a great scientist one day."

For the second time that night, Ema felt every single eye in the ballroom lock on to her.

Finally, she risked looking up at her parents. They

were staring down at her differently now—a glint of un-bridled pride shining through their shocked expressions. Františka and Josef had the same look on their faces. Even Dagmara's expression had turned approving.

Ema had dreamed of this moment, imagining how warm it would make her feel.

And yet, she felt nothing but cold, prickling dread.

29

Ema felt lost in the maelstrom of her own whirring mind as she watched the impresario lead the curators and headmistress through the black doors of the Moonlight Garden and out of sight. Every strange, unsettling, baffling thing she'd witnessed and learned over the past few nights was trying to push itself to the forefront of her consciousness: the whale skeleton, mausoleum, eyeball, Alois's hazel-eyed stare, tulip petals, masks, levitating tables, birdcage . . .

Each one brought with it a feeling of terror, or confusion, or shock, sadness, delight, tiredness, worry, anger, helplessness—Ema was feeling them all at once and growing increasingly overwhelmed.

Beyond this internal storm battering through her, she could half hear distant rumblings of disagreement coming from all around her.

"—the last three nights! How could you not have noticed Ema sneaking out?"

"Technically, sister, it was only two nights that I didn't notice. And that's because I've been worried about my missing cat—"

"You should have been worrying more about your missing niece—"

"Florentina is innocent, Matylda. I don't care what all this so-called evidence points to; I know she didn't do it."

"Silv, she's so very good at drawing people into her lies—"

"She's nothing like our mother! I loved Liliana very much, but I had to protect my children from those kinds of ideas—"

"Don't do to Ema what Mother did to you. Let her find her own way—"

Those voices were then drowned out by the distant chime of a cymbal, a faraway, vague clattering sound, and a couple of mutterings of "*Why is she sitting on that drum?*" and "*And why isn't she blinking?*"

As Ema tried to still the chaos inside her, it was the feeling of deep, stomach-churning sadness that ultimately pushed its way to the top. She pictured Silvie's moonlit face as she'd pulled that white tulip out from her sleeve, and the dark shadow that had pooled at her friend's feet—the same dark shadow of sadness that Ema had been running through in each of her nightmares. Instead of trying to push that uncomfortable sadness away, she seized on to it with every ounce of curiosity she could muster.

And just like that, the storm inside her cleared.

Whatever she was missing, it had been there in the graveyard with Silvie that night. Ema could feel the certainty of it course through her bones, like an electrical hum that set every nerve ending alight.

"Ema? Are you all right?"

The memory of standing outside that mausoleum was so vivid, Ema could almost feel the warm night air and the gusty wind that had blown around them.

A perfect white tulip for forgiveness.

There had been two tulips that night. And yet Silvie had insisted that Florentina hadn't left the one Ema had picked up.

"Beruška? What's the matter?"

Ema rocked at the memory of that gusty wind that had curled around her the moment she and Silvie had stepped inside Alois's mausoleum. It could have swept that white tulip off the tomb. And then when Florentina had arrived, that second gust of wind could have swept it toward the door—where it had settled neatly atop those moonlit footprints.

"Beruška, are you listening?"

Ema had seen another set of footprints as she'd followed Silvie toward Alois's tomb.

Someone else *had* been in that mausoleum before them.

There is someone whose forgiveness I need more than anything else in this world.

That someone else had been desperate to ask Alois for his forgiveness too.

Whoever that someone was, and whatever reason they had for killing Alois, Ema realized now that they felt *shame* for what they had done.

Again, Ema rocked . . . and blinked . . . until the memory of the graveyard dissipated, and she was back in the Midnight Guild's ballroom, sitting on a drum, with eight concerned faces all looking at her.

"Finally! She's back from her trance," Matylda said, as Valentýn and Ambrož stopped waving their hands in front of Ema's eyes.

"That wasn't a trance," Karel said swiftly, looking relieved as Ema blinked up at him. "You're just very tired, aren't you, beruška?"

"And in shock, no doubt," Milena added, pulling Ema into a hug.

As her mother's warm arms enveloped her, Ema met Silvie's narrowed gaze, then Františka's quizzical one. It wasn't tiredness and shock that had gripped Ema just then, and all three of them knew it.

"You're probably right," Ema said.

"We should get you home," Karel said. "And the rest of you, shouldn't you all be tucked up in bed too by now?"

Valentýn, Matylda, and Ambrož shifted awkwardly under Ema's father's neat-but-stern stare, and her uncle let out a long, weary sigh.

"Yes, I should be," said Josef—looking as if all he wanted to do was hang upside down in a cozy roost, wrap his wings around himself, and fall asleep.

Silvie was still staring at her, as was Františka. Ema could see them both trying to see past her nonchalant demeanor. She held her sister's quizzical gaze until, finally, Františka gave her a barely perceptible nod.

"Oh my goodness!" Františka cried, patting down her patron's cloak. "I've misplaced the gloves you bought me! Máma, Táta—I'm not leaving without them. Why don't we leave Ema to say goodnight to her new friends and you can help me search for them."

She tugged Milena away from Ema and grabbed Karel's arm with her free one. Then she nudged her mother toward Josef.

"It'll be quicker if we split our search. Isn't that right, Uncle?"

Josef eyed Františka suspiciously. Františka held his gaze a long moment, then flicked her eyes to Ema.

Josef eyed Ema suspiciously. Ema held his gaze too.

Josef plastered on a tired smile. "Sister," he said,

taking Milena's elbow in his own winged one. "You come with me. We'll search the moon for Františka's gloves. Hopefully they won't have been eaten by that moon goat, as I nearly was."

Karel shook his head as Františka tugged him toward Žofie's doorway. "But, we're not allowed—"

"Good thing they are all too busy solving a murder to notice us, then. Those gloves are my favorite. I can't leave without them."

As soon as the adults had disappeared into the hidden spectacle areas, Ema clambered to her feet.

Silvie was grinning now. "I know that look," she said. "You've figured it all out, haven't you?"

"Not all of it, no."

"Figured what out?" Valentýn asked. "What is there to be figured out?"

"I'll explain on the way—"

Ema made for Florentina's doorway, but Matylda blocked her path.

"Did your sister and uncle just *distract* your parents for you?" Her eyes widened in disbelief. "Wait, are you planning on going in *there*?" She pointed to the Moonlight Garden. "Are you planning on *interrupting* the impresario's meeting?"

"Yes and yes and yes," said Ema. "Now, keep your voice down and follow me—all of you—as we don't have long."

She ducked under Matylda's elbow, tugging Silvie along with her. Ambrož, Matylda, and Valentýn fell into step with them as they ran across the ballroom, toward the raven doorway. This time, it was Ambrož who skirted in front to block Ema's path.

"Maybe it's time we stopped sneaking about like this," he said.

Matylda came to stand beside him. "For once, Ambrož is absolutely right. We should just let the adults figure it all out."

"I never thought I'd say this," Valentýn said, also stepping in front of Ema, but facing his two much taller, much scowlier friends instead, "but the two of you can be such miserable milksops sometimes. We didn't get this far tonight by letting the adults figure it all out, did we?" He placed a leathery hand against each of their chests and pushed them backward, through the door — grinning beneath his bat mask at the look of surprise on their faces.

Ema and Silvie shared a silent chuckle as they followed.

They emerged at the top of the mossy stone steps, where Matylda and Ambrož gawked in open-mouthed wonder at the Moonlight Garden. Valentýn prodded the two of them in the back to keep them moving, and Ema steered them down a fern-lined path.

"Did Vendula build this?" Ambrož asked.

"She and Florentina did, yes," said Silvie. "Isn't it

wonderful? See what can be achieved when we work *together*, instead of bickering all the time?" At this she gave them a pointed look.

"What exactly is it we need to work together on?" Matylda asked, shrieking as they passed a feline skeleton peering out from behind a bush. She scowled at the resulting giggle from Silvie. "Ema comes out of a trance," Matylda continued. "Then makes some weird eye contact with you, and you seem to understand it when no one else does. Why are we here? Please explain. Oh saints—is that house made out of *teeth*?"

"We're going to use my secret science to find the truth," Ema said, turning onto a new path.

"You still haven't explained what that science is," Ambrož said.

"Her secret science is herself," said Silvie. "And it truly is a sight to behold."

"This is ridiculous," Ambrož said, shaking his head as if trying to dispel a dream. "I'm leaving."

"Me too," said Matylda.

Valentýn kept prodding them forward.

"It's fine, Val," Ema said, continuing down the path. "They're both lying. They have every intention of coming with us."

"How could you possibly know that?" Matylda asked. "Are you a mind reader?"

"Her uncle said she was like her grandmother, so

something like that runs in the family," Ambrož said.

Ema came to a halt beneath the ivy arch, peered down into the gloomy corridor that she had hoped never to see again, and let out a sigh. "I read faces, not minds," she said. "You each have several tells, but I'll start with the most obvious ones. Valentýn clenches his jaw when he's trying to hide something. Ambrož can't quite hold eye contact when he's lying, but your lies are the easiest to spot, Matylda. That chin of yours gives it away each time; the higher you point it, the harder you're trying to cover what you really feel."

Matylda frowned, then lowered her chin.

"What about that catlike trance you were just in?" Ambrož said. "You weren't communicating with some sort of demon, were you?"

"Why does everyone assume things like that?" Ema asked. "I was just . . . sifting through my brain. It gets a bit noisy and disorienting in there sometimes is all. These last few nights have been a lot to take in. But I remembered something.

"Those footprints in Alois's mausoleum . . . the white tulip that was already there before we got there . . . His killer had wanted to say sorry—"

"If you can read faces," Ambrož said, "surely you must have been able to see if Florentina was guilty just now."

"I was too flustered by Mr. Rivers's questions," Ema said glumly.

"You must have seen something, though," Matylda said. "Think. Did Florentina scratch her nose, or maybe she does a similar chin thing to me?"

"Don't forget Herr Finkelstein," Ambrož added. "Were you watching him carefully?"

Ema shook her head. "I don't—"

"If Frau Falkenberg and Herr Finkelstein are innocent," Silvie said, "then how would Ema have seen anything useful?"

Ambrož and Matylda both glared at her dubiously, ready to argue, but she leveled them with the kind of calming, silencing stare that only a true impresario could pull off.

"*Someone* in there is guilty," Valentýn said. "We should all care about finding the truth, no matter how much it might upset us. If we don't, then there's no hope for this guild. It'll tear itself apart."

"I'm going to go in there and try again," Ema said. "This is the only time I'll ever get to face all the curators in one go. If the killer really does feel shame about what they did, that should make them easier to spot. It's the only thing I can think to do."

"What if it doesn't work?" Matylda said.

"And why do you need us?" Ambrož added.

Ema turned to Silvie. "Remember Vodník?"

"I remember you nearly wetting yourself," Silvie said with an almost grin.

"The séance room has hollow walls, doesn't it?" Ema asked. "That's how Florentina made all those knocking sounds. There's space behind there, and contraptions too, isn't there?"

Silvie shifted uncomfortably but nodded.

"If my plan doesn't work, I'll need you to be ready to provide a—"

"Spectacle?" said Silvie, smiling knowingly. "We know the murderer believed in Alois's skills . . . you think maybe we can *frighten* them enough to reveal the truth to you?"

The sudden delight and anticipation in her friend's face *almost* banished the twisting knot in the pit of her stomach when she thought of the pride gleaming in her parents' eyes just a few moments earlier.

They had been proud of a lie.

It didn't count, no matter how much Ema wanted it to.

"Yes," said Ema finally. "So, let's go murderer hunting, shall we?"

30

The five of them tiptoed down the dark corridor like a train of silent shadows toward the glowing curtain door of the séance room. The closer they got, the louder the voices within that room got.

"Nowhere in that journal does it mention Herr Finkelstein or me," Florentina was saying, her voice full of bite. "Even if we were collaborating with him on that research—which we weren't—you have no evidence to even suggest we were."

"Then why keep it hidden, Florentina?" Ephraim Rivers replied in a much wearier tone. "Why not bring this to me the moment you found it? I'm the very person who should be investigating matters such as this! Why did you not trust me with it, if you are so innocent?"

"Because you're more concerned with quashing unrest in this guild than igniting it!" Florentina yelled as Ema and the others finally arrived at the door. "And you are far too trusting—if I didn't have the names of Alois's collaborators, I knew you wouldn't take my claim seriously. I knew that *one of them* would have the chance to worm their way out of trouble."

Ema shuddered as she came to a halt in front of the curtain. She could almost feel the animosity radiating from the room. By the wide-eyed looks on her friends' barely visible faces, they too were aware of just how *dangerously* deep and hostile the divide in this guild ran.

"I had my own suspicions about that night," Žofie Markova said. "My equipment *never* fails—"

"Yes, *your* equipment, Žofie," Florentina seethed. "The very equipment that killed him."

"The equipment *you* insisted I make for *your* ridiculous skeleton display. I should never have let you talk me into it."

"You hated him," Florentina spat. "All three of you made no secret of your contempt, nor did you ever shut up about how the guild needed to be rid of him and his kind. He was my mentor!"

"We already have curatorships, though," Aninha Carvosa said coolly. "You're the only one who got a shiny new position as a result of your *beloved* mentor's death. Not to mention the fact we do have clear evidence of you faking the skills you claimed to have."

"Do you have anything to say for yourself, Thibault?"

Kazimír Carvosa asked. "You're being conveniently quiet and gloomy, as always."

"What's the point in me saying anything?" the Astronomer replied. "You seem to have made up your mind about me already."

"QUIET!" the impresario roared.

Ema flinched. As did her friends.

The bickering beyond the curtain door stopped.

As the silence rang on, Silvie was the first to finally move—urging the others past the séance room door and squatting down next to a plain-looking wall panel. With a gentle push, the panel opened, revealing a dark and narrow space behind it.

One by one, Ema's friends slipped in through the open panel. Silvie went through last, pausing briefly to offer Ema one of her encouraging smiles. "They'll see you if you *let* them see you," she whispered.

And then the panel closed, Silvie was gone, and Ema was staring at the curtained door with itchy palms, a thundering heart, and a bone-deep certainty that what she was about to do would either fix everything or make it *much* worse.

Gingerly, Ema nudged the curtain aside and stepped through, into the shadow-strewn séance room. The curators were all sitting around the séance table, glaring silently but murderously at one another. Dagmara

Bartoňová was leaning against a crate of bones, watching each one of the curators closely with that cut-glass stare of hers. The impresario looked lost in a cloud of torment — his jaw clenched, his brow creased, and his eyes glazed.

Ema braced herself for their shocked reaction at her appearance, but not one of them looked her way.

"I think it's fair to say Florentina was right about one thing," Ephraim Rivers said finally. "I was far too quick — too trusting — to dismiss Alois's death as an accident. This journal changes everything."

Ema took another few steps forward, trying not to sway with the dread coursing through her. Still, no one looked up. Her throat felt closed tight.

"I have no choice but to reopen the investigation . . ." he said. "As a *murder* investigation. Florentina and Thibault, you are both suspended with immediate effect. I will be taking this journal to the police tomorrow morning, so I suggest you both find yourselves some very good lawyers."

In the heavy, angry silence Ema stood there, trying — and failing — to stop thinking about the pride that had gleamed in her parents' eyes just a few minutes ago. It wasn't too late to sneak right back out of the room again, before she made a fool out of herself in front of all these people.

But if she did that, she'd have failed Silvie.

No. She'd have failed *herself*.

What if Florentina Falkenberg and Thibault Finkelstein were innocent?

No matter how proud her parents had been at the impresario's praise of her, Ema would never be able to live with the thought of having unwittingly condemned innocent people.

Whatever the consequences, she had to at least *try* to find the truth while she had the chance. And she had to do it now—before her parents realized where she'd gone.

They'll see you if you let *them see you.*

Pushing all thoughts of her parents from her mind, Ema relaxed her shoulders and lifted her chin. She took a deep, steadying breath.

One by one, each head in the room turned her way.

They all blinked, as if Ema might have been a mere figment of their imagination. And then they all frowned when she didn't disappear as mysteriously as she seemed to have appeared.

"Ema?" Dagmara Bartoňová said finally. "What is the meaning of this? You shouldn't be here."

"Actually, yes, I should be." Ema's stomach felt like it might climb right out of her throat. And yet she managed to hold the headmistress's gaze as she stepped around the table to stand beside the impresario.

Ephraim Rivers tilted his head in question.

"Back in the ballroom," Ema said, with only the smallest wobble in her voice, "you said I had to be absolutely certain that the information I provided to you was true. And it was. But there's something I've missed—that we've all missed—I just know it."

"And how do you know this?" Dagmara asked, raising a single, skeptical eyebrow. "With your intuitive osteology?"

Ema tried not to think about the fact that she was ruining all potential for potential in the headmistress's eyes. "Yes," she said firmly. "I can feel it in my very bones. The very same way I *knew* that there was more to Alois's death than a mere accident, long before I found that journal. All I ask for is a few more minutes of your time."

Everyone was staring at her, but Ema could tell by their austere expressions that all they were *seeing* was a nuisance.

Ephraim Rivers's weary eyes locked on to hers. "A few minutes to do what, exactly, Ema?"

"Question the suspects."

The impresario's eyebrows shot upward. "You wish to *interrogate* Herr Finkelstein and Frau Falkenberg?"

"No," said Ema, trying to keep her voice steady. "I wish to interrogate *all* the curators. They *all* had the means and the motive, after all."

A rumble of groans sounded behind her, but Ema kept

her gaze fixed on the impresario and headmistress.

"I don't understand," Ephraim Rivers said with a confused smile.

"Twitchology, if I remember correctly?" Dagmara Bartoňová said, and Ema was surprised to hear far less scorn in the headmistress's voice than she'd expected—though her eyes remained inscrutable.

"I have some ability to read lies on people's faces," Ema said. "It's not a perfect science, but—"

"It's not science at all," Žofie scoffed. "It's nonsense."

Ema tried not to shrivel. Instead, she lifted her chin, held Dagmara's gaze, and summoned every atom of confidence she could. "It may seem implausible, or indeed ridiculous, to most scientists," she said, repeating the headmistress's opinions from that disastrous interview right back at her. "But I feel very *passionately* that it *is* science, not nonsense."

This time, Ema saw the tiniest flicker of curiosity in the headmistress's eyes, even though her expression remained wholly unconvinced.

"I appreciate your eagerness to help," Ephraim Rivers said kindly but tiredly. "But it's late—"

"Let her have her few minutes," Dagmara said. Then, when the impresario opened his mouth to protest, she added: "What harm could it do, Ephraim? Anyway, as I am apparently her official sponsor, I insist on it."

Ema swallowed down a hiccup of relief and gave the headmistress a grateful smile before turning to face the curators. The faces that greeted her all wore the very same mask of cynicism. Ema had just a few short minutes to try to see past those masks. Clinging to that thought, she stepped in front of Žofie Markova.

"Tell me a truth," Ema said.

The Dreamer pursed her red lips, narrowed her dark eyes, and leaned in close enough that Ema could smell a faint trace of fire and oil beneath her flowery perfume.

"I find you to be a fascinatingly absurd creature," Žofie said, with a piercing gaze that never wavered.

"Now tell me a lie."

"I'm hugely fond of cheese." ·

Ema watched a small twitch on the Dreamer's left eyebrow. "You're a woman who believes in innovation and progress, is that right?"

"Yes."

"Ghosts and belief in an afterlife . . . you believe them to be antiquated superstitions that do not belong in this guild. Correct?"

"Correct."

"And you believed that Alois's presence in the guild was holding the entire establishment in the past, so you wanted him gone."

"Very much so."

"Did you kill him?"

"I did not kill him."

Ema stared at Žofie's face until she'd seen enough, then turned to Matylda's parents.

The Illusionists stared hard at her but still offered up a reluctant truth and lie when asked. Ema could feel time oozing away, each second adding a tremble of urgency.

"You both believe in honest trickery," Ema said. "You make no false claims that your work is based on magic, but are instead thrilled by the science behind the illusion. Is that right?"

They both nodded.

"And just like Žofie, you were disgusted by Alois's work. As far as you were both concerned, his work took advantage of patrons desperate for a connection to their lost loved ones. It was dishonest and cast shame upon the guild. You wanted him gone. Yes?"

Again, they nodded.

"Did you kill Alois?"

"No, we did not," Aninha bit out.

"Of course we didn't," Kazimír half growled.

Ema watched their faces in turn, seeing none of the mischievous joviality they usually showed. Then, feeling the time against her, she turned to Herr Finkelstein and realized she needed to be quicker.

The Astronomer's almost-black eyes bored into her, but before he had a chance to speak, Ema felt a shudder as she glanced down at his dark shadow.

"You carry deep shame on your shoulders, Herr Finkelstein. Grief follows you everywhere you go."

She glanced down at the mourning ring on his left hand. He immediately covered it with his right. For a moment, those almost-black eyes widened in surprise, then hardened again.

"My grief has nothing to do with Alois Blažek," the Astronomer said coldly. "I played no part in his death."

Ema stared hard at every inch of his face a moment longer, then wordlessly turned to the Bone Sculptor. Florentina glared up at her defiantly, her bottom lip twitching and her nostrils flared.

"How did you convince Vendula Beranová to help you build that garden?"

"By showing an interest in her work. Then by impressing her with my ability to carve bones into any flower she wanted. But, mostly, by treating her as a respected colleague rather than an enemy."

"Why did you cheat your way into this curatorship, build contraptions to deceive your patrons, and lie about . . . well, pretty much everything?"

"I may have lied about many things," Florentina said. "But I would *never* have hurt Alois. I found that journal the night he died. And knew immediately that I needed to be in a position within the guild that would allow me to investigate what I suspected had really happened to Alois. I knew Ephraim would want another medium, and so I panicked and told him I could take over. It was a necessary lie, if I was to have any hope of getting justice for Alois."

"Why ask Herr Finkelstein for help? If you didn't trust anyone in this guild?"

"Thibault was Alois's friend. They disagreed over many things, and Thibault consistently refused Alois's offer to hold a séance for his late fiancée . . . but they respected each other. Like Vendula and I came to respect one another. I had no intention of telling anyone what I was up to, but after months of trying to find answers, I knew I needed help. With Vendula off on her expedition, he was the only one I felt I could turn to. And he was *new* to the guild. He didn't have years of resentment and grudges to warp his judgment." Florentina glared harder at Ema. "It turned out to be a perfect collaboration. If you hadn't *meddled*, we might have been able to solve it."

The ferocity in her voice made Ema flinch.

She stumbled backward, and a pair of hands caught her shoulders. Ema looked up to find the impresario looking down at her.

"Well?" said Ephraim Rivers. "Did you see anything useful?"

Ema could feel the headmistress's eyes on her, but she was too scared to look at them. She was also all too aware of the fact that Silvie would be able to see and hear her. And all too aware of the fact that time had run out.

She'd not spotted any lies.

The murderer's mask was flawless.

Ema realized she was trembling. "I can't tell—"

"Of course you can't," Ephraim Rivers said. "And no one expects you to be able to."

The kindness in his voice only made Ema's shame more potent. She needed more time; she needed to figure out what she was missing.

The answers were here, in this very room; she was certain of it.

As were her parents, Uncle Josef, and her sister Františka.

They stood in the doorway, shoulder to shoulder, looking at Ema with expressions that were half smile, half wince.

"I'm so sorry, Ephraim," Milena said. "She slipped away unseen. We'll take her home now."

"No," said Ema. "Please, I just need a few more—"

"Ema," the impresario said softly. "I am sorry that you found yourself involved in such an awful discovery. It is something that no child should ever have to encounter. But your time is up. I can assure you that you've done all you can. It's time for you to go home."

31

E ma turned back to the curators, getting increasingly frantic as she looked from one face to another. Why couldn't she see past the murderer's mask?

"Beruška, Mr. Rivers is right: you've done a wonderful job already," Milena said, reaching for her hand. "He can take it from here."

Ema looked up at her parents and knew that if she didn't leave right then, that last glimmer of pride in their eyes would likely disappear. She'd be left in the cold shadow of their disappointment once again.

And yet, she was so close to finding that missing link — she could feel it. Like being on the verge of a sneeze.

All she needed was more time.

"Ema," her father said in a warning tone. "Please listen to the impresario—"

"No, Táta, please listen to *me*."

Ema reached tentatively into her pocket, her heart

thumping increasingly harder. As soon as her hand touched the cool porcelain of the eyeball necklace, the temperature around her dropped, ever so slightly, and every hair on the back of her neck rose, one by one.

"I have another method I'd like to try." She held the eyeball necklace up, then lifted it over her head. "We are missing a key witness statement."

"What missing witness?" Dagmara Bartoňová asked, eyeing the eyeball suspiciously.

Slowly, Ema turned and lifted her gaze up to the portrait. Once again, a shudder ran through her, and she could feel the static in the air.

"Alois himself, of course."

The stunned silence that followed Ema's announcement was broken by the twin groans of embarrassed despair from her parents. As they reached for her, Františka jumped in their way.

"Máma, Táta," Františka said. "Perhaps you should listen to what Ema has to say."

Ema tried not to flinch at her parents' pained expressions. That glimmer of pride really was gone now, and she couldn't bear its absence. She looked quickly away from them, only to find the curators glaring at her in cynicism—except for Florentina, whose tear-streaked face held nothing but resigned despair. If her expression was a mask, it was a very good one.

"Did I hear you correctly?" Žofie Markova asked.

"You'd like us to *interview* the murder victim?"

"Perhaps painted faces speak to her too," Aninha Carvosa added with a scornful smirk.

Ema looked over to the impresario and saw that whatever patience and humor he'd had to offer her so far had very much run dry.

"Enough, Ema," he said softly but austerely. "You need to stop this now."

Ema shook her head. "No."

Her raspy whisper was punctuated by a low-pitched hum, and each lamp in the room began to flicker and buzz. As the entire room blinked in and out of light, Ema caught glimpses of the confused faces around her.

"Is the girl doing this?" the impresario asked.

"No," said Dagmara. "I am watching her closely."

All heads turned to Florentina Falkenberg and Thibault Finkelstein, who held up their hands.

"It's not them either," said Kazimír. "I'm watching *them* closely."

"Faulty circuitry, then," Žofie said. "It wouldn't do this if *I* had installed it."

Ema started as a figure appeared right beside her. Her mother leaned in close, and each flicker of light revealed the mortification on her face. Ema felt as if she might drown in her own desperation.

"Ema," Milena whispered. "Please, we need to leave now."

A searing-hot tear slid down Ema's cheek, but before she could respond, her uncle appeared.

"Milena," Josef said, putting a wing round his sister's shoulders. "Give Ema a chance to show you who she is."

Milena reached out and Ema braced herself, expecting to be dragged from the room. Her mother hesitated . . . then gently brushed away the tear from Ema's cheek, shook her head, and stepped back again.

The lights stopped flickering.

The sudden brightness felt as sharp and disorienting as the fear coursing through her. And yet, Ema felt herself standing straighter as, one by one, she looked each one of them in the eye—daring them to *see* her.

"Alois deserves to be heard." She turned back to the painting, feeling every eye in the room follow her gaze. "He demands it, in fact. Isn't that right, Alois?"

As soon as the words left her lips, the eyes in Alois's painting blinked.

Everyone, including Ema herself, sucked in a sharp breath of surprise.

It had happened so quickly, yet *undeniably*.

The eyeball felt suddenly heavier around her neck, and Ema's pulse quickened to a dizzying gallop.

"Alois?" Ema asked softly, her voice filling the heavy silence.

Once again, the portrait blinked.

This time, only Josef gasped.

Ema turned her gaze to the curators, studying each one in turn. Aninha, Kazimír, and Žofie had their arms crossed and their brows furrowed. Thibault Finkelstein was clutching the ring on his hand and seemed just as miserable as always. Florentina Falkenberg was staring up at Alois's portrait with tear-glistened eyes.

None of them, however, looked full of regret.

The murderer's mask was still flawless.

"A mere optical illusion," Kazimír said finally, his frown fixed.

"The lights *are* playing up," Žofie added.

Aninha nodded in cynical agreement.

Ema swallowed down the urge to panic. The truth *was* in this room somewhere. She just needed to tease it out.

"Alois," she whispered in a voice that gave herself goose bumps. "If you're here, please, let us know."

Silence hung like a thick blanket over the room. Everyone was staring at Alois, waiting for the next eye blink. When no such blink appeared, Ema saw a small, satisfied smile twitch at Žofie Markova's red lips.

KNOCK.

The noise was loud and hollow sounding and seemed to come from the crate of animal bones that the headmistress was leaning against. Ema watched in astonishment as Dagmara jolted away.

"Are you sure it's not the girl doing this?" Aninha asked.

"No, she isn't manipulating anything," said Dagmara, her composure restored as if nothing had happened. "I'm *still* watching her very carefully."

Ema met her sharp gaze briefly, then went back to studying the curators *very* carefully.

"Alois," Ema said. "We want to know what happened to you. We want to know the truth."

KNOCK.

Everyone swiveled to face the new noise, which came from a cabinet behind Ema's sister. Františka shrieked and leaped toward Josef, who tucked her under a leathery wing and looked around the room with wide eyes.

KNOCK. KNOCK.

Everyone pivoted to the portrait wall, as the force of the knocking tilted Alois's portrait.

KNOCK.

Even though Ema thought she knew the true source of the sounds, each one rattled straight through her. It took all her effort to keep watching the faces of the curators, who were no longer gathered in a convenient-to-study line. Aninha was rifling through the crate of bones, Kazimír was opening the cabinet doors, and Žofie was running her hand along the portrait wall.

Her parents were both staring hard at her but made no move to stop her. Ema found herself turning round in circles, trying to take it all in, and feeling that familiar hum of dread start to spread down each of her vertebrae.

"Alois, who did this to you?" Ema said loudly, trying to hide the panic in her voice. "You can tell me. I can make them pay."

Everyone was turning and leaping too much. The bone-itching unease spread down her arms and legs.

She couldn't watch them all at once.

It was impossible.

"The walls are hollow, aren't they?" Žofie said, banging her fist against one. She turned and glared at Florentina and Thibault. "You've built a—"

The Dreamer was cut off by the *SMASH* of a vase as it flew from a shelf and shattered by her feet. There was a yelp from Josef as several books went flying. A clatter as he and Františka ducked under the séance table. And a gasp as her parents ducked out of the way of an airborne bird skull.

Ema turned to each new clatter, shriek, gasp, and scowl—feeling the world spin dizzily around her.

This spectacle wasn't helping.

She was going to fail . . . again.

"Alois," Ema said, trying to still her whirring mind. "I understand that you're angry, but—"

SCREEEEEEEEEEEAAAAAAAAATCHHHHHH.

What sounded like sharp nails being dragged down a glass pane had everyone clasping their hands over their ears. It scraped away the last of Ema's equilibrium, making her tremble uncontrollably.

"Where are the other children?" Aninha asked. "Did they go home like we told them to?"

"Matylda?" Kazimír growled. "If that's you, show yourself immediately."

"And you, Ambrož," said Žofie crossly.

Ema watched helplessly and silently as the three of them began searching for her hidden friends. Every bone in Ema's body was itching now. All she wanted to do was crawl into a small warm nook, plug her ears, and close her eyes.

It was too much.

"STOP!"

The voice was shrill and commanding — and stopped the clamor in its tracks. It took Ema a moment to realize that voice had come from her own lips.

The room had also gone completely dark. It took Ema another moment to realize that was because she was squeezing her eyes tightly closed.

"Be *very* quiet," she said, unsure if she was talking to everyone in the room or to her own chaotic mind. "Let me listen."

In the dark silence, Ema felt like she could finally breathe again. And as she sucked in a deep lungful of air through her nostrils, she shuddered.

No murder could be *this* perfect.

She felt certain she'd already *seen* what needed to be

seen in order to solve the mystery but hadn't quite found the right perspective yet.

The white tulip, the falling skeleton, the static, the smell of burning flowers — she sifted through each detail, feeling the answer looming on the very tip of her consciousness.

Ema opened her eyes and looked up at the portrait of Alois, feeling an overwhelming sense of responsibility.

He *did* deserve to be heard.

She also felt certain that *she* was the only one who could give him his voice back — regardless of *how* she was able to do what she did. If one good thing could come of the bewildering enigma that she was, she wanted it to be this.

And with that sense of purpose, the uncomfortable hum coursing through her eased to a serene sense of lightness that had her striding toward him. Tentatively, she reached out and ran a fingertip along the painted version of the eyeball she wore around her own neck right then.

What wasn't she seeing?

This close, the shadowy lines on the wall that stretched out around him seemed almost vine-like. Instinctively, she reached out to touch one, holding her hand there as the static ran up her arm, and the vague smell of burning flowers tickled her nostrils. Ema stepped even closer still, until her nose was almost touching those dark, shadowy tendrils.

The shadows were *under* the paint, she realized.

She scratched at one, feeling the paint gather beneath her nail as it peeled away. Underneath she found a flaky, charcoal-like texture.

Scorch marks.

The kind left by a wayward burst of electricity.

If it could leave a mark like this on a wall, what would it have done to a person?

Ema bit back a gasp as her eyes trailed one of the vine-like lines down the wall, to the floor, toward a deeper, darker shadow pooled beneath a pair of boots. Instantly, she felt a crushing sense of regret, fear, and sadness that was not her own. Ema turned her gaze toward the person standing over that shadow and *knew* that this was the murderer.

It was written all over their face.

As soon as she realized this, every question, every pattern, and every cog clicked one by one into place. She'd had the pieces all along, but now they formed a picture so clear she couldn't believe it had taken her this long to see it.

"I know who did it," she rasped. "I know *how* they did it, and I know *why* they did it."

No one responded.

"You killed Alois," she said, feeling the truth of each word settle over her as she stared the murderer right in the eye. "And you killed Vendula Beranová."

All heads turned away from Ema.

All eyes locked on to the impresario.

32

Ephraim Rivers wore the most convincing mask Ema had ever seen. Every inch of his demeanor was carefully arranged to create a picture-perfect example of amused confusion, as if painted onto his face by da Vinci himself. But Ema could now see its weakness: it was too *curated*.

There wasn't a twitch of real emotion.

"Well, I wasn't expecting that finale from your little spectacle," Ephraim said, laughing with dazzlingly realistic incredulity. "And not just one murder, but two!"

She didn't need to see their faces to know that Ephraim Rivers had, in a single breath, made everyone in the room think her a fool. Not that they hadn't been thinking that already.

"Better a fool than a murderer," Ema murmured.

"Was it Alois who told you of my crimes?"

"You are telling me right now, Mr. Impresario. You wear the finest mask this guild has no doubt ever seen, but I can see through it. I *know* that it was you who killed them."

"You know it in your very bones, I suppose?" Ephraim sighed. "What peculiar detective skills you use. If solving murders is a burning ambition of yours, I'd suggest you stick to hard evidence, girl."

"I never wanted to solve a murder," Ema said truthfully. "And I have no burning desire to be anything other than myself: a scientist who seeks the truth. So, I'll use whatever skills I have at my disposal, no matter how implausible they might seem."

Ema cast her gaze across the room, to where Dagmara Bartoňová was watching her with those intimidating eyes. She could feel her parents watching her too but was too frightened to turn and look at them. If she did, she might lose her new sense of determination.

She couldn't afford to do that. Although *she* was certain that she'd figured out the truth, she still had the seemingly impossible task of convincing everyone of it.

At least she'd made them forget about her friends hiding in the wall.

There was still a chance she could make this work.

"Well," said Žofie Markova with a shake of her head. "I'll start with the most obvious flaw in your logic.

Vendula Beranová is currently exploring the Amazon rain forest," she said. "She set off many weeks before Alois's death."

"And who told you that?" Ema countered. "Mr. Rivers?"

The Dreamer's eye gave a small but noticeable twitch.

"I'm the impresario of this guild," Ephraim cut in. "Of course it was me who told them, as I've told them every other time Vendula has gone on one of her many expeditions."

"I think we've given this girl more than enough time to entertain herself," said Kazimír. "Let her parents go and put her to bed, so that we can get back to—"

"No," said Ephraim. "If I'm going to be accused of double murder, then I should like to hear the no doubt compelling evidence against me. Please, Emiliana . . . or Ema—whatever your *real* name is—tell us all the hows and whys of my supposed crimes."

Ema watched the tiniest, twitchiest smirk tug at the corners of his mouth. He was challenging her, offering her the rope with which he thought she would hang herself.

He had, after all, committed a seemingly perfect murder. But he'd made mistakes, Ema now realized with certainty. Mistakes he wasn't even aware of.

And so she smirked right back at him. "It would be my pleasure to explain every little detail."

They all stared at her expectantly.

"It all started several months ago," Ema began with barely a wobble in her voice. "Tensions were high in the guild, and several curators were calling for Alois's spectacle to be shut down. Now, Alois's motive for wanting to avoid such a fate is obvious—his spectacle represents his entire life's work. But Vendula's motive for helping him seems less obvious, seeing as she too was skeptical of his work."

Ema paused and took a shaky breath.

"However," she said, "Vendula liked Alois's acolyte, Florentina. She liked her enough to help her grow an underground garden. And she liked her enough to look at Alois in a kinder light and humor his request to help him conduct his research."

"That is a leap of speculation if ever I heard one," Žofie Markova said.

"Yes, it is speculation," Ema said. "But it is entirely plausible that Vendula is the 'she' who Alois references in that journal. If you really think about it, what did she have to lose? She was a scientist who believed in truth seeking, and whatever the outcome of their research, it would satisfy her need for truth. Either she could prove that her initial assumptions about Alois's skills were correct and this would only strengthen her argument that his spectacle should be closed, or it would help her see his work in a new light. Which leaves the other collaborator—you, Mr. Rivers."

Before anyone else could jump in with more accusations of speculation, Ema quickly plowed on.

"You, Mr. Impresario, had an obvious reason to involve yourself in such an experiment," she said. "It is, after all, your job to keep this guild running smoothly. Having several curators protesting against another is hardly that, especially when the spectacle they are protesting happens to be the guild's biggest earner. You saw proving Alois either right or wrong as a way to quell the rising hostility once and for all."

Ephraim Rivers raised a single eyebrow. "I am also the one who *authorizes* what research happens within this guild," he said with a faux-weary sigh. "Why wouldn't I just do that, if I was as keen to proceed as you insist I was?"

"Because you knew that if anything went wrong, *you* would be blamed for having been the one to authorize it," Ema said. "You agreed to it on the basis that it be conducted secretly. That's why Vendula—with her almost permanently bandaged hands—arrived here dressed as a patron, just in case. And it *did* go wrong, didn't it?"

She let the words hang in the static-filled air and tried not to scowl as the impresario schooled his features into the perfect veneer of bemusement.

"You tell me, beruška," he said blithely, with the tiniest twitch of satisfaction when Ema grimaced at his term of endearment. "This is the first I'm hearing of all this."

"It's all in that journal." She nodded to Alois's journal, lying there in the middle of the séance table. "But I'll spell it out for you, shall I?"

"Please do," the impresario said confidently; then he looked up at Ema's parents.

Instinctively, Ema did the same and immediately regretted it. Milena and Karel were standing shoulder to shoulder, with matching grimaces. As Ema turned back to the impresario, she saw the tiny smirk of satisfaction deepen. It seemed he could see her nervousness as clearly as she could see his nefariousness. And it was clear he intended to use it against her.

Ema swallowed down a heavy lump of worry.

She had no choice now but to keep going.

"'At first it was a great success," she said, flinching at the slight squeak in her voice. "You and Vendula were both amazed to begin feeling the presence of spirits. But this success came at a dangerous cost, because the only way you could achieve this result again was by using increasingly stronger electrical currents."

Ema walked to the séance table, flicked through the journal, and tapped at the page. The curators all leaned in, to where Ema pointed at a single line of elegant handwriting:

near-death experience

"At this point," Ema continued, flicking through a few more pages, "it was Alois—the one person who had the most to lose by abandoning this research—who insisted that you stop, that it was too dangerous to continue."

She showed them the page that said just that.

"He had no desire to risk harming anyone," she pointed out. "Not even to prove his point. But you, Mr. Rivers, with your quest for peace within the guild, and Vendula, with her now insatiably piqued curiosity, both insisted on continuing."

Ema ignored the convincingly amused scoff that the impresario offered and turned instead to face the headmistress.

"That's what it's like to be a scientist, isn't it?" she asked Dagmara. "Finding something in this world, or beyond, that mystifies you to such an extent that it makes your very soul burn with determination to find an answer. It's impossible to ignore, isn't it?"

The headmistress's eyes glinted, but she offered only a twitch of an eyebrow by way of an answer. Ema smiled as she turned back to the impresario.

"But research like *this*," she said, tapping the journal. "This is something else entirely. Proving the existence of ghosts, of an afterlife . . . of a legitimate way to contact loved ones—not only would this be unimaginably lucrative, but the fame and power that would follow would put this particular guild at the very forefront of prestige. As its impresario, you'd be unrivaled."

"Sounds irresistible," Ephraim Rivers said. "If only I'd thought of it."

"But you could not convince Alois to change his mind, could you? So you and Vendula carried on — without his help and without his caution." Ema paused, shaking the very image of what she knew had come next from her mind. When she spoke again, her voice was quiet and pained. "That's when it all went wrong. That's when Vendula died, isn't it?"

Ema heard the sharp intakes of breath behind her, but she kept her gaze fixed on the impresario's impervious face, waiting to see something — anything — to confirm her suspicions.

"As I've already told you," he said softly, "Vendula is on an expedition. She's very much alive, believe me."

"Everyone believed Silvie was at home all this time too," Ema pointed out, then turned to the curators. "It seems the mail here is a little unreliable, isn't it, Herr Finkelstein? Did Vendula ever reply to any of your letters?"

For the first time since she'd met him, Ema saw the gloom melt away, replaced with a wide-eyed look of surprise.

"And can we acknowledge the curious decision you took to hire Herr Finkelstein?" Ema asked, pressing on before anyone could interrupt her. "He's not the most obvious choice, is he? In fact, my parents were the most obvious choice."

Ephraim blinked. "Because he was—"

"Ah yes," Ema interrupted. "Because he was friends with Alois. *And*, I suspect, because he wears a mourning ring at all times—so clearly he believes in the afterlife at least a little bit. A curator who is both a scientist *and* a believer would be the perfect replacement for Vendula. Given a little time, I'm sure you hoped you could have convinced him to pick up where you and she left off. Perhaps, if you managed to convince Herr Finkelstein, he could even help you convince Alois to reconsider."

Ema ran out of breath. And as she looked around the room—at the ever-skeptical faces surrounding her—she realized she needed to both slow down and hurry up. When she continued, her voice was softer, slower, but with a rhythm she hoped would keep them hanging on her every word.

"Alois found out the truth. He confronted you about it. That's when you threatened him, hoping he'd promise to remain silent. But he didn't make that promise, did he? This left you with a difficult choice: keep your secret intact or keep your guild intact. You chose the former. Vendula's absence was easy to explain away. If Alois were to disappear suddenly, however, there would be difficult questions to answer. You needed him gone, with no questions asked."

As the impresario continued staring, Ema continued building the picture for them all to see.

"It was Florentina, and her anxious caution that her whale skeleton be thoroughly safe, that provided you with the perfect opportunity to get rid of him. You encouraged the curators to work together on a combined great spectacle . . . so that when something went wrong—as you planned for it to—everyone would feel culpable. No one would look at *you*."

The impresario's left eye twitched.

Ema pressed on.

"The safety chain was, after all, in easy reach of your podium. I know this, because I made that leap this very night. You took one of the damaged chain links that Žofie had discarded. And then up on your podium, as the lights dropped, you cut the chain."

Once again, Ema paused for a beat to let what she was describing form fully in their minds—as clear as it was in her own mind now.

"As soon as Florentina began moving the mechanism, the entire structure collapsed, straight onto Alois, whom you knew would be standing right below. And then when you got down to the ballroom floor and used your authority to demand everyone move away from the debris, you swapped the chain links, holding up the stolen, already damaged one, and declared it all an unfortunate accident. Is that enough detail for you, Mr. Impresario?"

She leveled him with a steady glare, as he returned a mirror image of it back to her.

"I'll admit, it's a much more entertaining and imaginative theory than I was expecting," he said, as if he were genuinely amused. "But no, it is missing quite significantly important details."

His voice was confident, his eyes were sincere, but his lips were pressed ever so slightly harder together. There was a slight chip in his perfect mask. Judging by the still-skeptical faces around her, however, no one else could see it. But a chip could become a crack, and with enough pressure, it could shatter completely.

"And what, exactly, am I missing?"

"Science, dear girl, is based on observable evidence, not on wild imagination and bone-deep intuition. Your little theory hinges on the supposition that Vendula Beranová is dead. And, well, there is no evidence that any harm ever came to Vendula, is there? And certainly no body. *And* there is not even any evidence that she or I were the ones working with Alois on this research of his."

Despite everything she'd just laid out, Ema could see they were still unconvinced—just like Ephraim knew they would be. After all, she'd proven herself to be a sneaky, deceitful, ridiculous little girl already.

The smile he gave her as he finished laying out the massive flaw in her hypothesis showed that he had every confidence his colleagues would continue seeing her in just that light.

The smile that Ema offered up in return let him know that it was she who had just trapped him.

"Except, of course, for the fact that there *is* physical evidence. Right here, in this very room."

And just like that, the chip became a crack.

33

I t was a mere twitch at the side of the impresario's nose, but it bolstered Ema's resolve. She couldn't help but grin, which made his nose twitch twice more before he managed to school his features once again.

"Headmistress," Ema said, in a strong voice she barely recognized as her own. "If you look inside Alois's safe, you will find a hidden compartment. It's somewhere near the back, and you might, like I did, receive a small electric shock."

Once again, the impresario's nose twitched. The more Ema stared at him, the more uncomfortable she could see him grow.

"You'll find nothing of the sort, I promise you," Ephraim said casually, though the smallest bead of sweat began to appear at his temple.

"Well, it was your idea to humor her in the first place, Rivers, so we might as well see this through to whatever end it has," said Dagmara, crossing the room with that determined stride of hers. "The combination?"

"One, two, twelve," said Ema and Florentina at the same time.

Dagmara raised a single eyebrow as she lifted Alois's portrait, set it aside, and twisted the dial. The safe door opened with a clunk. The headmistress put her hand in and patted around a bit.

Dagmara frowned. "There is nothing—"

"I told you." This time, Ephraim's smirk was plain for all to see. "Perhaps it really is time—"

"Oh, let me try," said Žofie, storming across the room, nudging Dagmara gently aside and reaching an arm into the safe. "Hidden compartments aren't meant to be *easy* to find—ouch! She wasn't lying about the static shock, at least."

There was a loud click, followed by the squeak of an unoiled hinge.

As Ema and Ephraim continued staring each other down, Žofie stuck her head right inside and emerged again looking ashen faced, clutching something in her hand. She slowly lifted her gaze to Ephraim as she held the object up for all to see.

It was a silver star brooch, and it was crisscrossed with dark, angry scorch marks.

Ema felt a bittersweet blend of sorrow and triumph at the sight of it. She waited for the impresario's mask to finally fall away, and for everyone to see the shame and guilt hidden beneath it.

Instead, Ephraim Rivers grinned.

"How, exactly, does Alois's ruined brooch prove that I killed Vendula?" he said, turning to Florentina. "And how convenient—again—that a piece of evidence be found in a safe only you had access to." Then he glared at Ema. "I think I understand what is going on now. How much did Frau Falkenberg pay you to put this little charade on? Or was it Silvie who put you up to it? What kind of sick and twisted conspiracy is this?"

His lies came so quickly and effortlessly, as did the picture-perfect look of outraged disbelief on his face as he glared accusingly at the Bone Sculptor.

"Alois was buried with his brooch," Florentina said quietly, her face pale with shock. Ema could see—quite clearly—that the Bone Sculptor had no idea that the brooch had been in there. "I *saw* him get buried with his brooch, as did all of us at his funeral."

"It's Vendula's brooch," Ema finally managed to spit out.

"Don't be ridiculous," Ephraim spat back. "It must be Alois's."

"No, Ephraim, it's not Alois's brooch," said Žofie. "His brooch was damaged, but not in this way. I removed the very tip of the star from the whale's skull when we cleared the debris. This can only be Vendula's—it's not like they are given out often." As the Dreamer looked up at the impresario, those dark eyes had a brand-new glint of suspicion. "Vendula would *never* leave without her curator's brooch. None of us would ever part with ours. Alois didn't, even in death."

"Alois must have found it," Florentina said, staring wide-eyed at the brooch. "He would have known the truth about her then—"

"It must be a fake," said Ephraim, cutting her off with a defiant, but not-quite-defiant-enough lift of his chin. "You, Florentina, could have easily had that brooch replicated. Convenient that you happen to own one yourself now, isn't it?"

Ema realized with sickening clarity that the brooch wasn't enough to condemn him. It had everyone's attention, though, and both Ema and Ephraim knew it.

If she was going to get his mask to shatter, it would be now.

She needed to dig under his determination to where she knew that guilt and shame lay. She could see it in the dark shadow beneath his feet.

"They were your friends," Ema said. "They were like family. You never wanted it to end this way."

His scowl remained rigid.

"Vendula's death was a tragic accident," Ema said softly. "You felt honor bound to her to not let her death be in vain—to continue the work she had given up her life for. You didn't want to cover up her death, but you didn't see any other option."

Ema watched as his shadow darkened further still, despite the unwavering look on his face.

"You didn't want to hurt Alois either," she said. "But if he told everyone what had happened, then everything you'd done and risked and endured would have been for nothing. What was it you said earlier? *Sometimes we must all break the rules in order to pursue vital work*? Is that how it felt to you? The work was too important to let anyone stand in the way, no matter how much you admired . . . or even loved . . . them?"

The shadow darkened even more, and Ema felt a churning, heavy, icy-cold despair wash over her. She shuddered, looking up at his unyielding expression with tears pushing at the corners of her eyes.

"I can feel it too now," she rasped. "That shame you carry. It feels cold, and suffocating, and so very heavy to bear."

His nostrils flared, and he sucked in a deep breath.

"You want to say sorry to them both," Ema pressed. "You yearn for the opportunity to do so."

She looked down to his boots, certain they were the very ones that had left those footprints in the mausoleum.

"You can say sorry to Alois *properly* right now," said Ema softly. "You can beg his forgiveness with words"—

Ema leveled him with a knowing stare—"instead of sneaking into his mausoleum in the dead of night to leave him a measly white tulip."

The impresario's mask shattered. His eyes widened, his brows rose, and he flinched visibly. "How did—" He shook his head, then forced his features into an exaggerated grin. "What on earth are you talking about?"

It was too late. His face was waging a war with his own emotions, and even he knew that he'd lost the battle to conceal it. He glanced nervously toward the others, and his strained smile slipped the moment he saw them all staring hard at him.

"Ephraim?" Dagmara said, her eyes now wide open in disbelief.

Ema turned to face the others, feeling them look at her in an entirely new light.

Aninha shook her head in disbelief. "It's true, isn't it?"

Florentina was shaking and crying, with Žofie's arm wrapped tightly around her shoulder. Kazimír's and Thibault's eyebrows were almost touching their hairlines, and Františka and Josef were staring open-mouthed at her.

It was then that Ema realized her friends were all standing in the doorway.

Matylda and Ambrož were both gawking.

Valentýn grinned. "That was—"

"Splendiferous," Silvie finished, her eyes glistening.

It was her parents' faces, however, that took every last bit of air from Ema's lungs. Her father's features were arranged in a neat configuration of awe, while her mother's expression flitted between surprise, fascination, and wonder.

They were all *truly* seeing her now.

And for the first time in her life, Ema felt no urge to push her shoulders up to her ears and run into the shadows to hide. In fact, when the impresario let out another one of his perfectly curated huffs of indignation, Ema found herself turning on him with a bone-thrumming sense of confidence she had never felt before.

"You can stop *acting,* Mr. Impresario," said Ema quietly, but with a commanding bite to her voice that made Ephraim Rivers wince. "You must be exhausted by it by now."

"I'm exhausted by *you*, girl. You are *ridiculous*."

"Don't you dare speak to my daughter like that." Karel seethed as he and Milena appeared behind her.

"You were absolutely right about her," her mother said. "She *is* shrewd, brave, and determined. Unlike you."

Ema leaned back against them, letting their warm arms envelop her.

Under the heavy weight of everyone's glaring, the impresario sank into his chair and averted his gaze, seemingly unable to look any of them in the eye.

The séance room fell silent for a long moment.

"I — um — "

They all turned to the headmistress as she opened her mouth, then closed it again, then blinked her eyes a few times. "It really is time you went home now, Ema," she said, finally back to her usual stoic disposition. "And it's probably best if Silvie stays with you tonight. We will take it from here." She turned away, paused, and turned back again. Her stare glimmered with something Ema couldn't quite work out. "I'll be in contact, Ema Vašková."

Ema may have nodded, or may have just blinked, but the next thing she knew there were four hands on her shoulders, giving her a delicate squeeze and guiding her to the door. Matylda, Ambrož, and Valentýn nodded and blinked in her direction as she passed them — their tired, baffled expressions a perfect reflection of how she herself felt.

As they made their way out of the séance room, Ephraim whispered, "I'm sorry," and then the curtain closed.

Then it was just Ema, Silvie, Milena, Karel, Františka, and Josef standing in the Moonlight Garden, in their outlandish outfits, surrounded by plants and skeletons.

No one spoke until they emerged from the hidden stone wall, into the narrow alleyway. Josef was the last one through, and he looked down at his man-bat costume and sighed.

"It's a bit late now, but I've left all my clothes in there."

"You look wonderful just as you are," said Silvie, yawning like a wild cat. "No more ridiculous than the rest of us, anyway."

Josef nodded and yawned in tired agreement. "At least the hat will keep my head dry as we walk home."

"It's not raining," said Františka, catching Josef's yawn and then passing it round the group like a wave.

"There'll be a short shower any moment," Milena said, nudging them along. "No avoiding it, I'm afraid, but it shouldn't last long."

No sooner had she finished her sentence than it started to drizzle.

The city was in deep sleep—house shutters closed like eyelids, the empty streets slumberous and still, and a warm blanket of darkness hanging overhead. The only lights were the streetlamps, which coated the mosaic sidewalks in a liquid gold glow. And the only noises were their dawdling footsteps and the occasional yawn.

They reached Big Old Town Square first, and as they stepped onto the shadowed cobbles that separated the Vaškov residence from the Astronomical Clock, Ema looked up at her uncle. The thought of him going back to an entirely empty home, after everything he'd done for her, was too much to bear.

"I'd like to stay at Josef's tonight," said Ema. "Please?"

Her parents frowned.

"How about we *all* stay at Josef's tonight?" said Josef.

Her parents blinked, then nodded tiredly.

By the time they arrived at Charles Bridge, the rain had stopped. The saint statues loomed over them from either side, watching the peculiar cloaked, winged, feathered, shuffling procession make its way along their ancient bridge.

Ema looked up at the full-ish moon and howled.

"That was the most impressive yawn yet," said Františka. "I suspect we will all sleep like the dead tonight."

*E*eeeeeeeeeeeeeeeaaaak!

It was a tiny, faraway noise that woke Ema the following morning—somewhere between the squeak of a bicycle wheel and the squeal of a deflating balloon. She opened her eyes, detangled herself from her own bat wings, and sat up, but the noise had stopped.

It took her a few crusty-eye blinks to realize that she wasn't alone in the attic room, and a few more to remember why.

Silvie was facedown on the pillow to one side of her and Františka to the other. Karel was asleep in the wing-back chair, and Milena was sitting on the end of the bed wrapped in a blanket, with one of Liliana's red journals nestled in her lap. The warm sun streamed in through the round window, basking them all in a golden glow that made Ema feel radiant with joy.

Squeak!

"What is that noise?"

For the first time since Ema could remember, her mother didn't jump at the sound of her voice. She merely turned and offered Ema a warm smile that *almost* hid the small crease of sadness between her brows.

"Your uncle must be oiling rusty wheels," said Milena tiredly. "He's been at it on and off since the early hours."

Ema crawled over to her mother and peered down at the page showing her mother's misfortune, now covered in fresh tear splotches.

Ema snuggled in beside her mother. "Josef's fortune never came true," she said. "Maybe yours won't either."

"Yours came true. And I think mine has come true already too—it doesn't matter how much worrying data I provide, or how many terrifying calculations your father makes, no one seems to want to listen to our concerns about the atmosphere. Which makes no sense because I just *know* I'm right about my hypothesis. I can feel it—"

"In your very bones?" Ema finished for her.

Milena gave her a wry smile. "If this misfortune is true, it means everything your father and I have worked on has been . . . futile."

The bed lurched violently beneath them as Silvie clambered over.

"Let me see that," said Silvie groggily, blinking her own crusty eyes as she took the journal from Milena and began to read. After a few moments of contemplation, she handed it back and shook her head. "Now I see where Ema gets her apocalyptic pessimism from. That's a perfectly splendiferous fortune to have been given."

"What do you mean?" Milena asked, looking as exhausted as Ema felt. "It's clearly a *mis*fortune."

The bed pitched and rocked again, like a ship in a storm.

Františka appeared behind them. "You were given a misfortune?" she asked groggily. "Let me see!" She mumbled the words as she read, then tutted. "I agree with Silvie. That's not a *mis*fortune at all."

"Perhaps you two aren't awake enough yet to read words properly," Milena said. "Here, let me. 'No matter how hard you work, no one will ever, in your entire lifetime, take your work seriously.' That is unambiguously, quite definitely, the most miserable misfortune if ever there was one."

"Nonsense," said Silvie. "It says no one will listen in *your* lifetime. That doesn't mean that no one will listen ever. Think about it: your work is so important that long after you're gone, people will still be talking about it."

"You are a maverick, just like Socrates was," added Františka, then her voice grew deeper. "*Education is the kindling of a flame, not the filling of a vessel.* You, dear Máma, are laying the groundwork for future scientists. You should be thrilled."

Ema watched something appear in her mother's eyes.

And then Karel was suddenly beside them too, also looking at the journal. The same something appeared in his eyes.

"Aha!" said Františka gleefully. "Look at that, would you? They both have the look of newfound wonder in their eyes. It is the same look Ema had when she saw her first duck."

All eyes turned to Ema again.

"I'm sorry it's taken us so long to see you properly, beruška," said Karel. "And I'm sorry we tried to force you to be someone you weren't. If you want to be like Liliana, then we won't—"

"I don't want to be like anyone other than me."

The windows shook as the attic room breeze picked up around them. "I swear this room never used to be so drafty," Milena said, wrapping the blanket more tightly around them. "I spent an hour this morning looking for the source of that breeze and found nothing."

Beside her, Silvie shivered, then silently mouthed: *Polter-granny?*

Ema shrugged nonchalantly.

Squeak!

The squeaky-wheel sound started again. A moment later, the door to the attic opened and Josef appeared, carrying a tray. It rattled as he walked in and set it down on the side table. Six mugs of steaming milk and six bowls.

Her uncle looked like he hadn't slept at all. Ema wished

she hadn't been so caught up in rescuing Silvie that she couldn't have helped him find Ferkel when he'd needed her to.

"I made us all breakfast," Josef said flatly. "Or maybe lunch. I'm not quite sure what it is, to be honest. I wasn't paying much attention while cooking. It might be edible, though, as it's mainly sauce." He walked stiffly over to the wingback chair and collapsed down on it.

Františka peered dubiously into her bowl. "What's *in* the sauce?"

Josef shrugged. "Sauce."

"Are we going to talk about what Ema did last night?" Silvie asked, slurping her milk noisily. "Because I have *a lot* to say on the matter. Wasn't she splendifer—"

"After breakfast," Milena cut in, eyeing Josef with worry.

"I should probably write to my parents and explain everything," Silvie said, suddenly much more solemn. "I was too scared to tell them what had happened to Alois in case they blamed me. They won't be happy to learn I ran away, but I hope they won't make me leave the guild—"

"Oh," said Josef glumly. "That reminds me." He reached into his sleeve and pulled a neatly folded letter out. "This came for you this morning, Ema."

Ema recognized the stationery immediately—it was the same paper Silvie had written on that night after their trip to the graveyard. She could even see the star seal. She sat there and stared nervously at it, making no move to take it from him.

After a few long moments, Silvie leaped from the bed and took the letter from Josef's fingers. "Shall I open it?" she asked, sitting down next to Ema again.

Ema winced, then nodded.

Carefully, Silvie pried the star seal off and unfolded the letter. Ema could feel the breath of both her parents and Silvie as they leaned in closely to read it with her.

> Ema,
>
> I'll get right to the point. You shocked, baffled, and downright outraged us last night. None of us have slept yet, as we pondered how on earth we should deal with you after all that transpired. I've avoided getting too involved with the guild's goings-on for years, and were it not for you I'd be merrily back with my pupils right now. It is clearer to me than ever before that you'd be an <u>awful</u> fit for my school. You are, frankly, the last person I would ever call a scientist.

Ema threw the letter to the floor and wiped a hot tear from her cheek. "I think I've read enough—"

"Oh, enough with the silly pessimism," Silvie said, picking the letter up again. "You're only just getting to the good bit."

"Good? She underlined the word 'awful' three times!

Máma, Táta, I am so sorry that I ruined my chances — "

"Silvie's right," Milena said, slurping at her bowl of sauce. "You're being silly. Now sit down and listen to the rest of it."

Silvie grinned, then began to read. "'You are, frankly, the last person I would ever call a scientist.'"

Ema groaned and buried her head in her bat wing arms.

"'And yet,'" Silvie said, with dramatic inflection. "'Even as I write these words, I recognize how very foolish, arrogant, and narrow-minded I am being in my assessment of you. What you did last night was not only mind-bogglingly implausible, but undeniably brilliant too. Every atom of my scientific mind is struggling to make sense of you, Ema Vašková, but my very soul burns — and yes, even my very bones strive — to solve the fascinating mystery that you present me with. Your parents were definitely wrong about the rocks . . . and I was wrong to dismiss you so callously. I sincerely hope you can forgive me.'"

With a small cough, Silvie reached for her mug.

"Is that it?" Ema, Karel, Milena, and Františka asked as one.

Silvie gulped the dregs of her milk, emerging a moment later with a white mustache. "No, but it's a very long letter, and my mouth has gone dry. Now, where was I?"

"Dagmara Bartoňová was begging Ema's forgiveness," Františka said. "Which I never thought I'd *ever* witness."

Silvie cleared her throat and continued. "'I still maintain that you are not suited to my school, for many reasons, but the most pressing reason being that my school does not possess a ghost-whispering laboratory, nor will it ever possess such a thing. You will not be joining your sisters, Ema. The unusual nature of your research requires an unusual approach, and so I hereby offer you my sponsorship to apprentice in the Midnight Guild, where I have reluctantly agreed to serve as impresario until a replacement is found. You will be under the tutelage of *all* the curators, working together in the pursuit of investigating spiritual phenomena in a safe, moral, and scientific manner. You clearly need some guidance on how to accurately verify these hypotheses of yours, using the proper scientific method. However, I am thoroughly satisfied by your passion, dedication, and, most importantly . . . your potential. That's all for now, sincerely tired, Dagmara Bartoňová.'"

"Does it really say potential?" Ema asked nervously. "Not potential for potential?"

"Just the one potential," said Silvie.

Františka grinned. "Coming from someone like her, it's a truly astonishing compliment."

Ema looked up at her parents, who both wore matching grins.

"Well," said Milena. "At least there's finally one of us in the guild's ranks now."

Ema beamed.

"Congratulations," said Josef from the corner of the room, and despite his clear heartbreak, he offered her a smile that warmed the drafty room. "I'm glad you found yourself."

"Thank you—"

Squeak!

"What *is* that noise?" said Milena.

Ema was on her feet, searching the room. "Well, it isn't Josef oiling bicycle wheels."

Finding nothing under her bed, Ema began searching the rest of the room. Behind the duck-foot mirror, under the dresser, inside the wardrobe. The squeaking seemed to always be coming from behind her.

Silvie appeared beside her, looking equally confused. "It sounds like it's—"

"Shh!"

Ema closed her eyes and strained her ears. When the next squeak sounded, her eyes snapped open. She hurried over to the wingback chair and nudged her uncle's legs.

"Move your feet."

"Pardon?"

"I need to look beneath your feet!"

Josef's eyes widened. He and Ema shared a knowing look.

"Oh," they said in tandem.

Josef jumped out of the chair as another squeak sounded. They both got down onto their bellies and peered under the chair. Farther back, under the cabinet behind the chair, was the source of the squeaking.

"Oh!" they said again.

"What are you two ohing about?" Silvie asked. She flattened herself down beside Ema and squinted into the gloom. "Oh!"

At the sound of her voice, a pair of bright yellow eyes opened and glared at them. Ferkel yawned a huge yawn, baring her huge fangs, then blinked and began licking the three tiny bundles of fur nestled on her stomach. The newborn kittens squeaked like a tiny, falsetto choir, their eyes tightly shut and their pink noses twitching.

"Oh," said Josef again, this time with unbridled joy.

"I guess we found your fortune right where Liliana said it would be," said Ema. "*You needn't go far, and you needn't feel bleak, for under your feet, you'll find all that you seek.*"

"I wore out a good pair of shoes searching very far and feeling very bleak," Josef said.

"But look at the glorious *fortune* you've found," Silvie said. "Although it looks like you'll be baking four times as many apology pastries before too long, so maybe it was a misfortune after all."

"Speaking of pastries," said Františka, after wedging

herself between Ema and Josef. "That orange kitten looks like a little furry apricot. You must call her Kolache! That sugary white one's a little Rohlíčky if ever I saw one. And the other one—"

"Look at his fur!" Milena said, as she and Karel joined the tangle of bodies on the floor. "Is he gray, or is he . . . blue?"

"A bit of both," Františka said. "How curious. He's—"

"A fascinating little enigma," Ema said. "Like—"

"Giraffes," said Silvie. "Or like you, Ema Vašková. His fur is the very same color as your eyes."

Ema grinned. "I wonder what other surprises he has in store for us."

"Well, he has the look of a rebel," said Karel. "I'd be surprised if he doesn't grow up to be the greatest mischief-maker of his time."

They all smiled as the gray-blue kitten yawned.

"And the potential for a ferocious roar," added Milena. "I've no doubt he'll be good at making *noise* as well as mischief."

"What are we going to call this little enigma?" Josef asked.

They all looked to Ema for an answer, who was staring at the astonishing little kitten in awe.

"He's perfect," she declared. "And I have the *perfect* name for him."

She named him Midnight.

EPILOGUE

Midnight arrived like a thief in the night—silently, purposefully, and without invitation. Moonlight caught the very tips of his whiskers, but the rest of him remained drenched in deep darkness. He soaked that darkness up—making him bigger, stealthier, deadlier—and surveyed his hunting ground with lunar-yellow eyes.

To a marauder less clever than he, the attic room would appear as it usually did: drafty, dingy, and dusty. But Midnight knew there was something very different tonight.

The dust had an unusual shimmer to it.

The darkness was thicker and chewier.

And the breeze that ruffled his under-chin mane smelled deliciously different too.

Twitching his nose, Midnight realized what that tantalizing scent was.

Adventure.

Tonight, he would catch his most elusive prey of all: the shadow-in-the-attic.

All that stood in his way of finally succeeding in that endeavor were the five smallish humans sitting on the floor with a glass bell in the middle of their circle. Their eyes were closed, their paws interlinked, and their furless faces lit from beneath by flickering candle flames.

What they were up to, Midnight did not know, nor did he care. But what he did know was that they mustn't realize he was there. And so he stuck to the shadows as he crept around them, leaping silently over a bundle of breeze-swept papers.

If Midnight had been able to read human words, he would have recognized the words "Shadowology" and "The Polter-Granny Hypothesis," but he was more concerned with making it to the bed without being seen or heard.

"My legs are going numb," said the Ear Fondler. "How long is this supposed to take?"

"It's been five minutes, Matylda," said the Kisser. "It might happen more quickly if you whined less."

"Silvie is right," said the Tickler. "We're not going to encourage any ghosts to come all the way back here just to listen to you grumbling."

"Thank you, Valentýn. Now, perhaps if we—"

"Shh," said the Quiet One. "I think I heard something."

Halfway across the room, Midnight froze—one paw lifted. He readied himself to run but was saved by the human with the moon hair. His human.

"Keep your eyes closed," said the Sneaker in a soft but commanding voice. "Ignore any noise other than the bell." Then, in a louder, more commanding voice: "We need empirical proof, Liliana."

The humans fell silent again, and Midnight swallowed a purr of relief. In three quick but noiseless leaps, he was across the room and up on the bedside cabinet. The shadow-in-the-attic was close; he was sure of it. He just had to follow his nose to find it.

Midnight was halfway across the cabinet when a teacup bashed into him, then clattered to the floor and smashed. Four shrieks followed in its wake, and Midnight bounded beneath the bed and huddled there, trembling. He watched as the circle of humans broke, and all but one of them looked to the shattered china in wide-eyed horror.

"What did I say about ignoring other noises?" the Sneaker said, her eyes still closed—except for the one dangling from her neck.

"Ema!" said the Ear Fondler. "That cup did not just leap off the cabinet by itself."

"Tonight's method of verification is the bell," said the Sneaker. "And *only* the bell. Now close your eyes and hold hands again."

Midnight waited until they were all back to their strange activity before edging his way forward again. He laid each paw down with careful precision, his whiskers twitching and his eyes darting in all directions, then poised himself at the edge of the bed.

It was then that he finally saw it.

The shadow.

It passed quickly across the floor and disappeared under the wooden legs of the hatstand. Every inch of Midnight tensed in anticipation. His hind legs wiggled beneath him, and then they launched him forward. He flew toward the shadow, his front claws outstretched and ready.

But when he was a mere whisker's breadth away, the hatstand's legs tangled themselves around him, and the shadow darted off again. As the careless hatstand teetered, there was a high-pitched squeak, then a fluttering of leathery wings. The bat launched itself upward, just as the hatstand crashed downward.

The racket covered the scraping of Midnight's claws as he scrambled to the safe shelter of the under-bookcase. He tucked himself into as small a ball as he could and peered out.

Four of the humans were on their feet now and huddled together.

"Surely that counts as empirical proof, Ema!" the Ear Fondler said.

"Matylda's right," the Kisser agreed. "Béla is too small to knock over an entire hatstand."

Midnight watched from the shadows as the Sneaker opened one eye and peered around the room. Midnight knew that look well—it was the same look she got just before she scolded and called him a kitten-beast. Instinctively, he pushed himself farther back—until he was so deep under the cabinet that he couldn't see anything but gloom.

The room fell silent, but Midnight didn't dare emerge from his hiding place yet.

His ears strained and his nose twitched and he waited.

When nothing happened, he inched forward.

Midnight's nose had barely emerged from under the bookcase when two large furless paws appeared out of nowhere, and he found himself suddenly airborne.

"Here's our empirical proof," the Sneaker said, holding him above her head and glaring up at him.

He let out a mewl of protest, then another one as a second pair of paws wrapped around his middle. Midnight found himself hoisted toward a new furless face.

"I think you mean empurrical proof," the Kisser said, pressing her lips against his forehead several times.

Midnight squirmed in her arms, finally crawling up onto her shoulder.

And then he froze.

"Is he all right?" asked the Tickler. "It's like he's

turned into a statue. Why isn't he blinking?"

Midnight could not have blinked if he'd tried to.

"What is he staring at?" asked the Quiet One.

The humans fell silent, and Midnight watched in unflinching fascination as the dark shadow settled into the middle of their abandoned circle. As the humans followed his gaze, a gusty breeze blew around them.

Then the glass bell rang.

AFTERWORD

This story is about enigmas.

It is also a story I thought I would never be able to finish.

Although I clearly *did* manage to finish it, and came to love it with all my heart, writing it felt like an endless journey through a dark tunnel. I'd managed to write one book already, so why was this one proving to be such an unsolvable dilemma, despite my devotion to it?

It was an enigma that had me asking: Where do stories *actually* come from?

Our brains, right? We think up some exciting plots and characters, mix them all together into a delicious story-soup, and then shout, "Bon appétit, readers!"

So why was it, then, that I couldn't get more than half-way through this story before realizing I had no idea where it was going? My story-soup was tasteless and undercooked.

Where was I going wrong?

Allow me to get a bit science-y with you. According to neuroscientists, we are only aware of about 5 percent of what happens in our brains. The other 95 percent of our "thinking" happens beneath our awareness. It is, therefore, no surprise that almost all of us struggle to make sense of ourselves.

The truth is, we are *all* enigmas.

I knew there was something deep in my subconscious that was stopping me from writing this book, but I had no idea what it was. So I went back to the beginning of the story—many times—and asked myself where this story was coming from.

Was it about exciting adventures at midnight? Was it about mysterious secret societies? Was it about someone being murdered with a whale skeleton?

No.

This story was about *Ema*—a girl desperately trying to understand a world that doesn't seem to understand her. A girl who is both terrified to be seen for who she really is but also so very, very desperate to be seen for that. She is stuck between those two realities, and I needed to find a way to unstick her.

And so, I really *looked* at her.

What I saw was an undeniable glint of myself in those candle-smoke eyes of hers, as she rolled them at me and said, "It's about time you acknowledged you are just as stuck as I am."

I realized that, like Ema, I have spent my entire life

feeling like I was an awkward fit for this world.

Like Ema, I made myself as invisible as possible.

Like Ema, I hid behind a mask and tried my best to act "normal."

So I put the story aside and went to a doctor, who gave me a fancy medical name to explain why I feel so different and out of place.

I am *neurodivergent.*

My brain is wired a little differently than most people's, and there are lots of very long lists of things that I struggle with—from attention, to noise, to social skills, and many other things.

What these lists never seemed to include, however, are things that my neurodivergence makes me amazing at.

I am endlessly curious and creative, and most definitely an outside-of-the-box thinker.

I can focus on things I'm interested in for hours upon hours upon hours.

I am stubbornly passionate about fairness and rationality.

These are all qualities about myself of which I am proud.

I have a feeling Ema, too, might be neurodivergent. She comes from a place deep inside me that had been begging to come out for thirty-odd years, so perhaps it was natural I wanted to write this into her character. But I was not *aware* of this as I was writing her. I was not *aware* that in writing her journey to self-acceptance, I was finally letting go of the shame I've felt from a very, very young age for not being "normal." As it was, it was *she* who showed *me* the answer to both the Ema Enigma *and* the Hana Enigma. Our experiences might not have been exactly the same, but the lesson we finally learned (to proudly embrace who we are) was.

But back to the Story Enigma. Where do they come from?

Some people think stories are just fancy lies. But I believe they are two fundamentally different things. Stories help us make sense of the world and ourselves. Lies do the opposite. And although sometimes lies can feel comforting and safe, if there is one thing I'd like readers to take away from this book, it is this: embrace the truth, no matter how uncomfortable or frightening it may seem at first or second or third glance.

So my hypothesis for the Story Enigma is that the most meaningful stories come from truth. Like Silvie says: *Fairy tales breathe truth into the world. They are more real than even you and me.*

Now, if you will, lower your voice and make it sound all mysterious and wise as you repeat this Socrates quote to yourself: "Let us follow the truth wither so ever it leads."

ACKNOWLEDGMENTS

This story would not have made it out of my brain had it not been for the support, patience, and unwavering devotion of my editors, Carmen McCullough, Maggie Rosenthal, and Naomi Colthurst, and my agent, Jenny Savill. Words cannot adequately describe my appreciation for you all. That goes for everyone at Puffin and Viking too.

Rosie Hudson — your energy and creative spark are bright enough to light the night sky. Thank you for helping me curate my school events and being as excited about my eyeball collection as I am. I hereby name you an official impresario of the Midnight Guild, and I can't wait to see what eccentric spectacles we can come up with for this book!

Speaking of spectacles, I'd like to thank Tamzin Merchant for taking me on a wonderfully bonkers adventure around Prague that not even Silvie could have dreamed up! I'll never forget those shelves of centaur legs and troll heads, the magnetic fur-gun, the fairy city we explored, and the room we *barely* escaped from thanks to that malfunctioning mechanical spider. What a day!

The *Everything Czech* Facebook group—not only have you given me endless delicious recipes to bake (Vanilkové rohlíčky is my absolute favorite), but you also came to my rescue when I was looking for some Czech superstitions. So, big thank-you to: Nikola Touchette, Lorraine Meiners-Lovel, Petr Hradil, Nicholas Morelli, Kathrin Bary-Schüller, Monika Pechacek, Yvette Nekuda, Barbara Moriearty, Marie Nwanyanwu, Wendy Kahle, Alexandra de Quimper, Olga Junek, Evelyn Funda, Monika Luksikova-Hickcox, Anna Buchman, Kuba Kubikula, Katerina Vlcek, Rafael Baieta, Ilona Norton, Rita Bella, Alexa von Alemann, Barb Waterhouse, Milada Nohel, Dagmar Benedik, Erica Viezner, and Joanne Semmler.

Aninha Bold—we may have come here from opposite sides of the world, but you really do make Bath feel like home. Your delightful mischievousness knows no bounds, and your feijoada is ALWAYS perfectly seasoned. I won't be letting you near any swords, though—we'll stick to music and dancing and arm wrestles instead.

Yasmin Rahman—I'm delighted you finally got yourself a cat-beast. I am also delighted that I am about to make you vomit at this soppiness: you are a very dear friend and I ADORE you. And Nizrana Farook—another delightfully mischievous friend I couldn't do without—I repeat to you what I said to Yasmin, but I know it'll make you smile, not vomit.

Emma Read and Hannah Rials Jenson, for the many writing and yapping sessions in BTP we've managed to squeeze in in between lockdowns. And for all my other author friends who I have missed spending time with, but whose camaraderie I have felt strongly across the vast expanse of the interwebs. You are all the BEST.

Jitka Němečková from ANA Prague, for showing me around your breathtaking city.

My big sister, Emily, for always standing up for me when I was growing up. And for climbing a tree in roller skates — giving me the inspiration I needed for the end of chapter 1. Mum, Dad, Kris, Ben, Tess, Nienke, Mark, Maddie, Kevin, Kate, Jane, Heather, Rachel — I'm grateful for you all and look forward to catching up on missed time together from these past two years.

Dylan — thank you for being the most patient sounding board that ever existed and for not only putting up with my hyperactive chaos, but for (somehow) finding it endearing. And Felix — not only have you grown to tower above me this past year, but so has your wit. I'm endlessly proud of you and only a little bit miffed that you're funnier than I am.

Thank you to the wonderful authors Katherine Rundell, Robin Stevens, Emma Carroll, and Cerrie

Burnell for your generous cover quotes for my first book. And all the bloggers and reviewers who took the time to read and recommend it too.

And, finally, I'd like to thank all the readers around the world who enjoyed *The Unadoptables* and sent me fan art, bookstagrams, and lovely reviews—all of which kept me motivated to finish this story for you too.